DreamGirl

DreamGirl

By Cyan Brodie

British Library Cataloguing in Publication Data
A Record of this Publication is available from the British
Library

ISBN 978-1-907335-35-8

This edition published 2014 by The Red Telephone
Manchester, England

All Red Telephone books are published on paper derived
from sustainable resources.

AUTHOR'S NOTE

This novel is a work of fiction and although certain locations in Edinburgh and New York do exist, the descriptions are for the most part fictionalised as are all characters and institutions portrayed within the story.

'I saw what I saw, I heard what I heard, and my soul sickened at it; and yet now when that sight has faded from my eyes, I ask myself if I believe it, and I cannot answer'

*Strange Case of Dr Jekyll and Mr Hyde
(Robert Louis Stevenson)*

7

DREAMGIRL

GIRL ONE

CHAPTER 1

HAVE you ever woken up to the echo of a scream? I don't mean the scream itself. Because that had already gone. Died in the mouth, or in the heart and lungs.

And no. Before you ask, it wasn't my scream. I know that when you produce a scream, a proper scream, it can make your throat hurt. Leave it feeling raw. But my throat was fine. I wasn't the one who had screamed – not this time.

It was some other girl – and all I could hear was the echo of her scream. Not a sound you would normally expect in this quiet corner of Edinburgh at 06:32 on a Wednesday morning. She didn't look like any of the kids from round here either but I didn't get much time to pay attention to her face.

What struck me was how thin she was. Not just skinny or anorexic, although I could see her ribs poking through her vest above her sucked in tummy, and her arms looked as if you could snap them as easy as breadsticks. She was thin like see-through thin. Her body seemed to blend in with the stained walls of the room. And her pale skin was greasy-looking as if she hadn't showered for weeks. Her underwear was smeared with dirt as well. Like one of them kids you see on TV in those adverts for 'Save the Children'.

I thought perhaps she was asleep. But then she whispered a few words.

"Levi... in Harlem... look, dese are ma jeans."

They were a horrible baggy pair; a grungy shade of grey and blue, discoloured with all sorts of filth down the front; creased, and worn into rips at the knees and backside. And there was a cheap-looking white plastic belt trying to escape from the loops. But then the man shape came into view and I didn't get a chance to study her face again properly. He held out two fingers as if he was

10

aiming the barrel of a gun and he went really close up to the girl and then...

That was when I woke up... when it woke me up.

This was still my bedroom. The same white wardrobe doors with the gold-framed panels. The fancy, curly brass handles. My navy blue leotard hanging off one of them. My can of 'Impulse' and my insulin kit on the dressing table. Photos of me and the other girls from dance class stuck on the mirror. Pablo the polar bear sitting on his chair with my green, chiffon scarf tied around his neck and one of my stripy, woolly bed-socks dangling from his foot. That dusty, purple lampshade suspended over my head. I could see two cobwebs like tight-ropes from where I was lying. The same faded blue wallpaper with that darker patch where I'd taken down my Jenson Button poster. My iPod nano on the windowsill. And the echo of someone else's scream still there flapping against the walls and the ceiling and the window blinds. Trying to get out.

"INSIDE your crack?" Lucy snorted with laughter.

"God, Luce! No!"

10:35 Wednesday. Break-time.

"Well, that's what you just said, Rubes. Somebody's fingers..."

"No I didn't. I mean, I didn't mean it like that. I was still half asleep and it just felt, well... that wasn't what I meant. It was like... like a sensation of someone's fingers."

"Shit, gurl, has anybody ever tried that? I mean, is anyone been doin' stuff like that?"

"No. I already told you, it was just some weird dream."

It didn't get any better when I got home. Even hinting at the nature of the dream to my mum was mega-stupid.

"What do you mean you had a 'sort of sexy dream'?

Was it about somebody special, a boy you fancy, in school?"

"Mum!"

"Well, it must have been about somebody."

"Look, it wasn't about anybody in particular, ok? Just some weird dream."

"All right, sweetheart. But..."

"It was more like a nightmare really. I mean, it was like I wasn't even there. Like it was happening to somebody else, some other girl."

"So what was happening to her?"

"Well. Somebody was touching her, you know.. . where they're not supposed to."

Mum's face suddenly a mask of dread.

"But I must have woke up real sudden 'cause I felt really spooked, and then I remembered something Aleesha had said to Lucy one time..."

"What have I told you? I don't want you finding out stuff about S-E-X from that pair."

"I haven't. Honest. It was nothing about sex."

"Ok. I'm just saying. I don't think you should listen to what the girls in the playground say."

The girls in the playground! Yeh, sure. When we play hop-scotch at break time. Huh. If Mum heard half of the stuff we talked about in the loos or in the changing rooms she'd have kittens.

"Ok. I won't."

"You know if there's anything you're not sure about in that department you can ask me."

I nodded, feeling the familiar burn of embarrassment as Mum prepared to launch into one of her mother-daughter lectures. I was glad I hadn't told her everything because she had already reached escape velocity and was off on a whole new orbit of her own.

"And funny dreams – they don't mean anything.

Everybody gets them. I remember when I was your age, my God." She was embarrassing herself, I could tell. "What I mean is, it's completely normal. And look, if there is a boy you are getting friendly with and haven't told us about, well..."

I began to cringe, realising we were on Chapter 5 of 'Dating for Dummies'.

"It's lovely that you've got yourself a boyfriend."

Note the space between both words.

"But you should wait 'til you're a little older. I really think you're better steering clear of situations that you're not ready to handle, love."

I should be so friggin' lucky.

"I mean, you're nowhere near old enough to have... or to do..."

"Mum, I know what fooling around is, and we're not. I mean..."

God, she was getting me all flustered now.

"I haven't even got a boy friend, ok? So just give it a rest."

"How are my two favourite girls tonight?"

Saved by Dad's arrival, or so I thought. I grabbed my bag but Mum still had her claws in me.

"You haven't let anyone?"

"Mum! I've already told you. There isn't anybody."

"Ok. I'm only asking."

"Well don't!"

"Asking what? Pinky?"

Dad checking we were both ok but making me feel even more uncomfortable. I was beginning to wish I'd never mentioned this dream business to anyone now. I just wanted to get away from them both and forget about the whole thing. Escape upstairs. Anywhere.

"Nothing, John. Just girl talk. Ruby's been having funny dreams."

I don't believe it. How could she?

"Mum!"

"Your dad's only..."

"You're doing my flippin' head in. I don't wanna talk about it so..."

"No one's saying you have to."

I could feel the word 'but' was about to feature.

"But, I mean, there's so many hormones flying around in this house. God, I can smell them outside in our garden sometimes."

I felt myself turning a darker shade of red. Dad calling me 'Pinky' for one thing when he knows how much I hate it.

Mum stood there at his side, nodding at his every word. It was like that Saturday morning when I'd answered the door to those Jehovah's Witnesses and there was no way I was going to escape without suffering a full blown sermon.

"Sometimes it can feel like your brain's been taken over by aliens. Your body as well. But it's only temporary. Ask Shona. You get everything back as good as new eventually."

"Dad, I know all about..."

"I'm only sayin'. It can feel weird. But it's all part of, well; part of growin' up."

Weird. This whole conversation was weird: Mum and Dad trying to tell me all about puberty five years too late.

"We're always here if you ever..."

"I know. Thanks, Dad."

I keep forgetting. 'Always' meaning 'Never'; never home, always at work or out playing golf.

PHEW. I was glad to retreat to my bedroom. Peace finally. I dug out my folder and started working on my

14

Statistics homework, still wondering how it's possible to dream about a place you've never been to, or about someone you've never met; something that's never even happened to you – that's never even crossed your mind. How did my brain come up with that all by itself – that feeling?

Pie-Charts.

TWO hours later I was stretched out on top of my bed in just my pj's varnishing my toe nails a dark shade of green. Once they were finished I sat up and rearranged my pillows.

Hmm. Neat feet!

I could feel myself getting agitated again just thinking about Mum and Dad. I couldn't possibly tell them everything. What I had actually felt. I hadn't even told Lucy the worst bit. It wasn't just dreaming that touch. I saw the man's fingers, like a pistol. They were gleaming wet, coated in some kind of disgusting, slimy gunge. Then they were inside me. These cold, clawing fingers; hard like steel. And they were digging into me as if he was trying to get a grip on my stomach or something so he could pull it right out of me. And it was the most hurt I ever felt for the teeniest tiniest of seconds.

Then…

I think it must have been just before I actually woke to that echo… the echo of the girl's scream. It was then he whispered he loved me. And that's what scared me shitless.

"SO, you ok, Junk?"

Aleesha and Lucy sitting at the same table as me. Lunch break. I normally make do with sandwiches and fruit but there's dance classes on Mondays, and on

15

Thursdays there's band practice after school so I need to have a proper cooked meal both days.

I'd known them both since I was twelve and first started dance lessons. They're a year older than me but we get on because we like the same sort of music and stuff. Aleesha doesn't go all the time now because her dad doesn't really approve. They're Muslims. But Lucy still goes. I actually had a crush on her once, to be honest, because she is really fit and is probably the most amazing dancer I have ever seen. But that was two or three years ago and I'm totally over it now, obviously.

"Yeh, Why wouldn't I be?"

Two shit-eating grins.

"Jus' askin'. That's all."

Aleesha fluttering her eyes and bobbing her face from side to side.

"So you had any more of them hot dreams, luvva, or what?"

"Hot dreams?"

"Well, uh-yehhhh," Lucy said. Huffing with contempt. "Like you tole me yesterday?"

For the best part of Summer term Lucy and Aleesha had begun talking like they were taking part in some trashy American TV show. 'Beverly Hills 90210' or whatever. Totally bizarre.

"No."

I so was not in the mood to go through all that again.

"Hey, Rubes. We all been there, hon. Right? Yo' motor's on fire, you gotta put out... or put it out." Aleesha's mouth like a sewer as usual.

"Lee-sha!"

Even Lucy's bottom jaw fell below the top button of her blouse.

"I'm jus' sayin'. I know how steamed up I gets."

16

"The answer's still no. And anyway, my dad said..."

"Yo what?" both voices now in stereo, one down each ear.

"He said it's my hormones," I whispered, realising as soon as I'd opened my mouth that it was a major mistake to mention his involvement.

"You tole this stuff to yo' ole man? Are you some freakin' idiot or what?"

CHAPTER 2

DAD was meeting Uncle Andrew for drinks at the golf club as usual on Friday night. I'd tried phoning Lucy but my call went straight to voice mail. Stacey was at a sleepover with Leslie Miller and Trudy King. I don't really get on with that pair because they're so into boys and always give me funny looks. They are such retards and Stacey's exactly the same whenever she's with them.

I don't do sleepovers. It's too much of a pain in the bum having to stick to such a strict routine: regular meals, two injections a day, checking my blood glucose and other stuff that's even more gross, and that I won't go into for now. When I was a bit younger my cousin Farran used to come and stay here. She's seen my Novopen and the rest of my kit. She thought I was brilliant the way I handled things. But she's not been near for the last eighteen months or so; long story.

Anyway, it was nice to have the house all to ourselves – just me and Mum now Shona was in college. I still miss having her around even though she can be a bossy cow at times.

I'd washed my hair. Then spent ages trying to straighten the fringe. Normally I would stay in my room until z-time, listening to my iPod or ringing round my mates. But tonight I was still a bit tensed up after the fuss of the last couple of days. I couldn't get the memory of that girl out of my mind. Levi's pitiful voice seemed to be haunting me no matter what I did. I needed to empty my head and chill out in front of the telly.

"What's this?"

"Oh, it's some film that's on. I'm only half watching it. Turn it over if you like."

"No. 'S ok."

"Want a drink?"

"No ta. Already had a glass of juice."

I sat next to her on the corner sofa and sank into the soft cushions.

"Feeling like some company? Just us two girls together?"

"Mum!"

She smiled, knowing she was spot on as usual. "Is your toe nail all right now?"

I nodded. I'd had an in-growing toe nail which had cleared up a couple of weeks ago.

"Let me see."

I slid my left foot out of its slipper and let her take a look.

"Ooh. I like the nail varnish."

I grinned, slightly embarrassed that she was seeing it for the first time.

"God, your feet are icy cold. Shall I give them a rub?"

I kicked off my other slipper, twisted myself so I was laid out with both feet resting in her lap, closed my eyes and let her fingers knead life back into my soles and heels. When Mum was pregnant with Struan I would lie next to her for hours on the old, collapsed couch we used to have. Struan, my baby brother who died when he was three months old. My feet would squirrel their way under that huge bump, and she'd rub them until I fell asleep. Like a contented cat.

Then there was the squeal of a police siren outside in our street.

"Oh, it's some film that's on. I'm only half watching it. Turn it over if you like"

And then a slamming door and sudden silence.

It was a huge, old Brownstone with walls streaked

19

black in places by a hundred years of city rain. There was a smell like the river, but cold as well. Muffled sounds like we were inside a narrow passageway. Clammy air all about us. Shoes slapping on stone steps. A screech from an old, metal grating being pulled to one side.

Sounds growing fuzzier; more distorted as if I was underwater.

Something loose clattering above my head.

A flickering light like when the tube in the garage sometimes doesn't quite come on properly no matter how many times you flip the switch. Coils of heavy chain and light-sucking puddles of oil on the concrete floor. A shadow thrown across it like a forgotten item of clothing.

"Levi... in Harlem... look..."

That poor girl again, her contorted face, close up to mine for an instant before she was yanked away just as quickly and I doubled up in pain.

"Ruby! What's the matter?"

I rolled away from Mum and wrapped my arms tightly about my midriff. It wasn't the snatch of the shackles on my right wrist that hurt. It was that sneaky punch.

The television was blarting twice as loudly in the background but I was still somewhere inside that cold, damp building.

"Ruby!"

I fought for air.

"Mum?" Saying it like I was only seeing this person for the first time.

"Is it bad tummy ache?"

No. Sore back. Sore from that blow to the kidneys that came out of nowhere.

"Did you do something?" I gasped.

20

Mum stared at me as I'd sworn at her all of a sudden.

"Me? What do you mean?"

"It felt like you just punched me."

"Punched you?"

I glared at Mum, half believing she might actually have attacked me while I was half-asleep. "That's what it felt like."

"Ruby, I was massaging your feet. That's all. You were fast asleep, then you suddenly woke up as if... well, as if somebody had stabbed you or something."

I shook my head, shivering involuntarily as I tried to get my thoughts into some kind of order.

"You were dreaming, darling. And you woke up all of a sudden and got a bit of a shock. You probably thought you were in bed, not down here."

She laid her arm onto my left shoulder and gently rubbed the back of my neck.

"Mhmm. I could hear a police car, and it was like there was somebody else inside the house."

She picked up the remote and snatched away the movie from the screen.

"It's this C. S. I. trash. You were listening to the telly but half asleep. That's all it was. All right now?"

I pulled up my t-shirt and tugged down the waistband of my track-suit bottoms. A patch of red, mottled skin on the right-hand side of my lower back was already beginning to turn yellow.

"Let's see."

Mum studied the bruise more intently.

"When did you get this?"

"Just then! That's why I jumped up. That's why..."

"Don't be silly. You wouldn't have a bruise as quickly as that if it had only just happened. Let me have a proper look." She pulled my shirt right up. "Turn round."

I felt her fingers pull my tracky bottoms down some more.

"Where did you inject this morning?"

Friday. My left-hand side this morning. I have to take it in turns: two jabs one side then two the other. The Diabetes Nurse says to keep changing sides so one spot doesn't get sore. But I never inject myself all the way back there where I can't even see properly, for God's sake.

I turned so she could study the slight roll of flesh on the left side of my waist. I pinched it and showed her the tiny prick-point of red.

It had been Dad's idea of a joke calling us 'Pinky' and 'Perky'. Me and Shona. I was 'Pinky' of course because I had literally turned into a pin cushion. And once my diabetes became common knowledge they all started calling me names at school – mostly 'Junk' or 'Junkie'. But I actually prefer that to 'Pinky'.

The skin was no more inflamed than usual.

"Here. See? Same place as Wednesday."

I twisted my head to take a closer look at the bruise again. I could almost see the indentations of two knuckles impressed into the tissue, but that was probably my imagination working overtime.

"I think the doctor ought to take a look."

"It's only a bruise, Mum."

"Yes, I know. But your kidneys; it might be something to do... I don't know. Your blood-sugar levels? Perhaps the dosage needs checking. Are you sure you didn't knock yourself in school? Gym perhaps? And then forgot about it? It's easily done."

I shook my head. I would have remembered. The pain had been devastating for a split second, sucking all the energy out of my body as my legs spasmed in shock. Then I thought back to the first dream. That same girl, Levi. The

22

feeling I'd had when that one ended. What he'd said. And now, bam! First he loves me and now he hates me. It was nuts!

Mum had wandered off into the kitchen.

"Mum?"

"Yes, darling."

She came back with the cordless phone.

"Oh. Phoning Dr Kerr now?"

She nodded.

"Better had. I'll leave a message. See if he can fit us in early next week."

I nodded dumbly. Us. When she really meant me. More prodding and probing.

"Mum?"

She stared through me as she waited for the 'beep'.

"Mm? Hang… Oh, yes, this is Tricia MacGregor, Fingal Gardens. It's nine-fifteen p.m. Friday the 19th. I'm leaving a message for Dr Kerr regarding my daughter Ruby…"

I let her continue talking machine-speak and headed off into the kitchen in search of some crisps.

She finally followed me through, nodding her head as if to prove to everyone watching what another fine job she had done. Bless her.

"What was it you wanted, sweetie?"

"Oh," licking salt off my fingers. "Nothing important. Just something for our Geography homework. Mhmm. You ever heard of a place called Harlem?"

I didn't get much joy. Mum's no geographical genius. She thought it might be some place in America, close to New Orleans but wasn't certain. She dug out an old, battered atlas from the cupboard under the stairs where she keeps her recipe books and a couple of Catherine Cookson novels.

I checked in the index but couldn't find anywhere called Harlem. I'd imagined it being somewhere in America as well. There'd been that dream with the sound of the police siren – but maybe that was the TV film taking over or whatever. I couldn't decide what I would do if I found it anyway. Would I suddenly remember being there? In another life perhaps?

Unlikely, seeing as there was no such place.

"Anything?"

"Nope."

"You could try the internet... it's bound to be on there."

"Yeh, I s'pose."

I was too knackered to be bothered. Mum said I looked dreadful and told me to try and get a proper night's sleep. So I kissed her goodnight, checked my blood glucose level then took my time getting undressed. Putting off climbing under the duvet. I don't mind admitting I was a little nervous what demons might be lying there in wait for me.

I almost wished Shona was still at home and I could creep into her bed for just the one night. Like I used to do when I felt a bit lonely or fed up with my lot in life. Sneak into her room and smush up next to her. She always pretended she was asleep and hadn't noticed but a couple of minutes later I'd feel one of her arms wrapped across my belly. I missed her more than I thought I ever would; obviously more than she missed me.

It was her first year in college and to begin with we had kept in touch almost every other day. But now she actually owed me a couple of e-mails, and I don't think it was because she was too busy with her studies. Probably partying or messing around with her latest guy. God! Why did everything always come back to guys?

24

I eventually slid in between the sheets, snuggled into my pillow and folded my knees up to my middle. Trying to think of any boy in school that I might want to share the night with. God. As if there was anybody I fancied enough to fantasize about. I'd even gone off that Luke Moffat in the Upper Sixth; although I'd once had him down as a Fittie McVitie.

What a laugh.

CHAPTER 3

SATURDAY was a glorious summer's day – shafts of sunlight flaring between the slats of my window blinds long before six – but I was in no hurry to get out of bed. Still feeling a bit yucky, actually. I was supposed to be staying overnight at my nan's in Penicuik while Mum and Dad went off to some grand dinner dance at the golf club. Prize-giving. Speeches. Blah-blah. They were going to make a night of it.

But then just before nine o'clock Nana phoned to say she was under the weather. Trouble with her hip again. Mum came upstairs to check how I was and decided I'd be better staying home.

"I don't know what to do about tonight."

I couldn't see what the problem was.

"You can still go out. I'll be ok. I mean, if I'm no better I'll probably have an early night."

But Mum wasn't so sure with the dance not due to finish until the early hours. She was actually planning on missing out; staying home to babysit me, for God's sake.

"Just go and enjoy yourselves. I'll be fine, honest."

So… ten hours later and with a list as long as my arm of dos and don'ts here I was. Home alone and bored senseless. Suddenly the whole night stretched ahead of me with the house to myself and I just didn't feel like taking full advantage.

I could choose any DVD I wanted to watch. Eat popcorn 'til it came out of my ears. Well, perhaps not. We all remember the Great Dunbar Exploding Popcorn Incident in this house. But I could play my CDs on Dad's hi-fi full blast. Dance around the lounge in just my undies. Sing at the top of my voice.

Pah. What was the point? I still felt a bit wonky, and none of my mates were here to share the fun so it was all a complete waste.

I ended up watching 'Twister' for the hundredth time. It looks much better on the flat-screen than on my laptop – with the room lights turned off and the volume up to +20. I still laugh every time I watch that woman in the back of the pick-up talking on the phone to her friend telling her to stay calm and practice how to breathe – then saying she has to go now because 'We've got cows'. She's just seen a cow flying past – then another one flies past; except it's the same cow going round for the second time.

I'M such a party animal. I was up in my bedroom soon after ten. On a Saturday night! What a saddo! I didn't dare ring Lucy or Stacey and let them know how bored I really was. I checked my blood for the hundredth time (8.5 – which was probably a bit high but would start coming down once I injected). Then I decided to plug in my laptop and get changed into my pj's while it loaded.

Then I clicked the broadband connection button and checked my e-mails.

You have **0** new messages.

No surprises there as I'd already checked it at tea time. There had been two – one from Nana saying how sorry she was that I'd not be staying the night, and one from Shona telling me all about her latest bar-tending job – that's four nights a week she's working now – and her weekend plans. Shopping for knee-length boots then off to some glitzy nightclub later. Her and her bezzie mate, Laura, and somebody called Harvey. So much for studying hard for her exams.

I decided I should go searching for my own Harvey.

FAVOURITES - PERSONAL - CHATTERTEENS

I'd only been on this site once before, about a month ago after Lucy told me all about it but I couldn't really make head or tail of it.

To begin with everybody on here had made-up names and their own little personal picture – one was a St Bernard dog – one just a pair of legs in stripy socks – Taz – some kind of fairy – a vampire bat.

Lucy's was a pair of red lips.

I'd chosen a pink starburst to go with my name – *pinky*. Yes, I know. Me picking a name I hate. But I honestly couldn't think of another one to use – *junkie* wouldn't really be very appropriate if I wanted to find some fit guy.

Lucy's on-line name is *sexylegs*. I would never have the guts to use one like that. There must be all sorts of pervs after her.

As for the chat itself – a load of messages appeared as lines of one-way conversation alongside each little picture. Most of them seemed to be chatting to nobody in particular. It was impossible to keep track because the page scrolled up so quickly. And those I did manage to read didn't make much sense. Tonight was just as bad. There was no sign of Lucy on there. Just a load of losers like me.

pinky	has entered the room
groboy	has signed out
nubile15	has rusty bin in tonite anyone?
honchoZ	any 13 y o girl looking for 1-to-1 fun PM me now
crazylily	has entered the room
jozy	hi evrybody

crazylily	anybody wanna chat////
pervydad	9-14 y o girls in lycra get in touch

Eeeewwh. Get a life! This was meant to be a chatroom for teens but I knew there were more weirdos on here than normal people.

crazylily	has signed out
pinky	anyone here from Scotland?

Nothing. Just a load more random messages and meaningless snippets of nonversation. I was invisible. Then a little box appeared in the top left of my screen. I'd not seen one of those the last time I was on here.

Bigbob	would like to chat with pinky

OMG. I panicked and clicked on the IGNORE button straight away. Bigbob sounded like the name of a 40-year old truck driver.

Bigbob	would like to chat with…

Ignore again. I was ready to sign myself out and scrunch under the duvet – maybe ring Stacey for a desperate goodnight chat. Then…

Duke_$	would like to chat with pinky

I thought it through for about ten seconds. We're not even chatting are we? Just typing words to each other. I don't have to let him know who I am or where I live or anything private like that. And I can stop chatting whenever I want to – just click out and switch everything off.

29

ACCEPT

Suddenly my name was inside another little box of its own.

    Duke_$ hi pinky
                         whats yr asl

Oh, great. My first ever on-line chat with a real person and I can't even understand the language.

    pinky   im sorry
                         whats asl
    Duke_$ hehe
                         age sex location
    pinky   oh right
                         16
                         female
                         in Edinburgh in Scotland
    Duke_$ oh cool
                         and whats yr name
    pinky   Ruby

Already I'd broken every rule in the book. But he was such a fast typist. He didn't give me time to think.

    Duke_$ hi Ruby
                         you have a pretty name
                         I'm Stefan
                         23 years old
                         from the Netherlands
    pinky   wow
                         hiya
                         how r u

Duke_$	I'm good -
	even better for meeting you
pinky	hehe

He was funny, and Stefan – that's such a cool name for a guy.

Duke_$	so you are at school still ruby
pinky	yeh
Duke_$	and what do you study
pinky	oh, all sorts
	I like English and music most
	play in the local band -
	and I do dancing
	and drama
Duke_$	wow
	you sound a really talented chick

OMG. For some reason I could feel myself getting short of breath. Am I really a chick?

Duke_$	I am also a student - in Amsterdam
	studying sociology

Wow, he was an intellectual. He'd take about ten seconds to realise I was just some dumbass school kid and then it would be goodnight Ruby.

pinky	that sounds hard

How lame am I?

Duke_$	hehe
	good one

31

pinky	So do you always come on here on a Satday night
Duke_$	No - sometimes I go out to a bar with friends have some drinks and talk a smoke maybe

I hate people who smoke but I needed to try and act a little more mature.

pinky	o I love the bars they have in Europe even children can go out at night for a drink with your mum and dad
Duke_$	I guess that's a good point so where in Europe have you been?
pinky	belgium
Duke_$	I like Belgium it is very close to where I grew up they have good beer what part did you stay?
pinky	Blankenberge we had croque monsieur? and we went to Bruges as well and on a canal trip
Duke_$	yes Bruges is very pretty so tell me ruby what do you look like

Why was he wanting to know stuff like this? Hmm.

pinky	5 foot 6 long auburn hair blue eyes quite slim I spose

32

Duke_$	what is auburn
pinky	you know - reddish brown
	with lighter streaks
Duke_$	you sound very pretty
	my hair is a little darker
	but short - I have Grade 1?
	otherwise I am quite a hairy guy
pinky	u got a beard
Duke_$	well yes
	but my body is very hairy

I stopped typing. Picturing this strange man's naked body covered in hair. Perhaps I should log out while I could, but I didn't want him to think I was being immature. He was a lot more polite than most of the morons I'd seen on-line.

Duke_$	girls your age don't like hairy
pinky	hehe
	depends
	I quite fancy Justin Timberlake
Duke_$	I guess he's a hunk!!
pinky	so do you have a girlfriend

I cringed. I couldn't believe why I wanted to know anything so personal.

pinky	sorry thats none of my business
Duke_$	that is ok
	not at present no - but I did have
	up to 4 months ago
pinky	sorry for being so nosy
Duke_$	nosy?
pinky	asking private stuff

33

Duke_$	that's fine
	you can ask me anything
	then I can be nosy too
pinky	hehe
	what about
Duke_$	well I am curious
	a pretty girl like you
	do you have a boyfriend
pinky	OMG no
	not really into boys yet
Duke_$	that's ok
	you are still very young
pinky	but I have had a couple of snogs
Duke_$	what are snogs??
pinky	kisses
	with a boy I was dancing with one time
Duke_$	hehe
	oh that's cool
	and did you like it?
pinky	I spose so
	it felt ok really
	- it was cool
Duke_$	and the boy too
	did he like
pinky	yes
Duke_$	he told you?
pinky	no way
	but I could tell

This was getting a little weird but I couldn't seem to stop myself typing more brain garbage.

pinky	he was pressing against me
Duke_$	what?? press??

34

	was he hurting you??
pinky	nono
	but mum told me about boys
	how they get turned on
Duke_$	I understand what you say now
	hehe

My throat and mouth went suddenly dry and my brain was screaming at me to get out of there before I wrote something even more stupid.

Duke_$	you should feel flattered
pinky	OMG
	I can't believe I told you all this stuff
Duke_$	it's ok
	you should not be embarrassed
	boys have no control
	over things like this
	it is a normal reaction

It was exactly the kind of lecture Mum and Dad keep coming up with – but we were two grown-ups talking about grown-up stuff so it felt different.

Duke_$	especially with a pretty girl
	a girl who is sexy
pinky	hehe
	don't think so
Duke_$	maybe when you are older
	you understand sexy

I blushed. Stupid cow or what?

| pinky | probably |

Duke_$	so can I ask you
	a very personal question?
	if your breasts are big or small?
	or perhaps you prefer not to tell
pinky	I'm blushing but.
Duke_$	oh sweet ruby
	I don't mean to embarrass you
	don't tell me anything else.
	ask me something
pinky	34
	34 B
Duke_$	right
	I know what that is
	so now I understand
	why the boy was turned on
pinky	but we didn't do anything else
Duke_$	no
	you are still very young and
	you have given him a
	wonderful memory
	I am sure
pinky	don't know
	cos im just a stupid schoolgirl
Duke_$	ruby, listen to me
	you are very sweet
	and I can tell you are very bright
pinky	thanx

I was blushing all over again.

pinky	it's nice to be treated like a grown-up
Duke_$	hehe
	you are welcome
	so maybe we can chat again sometime

pinky	ok
	I shld go to sleep now anyway
Duke_$	ok ruby
	I will say goodnight
	sweet dreams
pinky	you too Stefan
	u have a cool name
Duke_$	hehe
	goodnight ruby
pinky	goodnight
	xxx

Three kisses, honestly. I logged out and snuggled into my pillows. My heart was pounding and I felt ridiculously thrilled. Nervous as well – that next time he might start talking about stuff I couldn't possibly relate to. Serious stuff about sex and things that only boyfriends and girlfriends talk about. I hate feeling like some feeble kid who doesn't know enough about anything.

'Sweet Ruby.'

Nobody ever called me that before. Even remembering that bit made me feel marshmallowy and warm all over as if my whole insides were expanding through my skin. I tried to get comfy and think about what he might look like, trying to focus my dream radar on some gorgeous guy with a hairy chest and big, strong arms. But, of course, it's impossible to pick and choose what you are going to dream about...

CHAPTER 4

*I'M beginnin to welcome da noise evrey day an da smell
uh garbage dat carry in when he open da door. It a
remind dat da outside world still dere. Dat cool breeze fuh
a moment to clear da smell uh dis room. Dis bad smell.
Dis smell is me.*

*I miss to be home. Mom an Effie an Mrs Sopel next
door. I miss to hang round wid Kitchie an da boys in st
Nicks park. Jay an sammy from special English class. Dey
must all be wonderin where I get to.*

*I member seen man follow me from lights outside ice
cream store an my mind tick over wid next step den he
grab me. A bad burn an stingin like somthin live crawlin
upside me an den my nose done bleedin all down my front
an over my jeans. Den I feel engine vibrations through da
floor an da gentle sway wid truck as it moves. I bad scare.*

*More bad scared when he took me in dis room an I
start cryin til he say to stop. Da man spoked with velvet
tone dat first time. Den he fastnd dat chain on ma riss an I
knowed I gonna be dead maybe soon.*

*I stink worse dan any bag lady. So hot in here cos dere
no any air condition. My pants grey with dirt now an can
hardly make out da little rosebud patterns on dem no
more. Dey stick to me like second skin. Vest all crease an
stain as well. My turquyze bra – well he torn dat off first
night an aint seen again. He said I much got nuttin up top
half to put in it anyway. An he tooked off my sweat shirt an
jeans an dey layin on floor still like a pool uh laundery.
My shoes nowhere now.*

*I no wash any my hair since I been here. No shower –
a face cloth in bucket. But he say he dont care bout smell
or ma dirty skin. No mind any dat. Den he run his hands
over me an... His hands an His fingers touches me. An dat*

firs time when he cut me wid a knife. Say it won't hurt but I His now. Tell me he loves me an I more scared dan ever.

An I starts believin some other fifteen year old girl das be in dis cellar – not me. I try coverin my ear – but all dis time I hear her sob an her whimper. An dat machine noise shaking trou floor into every bone my body.

Den dat one time when I fall asleep I dream real nice dream. Bout another little girl close by – like a lily grow in a desert. Feel so bad to wake her cos she look she have such nice sleep. An I nuttin I could gave her. Nuttin down here worth a dented cent except dat fancy white belt on my jeans. Belt I borrow off Effie widout her knowin.

"Who you tink you talkin to, gal?"

He got ears like bat, an I only whisped tree four word. Now he snatch away my denims from my hand an says dey nuttin but trash. Den he dere in my face, crowdin me, makin me feel small an worthless like he always does. Fingers like gun barrel comin right at me.

"You want some more a dis?"

An his other hand punch me hard an I feel my head swimming against dark tide revoltion. Part him inside me an I all shrivel up like dead flower an his arm press gainst my troat an my eyes drownedin in so many tears an I prayin hard prhaps to not wake up an it growin more darker…

CHAPTER 5

03:12 on my bedside clock. I gasped awake, fighting for breath. I couldn't move. There was someone inside my bedroom, someone inside my head listening to my heartbeat and aware of my every thought. I didn't dare close my eyes again because I knew he was waiting for me.

Shudder.

I heard every creak inside the house, every stalking shadow as it stepped upon the stair, every layer of congealing air as the heat of the day slowly cooled into the walls of the house.

Levi had reappeared. But this time there was no scream, just muffled sounds that didn't sound particularly pleasant. And before I knew it I was staring into her eyes and drowning on poisoned air, suffocating in my own bedroom with no way to draw in breath as something coiled around my throat.

My eyes were gritty and I itched all over. My stomach felt queasy like it sometimes does after a hypo, as if something churning inside me was trying to escape. The warm, shortbread scent of my skin had turned sour. I was desperately hoping Mum and Dad were home but too terrified to sneak a look outside my bedroom. Then I heard a toilet flush somewhere in the house. Thank God.

I must have finally gone back to sleep because light was showing through my blinds the next time I opened my eyes. Birds were busy outside making bird noises in the branches and tweeting each other while there were no humans about. But it didn't feel the slightest bit summery. Sunday mornings in June should not be tainted by such darkness. To be honest I felt as low as I can ever remember feeling.

For one thing there was poor Levi. I'd never met her, never seen her in real life. Had no idea where in the world she was from. Yet I was convinced she must be a real person and I was trying not to imagine what she had been going through in her final moments. Oh yes, I knew for a fact that the poor girl was dead. I felt that tightness around my throat as her last breath gusted through my body: a cold gasp of despair leaving a trail of poisonous fumes. Like a ghost rushing to escape life because life was so shitty.

Then there was Mum and Dad trying to be cool parents and making a hash of it. Making me wish they could be just like everybody else's parents – there in the background like a comfy sofa or a set of kitchen cupboards. Making no demands.

And my so-called mates. Stacey, who had been my BFF right from junior school. She was changing into a right mare. Lucy and Aleesha suddenly acting like a couple of cows as well. Putting on the phoney talk and taking the piss about my erratic hormones and the fact that I've never actually been with a boy.

Plus now there was Stefan. One more unknown variable in the chaos of my mathematical life.

$$l \pm (m + d) = (s + l + a) \pm s$$

I was a simultaneous equation with neither side ever likely to balance. Just like this diabetes. This ticking bomb hidden deep inside my body that seemed to rule my life. A little too much sugar, or not quite enough, and my body would start fighting back. Ok, I'd got things under control, but now and again it would catch me out. Creep up on me and punch me in the guts like in that horrible dream.

How come my life is always such a mess?

CHAPTER 6

THE telephone call came from upstairs. Detective-Investigator Reuben Garcia was about to type up a report on the latest stabbing on West 88th Street. Yet another gang-related crime. The latest scourge to hit the city, it seemed. But now the Chief wanted him to drop everything and take a look at a pair of trousers. It made no sense. But after seventeen years' service at the 24th Precinct, Garcia realised that only a fraction of his work made sense.

He grabbed his coat and made his way to the front desk.

"You got something for me, Baker?"

"You mean the broad that found the pants?"

"Yeh. A name? An address? Some kinda clue so I can get this over with then go back to doing my job?"

Baker scratched his head with his pen. Searching for the 'Replay' button.

"Sandler Hall. I've got the apartment number right here in the log. 'Glava' – that's what he said it sounded like. 'Glava'. 'Glava'. That's what's here in the log."

"What language is that meant to be?"

Baker continued to scratch.

Garcia shrugged and took the evidence bag into one of the Interview Rooms, collecting Iversen en route.

Karl Iversen was a relatively new recruit to the Bureau. He'd worked his way through college, and although he'd been Garcia's partner for less than twelve months he thought he knew it all. He treated the job like he was on a one-man mission to save New York. It hadn't taken the rest of the squadroom long to start calling them Batman and Reuben.

"What we got here, Reub?"

"Just somethin' of nothin' by the look of it. This broad

42

phones in this morning, says she wants to report a suspected homicide. It turns out her dog sniffed out an old pair of blood-stained denims down by the river."

"Is that it? We got nothin' better to do than handle this shit?"

"I know. But it was the Chief who took the call. Don't ask me how or why. Desk sends a squad car all the way out there. Some jumpy broad walking her mutt down at the Grant Memorial. And she's standing there waiting for them, guarding this pair of trousers like as if her life depends on it."

"Somebody's cast-offs I'd say. People dump all sortsa crap out there. What did she expect us to do with them?"

Garcia's waistcoat bulged as he gave a shrug.

"Who knows? She made some big deal about there bein' blood all down the front. So the uniform bags them and brings them in here. The desk sergeant was gonna dump them in the trash but there was no chance of that with the Chief on the case. Then some bright spark from Juvenile remembers readin' a bulletin from 26th about some young runaway. Reported missing nearly a month ago. Last seen wearin' torn jeans with a fancy white belt just like this pair. So…"

"…they could be hers. And they expect us to find her?"

"Nah. I reckon if these were hers then some low life's probably tricked her out of them before doin' the business. Left them in an alley somewhere. Then some derelict's found them and wore them 'til they fell apart. They're gonna stink this place out as soon as I open the bag, I just know it."

Garcia fished out a pair of crumpled denim trousers, torn ragged and stained ruby red from the crotch down.

"That sure looks like a hell of a lot of blood."

"Mhmm. Get back to the Desk and have Baker tell you all he's got on this broad."

43

Garcia let the trousers fall onto the formica-topped desk in a puddle of grey, blue and red misery. There was a strong smell of urine, stale sweat and the damp, tidal air fresh off the river. He poked his pen into the pockets but found nothing more.

No one seemed in a hurry to answer the internal phone when he tried to reach Harper in the labs. Then Iversen came back in, shoving the trousers to one side as he sat at the desk causing the cheap, white plastic belt to slide free of its loops and fall to the floor like a coiled viper.

Both detectives flinched.

Garcia hung up. "Shit. Where is everybody?"

"I've got that name," Iversen laughed. "I was guessing Baker must have wrote it down wrong."

"He said Sandler Hall."

"Yeh. That's right. Corner of Amsterdam and 122nd. And then Glava."

"Is that supposed to be the broad's name or what?"

Iversen's grin grew wider.

"Sure. It's the way they talk up there on the Gold Coast. Old money, Reub. She must be old New York blood. It's 'Glover'. Found her name easy enough. She's on Columbia's books."

"Ok. Get Baker to telephone her. You and me should maybe go and pay the lady a visit."

Outside, the muffled wail of a squad car's siren could be heard trailing up Broadway, fading into Harlem like the death scream of a banshee. Within less than a minute all that remained was the echo of its passage.

PROFESSOR Glover wasn't particularly surprised to find two detectives outside her apartment on a Saturday afternoon.

"Was it one of you two gentlemen who telephoned me just now?"

"No, ma'm."

"That would have been the Watch Sergeant. Letting you know we were on our way."

"Really. Well, it's very thorough of you. But I don't know what else I can tell you…"

"We need to follow up a few things, ma'am. That's all."

Garcia took over, formally identifying himself before asking if they could come inside.

"Of course. It was blood then?"

"We'd rather not go into that. We just need you to tell us as much as you can about how you came to find the trousers."

She smiled rather like a pedigree greyhound.

"Quite. This way gentlemen."

She led them through the apartment: solid beech floors, thick rugs, expensive artwork and antique furniture one would normally associate with a 5-star hotel.

"It was round about 07:45 yesterday morning. I had a funding committee meeting scheduled for ten so I took Marlon out for his constitutional a little earlier than usual."

Marlon – a cross between a rat and a lapdog – lay panting on a sequined footstool. Iversen ruffled the pouch of skin beneath its receding chin.

"Do you always go that way?"

"Well, it is so convenient. I generally take him past the Riverside Church as far as the Park. And I have always thought it a safer place for a woman to walk her dog unchaperoned; compared to, say, Central Park."

"Quite. And you found them where?"

"We were close to the Memorial when Marlon started whining. Pulling at his leash."

The dog looked as if he barely had the strength to pull

45

his shadow along behind him.

"He made a beeline towards one of the park benches then started snuffling underneath it and growling. I knew that something was not right. He tugged it free before I could restrain him, and that's when I saw the bloodstains."

"You picked them up and…"

She wrinkled her face as if a sudden stab of headache had snatched at her cranial nerves.

"I had gloves on, of course, but no. Most definitely not. I pulled Marlon away, gave him a titbit and just kept an eye on them while I called one of your colleagues. The Chief happens to be an old friend. It's just that I was on my way to the University so I couldn't wait around for long. As soon as your officers arrived I gave them my details then had to excuse myself."

"That's fine. We understand."

"I wish I could have been more helpful. It's just, well. It looked like an awful lot of blood to me, you know."

"Yes, we know. But as you'll appreciate, we can't say more at this stage. There's no crime been reported to the best of our knowledge that can be linked to what you found. It might just be kids fooling around."

Iversen stepped forward and handed her his card. "If anything else comes to mind just telephone me. Any time. Day or night. We're always at your service."

Garcia closed his eyes and took a deep breath as he began to count to ten.

"You did the right thing. You didn't go through the pockets or anything?"

"Good gracious me, of course not. Whatever do you take me for, young man?"

BACK on the street Garcia relit his half-chewed cigar as he prepared for the drive downtown.

"Your knight in shining armour act didn't go down too well back there. What were you looking to do? Score brownie points with the Chief's lady friend?"

Iversen's face flushed briefly. "No. Just being polite, that's all. So what do you reckon? Are we dealing with a homicide?"

Garcia let out a huff of blue smoke.

"Maybe. Maybe not. Somebody losing that amount of blood, you have to expect the worst."

Iversen flashed a smile like a shark scenting blood. "So we might get lucky and have a body turn up."

Garcia grunted but didn't share his partner's twisted optimism. Sometimes he hated his job.

CHAPTER 7

08:15 and my bedroom still held faint traces of that nightmare. Like black cobwebs you might see in one of those spooky houses in horror movies. Though they were more like floating flecks of charred paper from a bonfire than spiders' webs. I fought my way through the haze to reach my bedroom window. I was desperate to open it wider, to let out the smell of sleep. The stench of damp air and stale body odour was everywhere. On my skin. In my hair. I needed a shower sometime soon.

But first I stared down into our street, lazily scratching at my belly and trying to bite back a yawn. It felt as if a twister had blown through the house and turned everything on its head while I slept. But out there nothing had changed. Everything still looked completely normal.

Inside my room it was different. The sensation of someone's hands around my throat, salt drying on my skin. I itched all over as if I had heat rash and I was expecting my blood-sugar level to be all over the place. But when I checked it wasn't much higher than normal. I went into the bathroom, had a wee and took my insulin jab then tiptoed downstairs in search of some breakfast.

It was still early for a Sunday but Mum was already up, sitting at the kitchen table in her dressing gown, nursing a mug of black coffee and gazing into space.

I pecked her on the cheek. She hadn't washed all of last night's make-up off her face properly so I assumed it really had been a late one.

"Were you ok last night? Sleep any better?"

"Better? What do you mean?"

She seemed to be searching my face for clues. "Well, just wondering. Any more nightmares?"

I turned my back on her and opened the fridge door –

48

in raptures as the cold sucked all the heavy heat from my body and wiggling my bare feet on the cool floor as I savoured the blissful moment.

"No. But I kept waking up. It was so hot, that's all."

"It was."

"And I kept tossing and turning."

"I know. Me and your dad were the same. We just couldn't get off to sleep."

I filled a drinking glass with cold milk and decided I needed more than just a soothing blast of arctic air.

"I could do with a quick shower. Is Dad getting up?"

"God, no. He had a bit too much to drink last night. He was snoring like a chainsaw when I got up to go to the loo. I've left him to it."

"Good."

"Anything special planned for today?"

I had no idea.

"Mooching about here I suppose. Finishing my homework."

I still felt shell-shocked by the dream, if that's what it was. I wasn't too keen on going out anywhere.

"Well, we're going to see Nana Mac after lunch. Thought we better had seeing as she's feeling poorly, but you don't have to come if you don't want to."

"Ok. I'll see."

I had other things planned so it was unlikely I'd be joining them. It was time to sort out this Levi business once and for all.

CHAPTER 8

REUBEN Garcia's hangover was the real thing. Not a hazy impression of dark cobwebs, charred newspaper and stale air but a pounding throb at the back of each eyeball. Too much beer and bourbon the previous night and a crowded bar filled with the fug of cigarettes and cheap cigars.

Now a familiar buzzing sound added to the feeling of nausea. He checked the display on his cell phone. 04:17. It could only be bad news.

"Garcia."

"Reub. It's Karl. Sorry to disrupt your beauty sleep but there's a body turned up that might be the one. A young girl. Looks like our runaway."

"Right."

He could picture the excitement on the young detective's face. Relishing the role of senior officer on a homicide scene for once.

"Not gang-related according to the uniforms. Superficial cuts to her body and a plastic bag tied over her head. Looks no more than twelve or thirteen."

"You still there now?"

"Yeah, but I'm heading back to the station. The blue van's just turned up so we're about done here. Just thought I'd let you know."

"Ok. Let me wake up properly and I'll meet you in about an hour."

IVERSEN took out his spiral-bound notebook and read through his notes.

"Levi Washington. 15 years 10 months. Reported missing 17th of May. Her mom called it in."

"Have her folks been informed?"

50

"There's a patrol car from 26th on the way there now."

"26th?"

"It's just a courtesy thing – they're calling to inform the mom because that's where she reported her missing."

"Fine. Who d'you say's doing the P M?"

"Gina Harper. Said she'll let us know soon as she's taken a closer look. Tuesday morning at the earliest, she reckons. She thinks the cuts to the body were done a couple of weeks before the kid died. All the signs point to death by asphyxiation."

"And we're pretty sure it's this Levi kid?"

"Everything matches the description. Just need her parents to confirm the identity."

Iversen passed his partner a matchbook-sized photograph of a young girl. It had been taken in one of those cheap photo-booths they have at most subway stations. Her dark hair tied up in a top-knot with cornrows either side. Eyes alive with mischief. An obvious overbite made her look younger despite a sloppy attempt at applying lipstick. Still naive enough to care about her appearance yet not bother checking her handiwork too closely.

"God, what a way to spend a Sunday. Who found her?"

"Someone reported a body in the river at 02:05 this morning – college students on their way back from a late-night party. A Matthew Fraggard, his date Simone something-or-other, some fancy French name, and another girl, Amy Grossman. They'd taken a short cut to the river because this Amy had to stop and take a leak. She finds a spot between the rocks and just as she's about to pee she sees this body at the edge of the water."

"Ouch."

"Yeh. She freaked out. By the time the squad car

turned up the three of them had sobered up and were pretty much desperate to get home. Their statements all match up. We'll probably need to check with the frat house where the party was held. But if the three left close on 01:30 that just gives them half an hour to walk the distance and stumble across the body."

Garcia passed the photo back to his colleague.

"Been dead long?"

"Gina estimates less than 24 hours. But like I say, she's not started working on the body yet. Forensics did a quick ground search but it looks as if the girl was killed elsewhere then dumped. Still wearing the same underwear as her mother reported. Looks skinnier, but we have to assume she's been living on the streets for the last month or so."

"Is that what you really think?" Garcia's voice a growl.

"I'm just saying. She was reported missing end of May. So..."

"But where was she heading?"

"Supposed to be on her way to a special, out-of-hours English class. Public School 180. Down on West 120th. Not that far from where she was found. Not the brightest candle in church, but a good girl her mom said."

"So there's your first clue. Not the kind of kid to suddenly take it into her head to run away from home, was she?"

52

CHAPTER 9

I knew all about 'Wikipedia' and 'Google'. Every kid with a laptop and homework to do sooner or later knows how they both work. But Dad had loaded 'Google Earth' as well – which is really cool because you can actually visit anywhere on the planet. Pretend you're flying overhead or even driving down some of the streets. Our house is on it with Dad's van parked on the road outside. You can actually see him in our front garden talking to Mr Dawson next door – on display for everybody in the world. I was tickled pink when I spotted them.

There's the flats where Nana Crozier lives on Morningside with a gang of lads hanging round on one of the corners. One looks like Kenzie, Aleesha's brother. But it's not that easy to tell because the face is blurred out. Stacey's bungalow on Dulwich Drive on the other side of the golf course looks a bit dingy because the pictures were taken before they had their new conservatory and block paving done. Her mum and dad must be gutted.

But I hadn't gone on here to nose around even though I just love it. I was curious about Harlem.

I was wondering if I could 'Google Earth' it and find
a) if there was such a place, and
b) whether I'd recognise it.

So once I'd put clean sheets on my bed, had my shower, got dressed and had some toast and peanut butter, I announced I was going upstairs to do my homework. Which is what this was in a way.

I typed in the word '**Harlem**'. Not expecting to find much, if I'm being truthful.

But I did. I found more than I had bargained on, and it gave me a bit of a shock. Suddenly I understood why I'd been having those weird dreams. It all made sense in a creepy kind of way. The dreams had begun round about the same time I'd started chatting to Stefan.

Stefan, a hairy, 23 year old guy who lives in the Netherlands, who has a thing for young girls, knows my name, where I'm from. What size bra I wear for God's sake. He had to be involved in it somehow but I couldn't figure out why. Levi was trying to warn me in her own way, bless her. There was the evidence right in front of my eyes.

'Haarlem : The Netherlands'

CHAPTER 10

THE following week began a little more calmly. No more dreams. Just a niggling feeling at the back of my mind that this Levi business wasn't over with. Not yet.

I'd finally got round to phoning Stacey on Sunday evening. She was quite chatty because I'd not seen her since Tuesday afternoon. Bragging about her wild weekend as usual. I told her about the nightmares in passing. About waking up with that weird voice in my head. And how I thought Levi might have been murdered. I mentioned Stefan as well – told her how I'd met him on some internet site and was beginning to think that he might be a little creepy.

I'll admit I didn't go into much detail. Didn't tell her I'd given him my life story.

Stacey spends hours on the internet. She's forever on Facebook. So I suppose I was expecting her to laugh and tell me to stop being such a drama queen. But instead she got quite snotty. Asked me if I was trying to attract everybody's attention. Because it was so obvious I was making it up. I would have told Mum and Dad if I was really serious about any of it – or even the police.

I let her go on a bit longer then said I was tired and had to get ready for bed. I assumed it was her way of getting back at me because I can't be doing with writing stupid online comments to people I see most days in school anyway – reading every single tweet detailing their boring existence from dawn 'til dusk.

Anyway, I couldn't go to the police and tell them I'd had a dream about some girl who I believe has been murdered in Haarlem. They would think I was some loony. And how could I tell Mum and Dad I'd been in a chat room flirting with a 23 year old guy? I mean, what would Stacey have done if she was in my shoes?

Exactly.

TUESDAY after school Mum took me to see Dr Kerr. Even though my bruise had pretty much faded away she still wanted to be on the safe side. If you ask me she makes too much fuss about my diabetes.

I had to take the usual sample of my wee as well. Ick. And I took my Diabetes Diary where I log all my daily blood-sugar levels. Sometimes I feel like a clapped out car that has to be serviced every few months just to keep running.

Anyway, he said my glucose levels seemed to be under control despite one or two highs. Then he took some blood as well and said that everything looked ok. Said if I noticed any other signs of fresh bruising I should get in touch, but as far as he could tell there was nothing to worry about.

ON Wednesday afternoon Stacey started having a right go at me after school in front of Leslie and Trudy. Asked me if I'd been sexting more perverts recently. I told her no. But she kept going on about what a loser I was. It made me feel like it was my first week at Pentland all over again. The older girls picking on me just because they could. Five foot seven in my wedges suddenly cut down to a measley six inches. Three against one. In the end I told her to do one. She gave me a bit of a pitying look and I could hear the three of them having a right laugh – high-fiving each other as they set off towards home. As if I care.

I hung around the gates for about five minutes until I was sure they were gone. A nervous feeling that they were out there waiting for me. Or someone else maybe, waiting to grab me and carry me off goodness knows where.

THURSDAY band practice was cancelled because Mr Butterfield was away on a course which was a bit yawn. Then Friday after school I went swimming with Mum and Aunty Grace. Farran's mum. She never has much to say about Farran any more. I suppose she's used up all the words she can – making excuses for a daughter running away from home at 17, living in a squat with some dope-dealer and turning into a heroin addict. Mum tries to take her out as often as she can: shopping, keep-fit or just for a coffee. But she always looks as if it's her fault Farran turned out the way she did.

 I normally love swimming. But this Friday. Huh. I freaked out. I've no idea why, but as soon as I got near the deep end I felt all the strength go out of my arms and legs. Like air let out of a tyre. I couldn't keep my eyes and nose above water. Didn't even try to. I sank. No attempt to save myself. Shapes coiling on the currents, reaching out for me like the tendrils of some sea creature. A smell of salt water not chlorine. Something dark over my eyes. That familiar tightness around my throat. And fingers scratching at the plastic bag covering my face. Levi's bone-white fingers. I gagged as my mouth filled with her scream, and… thrashed to the surface desperate for air.

 No one noticed a thing. Mum and Aunty Grace splashing away in the shallow end with not a care in the world. Some kid with goggles and freckles giving me a funny look as I climbed onto the edge of the pool. I sat with my feet clear of the water, blew air from my nostrils and tried to wipe the memory from my stinging eyes. It had felt like someone else was in control of my body. Somebody else controlling my mind.

SATURDAY morning Stacey phoned me, said I was forgiven for being a mardy bitch, and asked me if I wanted to go up town with her after lunch to help her choose some new outfits for her holidays. I'd rather have stayed home. Somewhere I could feel safe. The thought of going outside and possibly having another funny turn terrified me. But she twisted my arm in the end. Said some retail therapy would cheer me up. Of course, she just wanted to show off how much spending money she had. She was off to the Canaries for ten days at the end of July. I suppose I'll be off to the caravan at Dunbar with the rents. But I don't mind really. I just wonder whether Shona will be coming with us this year. Somehow I think not. It'll be dead without her.

SATURDAY night I finally did what I'd been thinking about doing all week. After getting changed for bed I decided to get back in touch with Stefan. If he was still in circulation. There was a chance he might ignore me anyway. He probably thought I was just another stupid kid messing him about for a dare maybe, not too fussed about keeping in touch even though I promised I would.

I hung around for nearly twenty minutes watching the electronic blether spill across the screen of my laptop like dirty dishwater. There was a lot of really mean stuff – boys saying they would wank off on their webcams if any girl wanted to watch. And a girl called *missymeow* saying she'd do the same for any guy who wanted to join her on yahoo. It was all so sordid.

Then out of the blue…

Duke_$ would like to chat with pinky

There he was. I didn't give it a second thought.

ACCEPT

Duke_$	so hi ruby
	how r u tonite
pinky	im good really good
	thought you might have forgot me
Duke_$	hehe of course not
	so how have you been?
pinky	v busy in school
	studying 4 exams
Duke_$	ok - I also have exams
	which finish next week
pinky	right
	so you aren't out tonight
	with yr friends
Duke_$	not tonight
	I stay home to study
	have a little drink
	perhaps a smoke later
	chat to my friend ruby
pinky	hehe
	don't really like smoke
Duke_$	it's just a little weed
	you know what that is
pinky	drugs
Duke_$	yes
	it is no big deal
pinky	really???

Duke_$	but no
	there are many cafes here
	where you can smoke openly
	or even buy cookies
	with hash inside them
pinky	wow

A weirdo and a druggie as well. I knew I should get out of there, but he was like a toothache to me. I just had to keep probing my tongue against the nerve until the pain was so overwhelming that I'd get the message to stop.

pinky	so you like smoking weed
Duke_$	it helps me to relax
	chill out
	you know chill out?
pinky	yes - that's what I do
	to my music sometimes
Duke_$	that's a good way too
	just lying in bed
	smoke a little bit
	you know - with not a thought
	in your head - floating
pinky	right
Duke_$	don't you do that
pinky	OMG no
Duke_$	hehe
	I mean lie in bed
	just relaxing
pinky	sometime
	and empty my mind
	coz theres not much in there
	lol

Duke_$	hehe
	so tell me ruby
	are you in bed right now?
pinky	yes

My built-in creep radar knew how his mind worked. I could sense he was more interested in what I was doing than in chilling out. It was a wee bit scary. This man so focussed on a strange girl he had never met. Never would get to meet. Yet it made me feel I was in control of things as well. The power I had over him gave me a thrill, to be honest.

Duke_$	and what are you wearing
pinky	just my t-shirt
Duke_$	right
	nothing at all underneath
	so it is hot with you also is it
pinky	has been, yes

Hot? I could feel my face burning up just waiting for what he was probably going to ask me next. He was such a sleazebag. I can't imagine why I found him so charming the first time we chatted.

| Duke_$ | do you have windows messenger |

Do I what?

Duke_$	on your computer
	it's a program
	I use for live chat

Live chat? Gulp.

Duke_$	it is better than this
	chatroom
	more private
pinky	no
Duke_$	you should try it out
	it is free
	then maybe we could chat with each other
	whenever we want to
pinky	is that what you want?

So much for being in control of the situation. I felt like a puppet – with someone else controlling my brain and my movements all over again. Mental or what? My eyes glazed over as he told me what I had to do. Meaningless words appeared on the screen. Letter by letter as his fingers tapped on his keyboard. Fingers that could crush my throat as easy as wringing out a dishcloth.

Duke_$	do you have an e-mail address
pinky	mhmm yeh
Duke_$	good - you will need that
pinky	ok
Duke_$	then once you have an account
	you will need my e-mail address
	to add me as a contact

I was getting increasingly out of breath. Praying there'd be a power-cut or something so he would just clear off.

| Duke_$ | dukes@spazmoid.nl |

It had to be some kind of trap. I scribbled it on the back of my magazine anyway but I had no intention of ever using it. It all sounded pretty bogus. As if he was just trying to get hold of my e-mail address so he could find out where I actually lived and other stuff like that. Like one of those computer hackers who send you spam and steal your bank account. Or worse.

pinky   I can do all that tomorrow
             and then perhaps we can chat again
             tomorrow night
Duke_$ yes for sure
             you know ruby
             you never have to do anything on here
             you don't want to
             you know that don't you
pinky   spose

But I didn't. I was floundering in the deep end again with something covering my head and a couple of lead weights round my ankles. There was no way I could handle all this new stuff right now.

Duke_$ sweet ruby
             let's just chat for now
             you don't have to change anything for me
pinky   ok then
Duke_$ so what did you do today
pinky   went to town
             shopping with stacey
             got some new clothes
             for the summer
Duke_$ girls like to shop
pinky   mhmm
             but I only spent like 18£
Duke_$ ok - is that not very much

	I guess no
	so what did you buy
pinky	oh just a summer top
	yellow with a lacy panel
	and a swiming costume in the sale
Duke_$	very nice
	a teeny bikini???
pinky	OMG!
	never!!!
	Its a 2pce but the bottoms are like shorts
Duke_$	you look very sexy
	in them I am sure
pinky	hehe
Duke_$	what colour
pinky	blue and orange
	a bit dazzly
Duke_$	sounds cool
	I can just see you in my head
	walking on a beach
pinky	ooh
Duke_$	I am just teasing
	I am sure you look very pretty
pinky	well - I don't know
Duke_$	it would be good to have
	a picture of you wearing them
	perhaps one day
pinky	right

In your dreams, slug-brain. What a creep. He had no shame.

Duke_$	it is good you got in touch
	so is there anything
	you wanted to ask me

64

I couldn't think. I wanted to get away from him to be honest but I didn't want to seem rude.

pinky	your name Duke_$
	are u really a duke?
Duke_$	hehe - nonono
	it is after a part of Netherlands
	where I grew up as a boy
	Duketown
	what we also call
	's-Hertogenbosch
pinky	yikes
	is that German
Duke_$	hehe
	no it is Dutch
	what we speak over here
pinky	oh. course
Duke_$	it means
	Woodland of the Duke you see
	very pretty countryside
pinky	but you live in Amsterdam now
Duke_$	one of my sisters and her family
	she still lives there
	but I live closer to my college
	in the north
	about 100 Km away
	a place called haarlem

And that's when I shut the lid of my laptop. I know you're not supposed to turn it off like that because it could crash or something. But he'd more or less admitted it. He had to be behind all this Levi stuff. Suddenly my bedroom felt colder than the coldest Arctic night. Cold enough even for Pablo my cuddly bear to shiver under all his fur.

Stefan was someone who could kill without a second thought. He was nothing less than a cold-blooded monster. A drug-fuelled fiend who had probably met poor Levi in one of these chat rooms, found out where she lived then murdered her. And now he had me in his sights.

CHAPTER 11

GARCIA stood watching the tide wash over the rocks at the Hudson's edge. The only thing left to mark what had happened was a ribbon of crime scene tape flapping in the breeze. Snatching at the passing squalls as it tried to break free of its moorings.

Behind him the weight of his promise seemed to hang above the buildings like a thundercloud. All those skyscrapers and apartment blocks and congested streets and traffic. All that humanity prowling to make a living. He didn't know where to begin to look.

They'd visited Levi's family late Tuesday evening after the post mortem was completed. Garcia warned Iversen not to repeat his super-hero act – but for once his partner was subdued. Both disheartened as they watched the young girl's family disintegrate before their eyes. The silence filling their apartment like contagion. Only the older sister, Effie, was coherent enough to verify the information they were after.

Levi was a good kid. A little slow off the mark when it came to schooling, and as snarky as any teenager when she wanted to be. But there were no boys on the scene. Not in that way. No rows at home. Nothing that could have made the family suspect her disappearance had been voluntary.

"She was snatched, Mr Garcia. Der ain't no other word for it. Somebody snatched ma baby sistah and killed her for no reason an' we ain't never gonna see her again."

And so he'd promised. Promised he would find whoever was responsible. Find them and remove them from the streets forever. It was the least he could do. But five days later and they were no nearer catching anyone. Iversen had visited the school and spoken to her teachers and friends. Garcia had organized squad cars to canvass the stores and offices between Lennox Avenue and Riverside. But it was hopeless. No one reported seeing the girl. She was just another blank face in the crowd.

The river always looked most sinister at this time of night. Dark shapes coiling beneath its surface like tendrils from some malignant growth desperate to reach dry land and claim Garcia as its prey. He wondered what kind of creature could evolve that would do such a thing to an innocent young girl. It had to be a man. But as the lights came on behind him illuminating every window from Manhattan to Union City across the water, his promise grew bitter in his mouth. Over eight million people in New York city alone. How could he find one man amongst all of them?

His only hope was that the murderer might strike again. Leave a clue – something new for them to work with. But he cursed the thought the moment it came to mind. The last thing he wanted on his conscience was another dead girl.

DREAMGIRL

GIRL TWO

CHAPTER 12

THE school holidays started quietly – rather boring actually because Lucy was working most days and Stacey was away on her holiday in the sun. Even though I don't see as much of her as I used to, Stacey's always the one I phone for the latest goss. And although Shona was back home for the summer she was hardly ever in. Too busy catching up with her old school mates, giving them all the dirt on her love life in Leeds.

Lucy had mentioned we could meet up whenever I wanted something to do. Perhaps go into town with her even. But when she wasn't stuck behind the till in Lochend newsagents she was usually with Casey. Her ned of a boyfriend. Still, I figured that she might enjoy a little female company. Someone to chat with between snogging the face off him and struggling to keep his hands under control.

So Friday morning I sent her a text asking if we could meet up later. She said it was her afternoon off so she'd be waiting for me at the Park any time after six. Although I'd mentioned to Mum that I was meeting one of my friends in town I didn't tell her it was Lucy. Mum thinks she's a bad influence. Which I suppose she is. She told me to make sure I was home by half eight and to take my mobile with me and ring her if I needed picking up.

I put on my glittery denim shorts and a new blue sleeveless top. I also took my little back-pack with a water bottle, my mobile, some bits of emergency make-up and my rations. In case I have a hypo or something. That's when my blood-sugar suddenly gets too low. I could collapse into a coma. So I never go anywhere without a bar of chocolate: something sweet. If I need a sudden sugar boost I'm prepared.

Lochend Road isn't that rough even though the council flats look pretty grotty from the outside. Lucy lives with her mum on the second floor overlooking Lochend Park so they've got a nice view over the pond and the trees. It took me about half an hour to walk there from our house and she was waiting for me by the park railings, grinning like a loon as usual.

"Hi girlfren. You look amazin', doll."

I felt a bit bare but it had been such a lovely sunny afternoon. She was all covered up in baggy tracky bottoms and a grey NEW YORK CITY t-shirt.

"Thanks. I'm tryin' to get a tan."

"Ho. Should do same as me, gurl. Get it from a bottle."

We went through the gates and crossed the wooden causeway onto the island at the far end of the park where most of the ducks are. There's even swans out there sometimes.

"So whatchu bin up to?"

"Not much. An' you?"

"Still workin' ma butt off. Went to the arcade with Leesha this afto. She an' Lauren an' Zoey come to the Youthy las' night. Good laugh, I tell ya. You should hang round wiv us more."

That was unlikely to happen seeing as I had to be home by nine most nights before I turned into a pumpkin.

"Caseeeeeey!"

Lucy screaming at the top of her voice as soon as she saw the group of boys sat at the water's edge.

I recognised the other two schemies with Casey. John Kerr or Jaker, Aleesha's on/off boyfriend. And Midgey Garrett who got suspended from Pentland last term for trying to set fire to some lockers. They were passing round a green bottle and I could see a couple of empties on the grass nearby.

71

Casey leapt up and ran to meet Lucy, wrapping his arms round her like an octopus. It made my flesh crawl watching his hands as they grabbed her butt and started squeezing her bum cheeks together. She didn't seem to mind one bit.

The two by the pond looked as if they'd like to do the same to me. One gave a wolf-whistle and the other started eyeing me up making me feel totally creeped out.

Lucy finally wriggled free of Casey's tentacles and crouched down alongside the neds.

"Hi, hen. Come an' sit wi us."

"Leave her, Jaker."

"Ye gaunnae rest yir arse next tae mine, ur ye?" Midgey. Scrawny as a skeleton and stinking of cigarettes.

I gave them both a wide berth and settled next to Lucy, my feet inches above the waterline.

"Any ay youse want some Buckie?"

Jaker passed the bottle of Buckfast to Lucy. She took a swig then passed it back.

"What aboot the wee lass?"

She looked at me. I shook my head.

"She can't. Medical reasons."

Midgey sniggered. "No expectin', is she?"

"Shut it, you pillock. It's diabetes. She's not allowed anything with sugar in it."

Well that wasn't strictly true, but who cares?

"Och, I get it. Some stupid girly diet she's oan? Ye're awright as ye are, pet. Fine pair ay tits an' a nice wide arse."

"It's nothing like that," I snapped. "Alcohol would really screw me up."

"Huh. That's the general idea, pigeon."

I didn't respond to their pathetic laughter. I was debating whether or not to tell Lucy I was going to

72

disappear. Leave her to hang around with these douches if that's what she really wanted. I had better things to do. Though I had no idea what.

Then Casey squeezed in between us, took a tin from his jacket pocket, removed a roll-up cigarette, tapped it on the lid, lit it up and passed it round.

"Who's first on?"

Jaker took a drag before passing it to Midgey. Lucy was last in the queue. I could sense she was on edge. She held it between her fingers, sucked really slow and held in the smoke for as long as she could. Finally she removed it and looked at me, face tilting to one side with a huge grin that looked in danger of sliding off the edge of it.

"Ye wanna drag, Junk?"

I don't smoke. Never even tried it. Couldn't see the point.

"No ta."

"Just have one puff. Go on. It'll help ye chill out. I'm tellin' ya, girlfren, ye need to loosen up."

Lucy's eyes were bulging and her voice sounded like she'd developed asthma all of a sudden. It dawned on me what it was they were smoking. Chilling out. I thought back to what Stefan had said.

"It is no big deal."

Mum and Dad would kill me for sure if they ever found out, but I didn't want to look like a total loser. I swallowed hard and reached across for the spliff, being extra careful not to squash it in case it fell apart. The end was all soggy with everybody else's spit. What the hell.

The four of them laughed as I raised it to my lips.

"Is thit yer first, is it?"

Lucy nodded, laughing the loudest. "Oh yeh. Rube the nube."

I didn't give a shit. I was right there. Sprawling on the sloping paving slabs at the water's edge. Flecks of sunlight sparkling on the ripples between my feet. A starry sky lost underwater. Bliss in an instant.

The buzz inside my head grew in intensity and before I knew it my fingers had hold of the joint again. I sucked at it like a baby at her mother's breast. A long, long suck like I'd watched the others doing. Heavy warmness infiltrating my brain and sweetness and claustrophobia. I reached down to unfasten my trainers. Whoah. They seemed a hell of a long way down. Then I slipped my feet out of them and rolled off my sports socks.

"Rubes?"

My eyes locked onto Lucy's.

"What ye doin', gal?"

"She looks like she's gettin' ready tae hoof it across the pond."

I grinned like some cartoon character. That wasn't such a bad idea.

I slid my toes into the water and wriggled them. I was filled to bursting with giggles but managed to keep everything under control until it was my turn yet again. This time I began to cough, and the cough became a laugh that didn't seem as if it was ever going to end.

I had escaped into a loop where time kept repeating itself. The wind had picked up as the shadows lengthened but I was in my element. I was a mermaid on the beach at Dunbar. I had no feet any more since they had disappeared under water. My legs had shrunk to half their length beneath the surface and swelled up like pink balloons. What was that all about?

Casey had one of his hands down the back of Lucy's trackies but he wasn't doing anything else as far as I could see. Lucy was too spaced out to be bothered either way.

The two neds were steaming with drink and deep in conversation about football.

I took my mobile out of my back-pack. 20:47. The numbers didn't signify much but I knew I was seriously late.

"I've so gotta go," I muttered.

Some bloke walked past with a dog. Tut-tutting at the very thought of us being there. Jaker and Midgey had started skimming stones across the water, whooping with delight then arguing about which one had travelled the greatest distance. Jaker gave the old tosser the finger and told him to keep his neb out. I shrieked with laughter, Lucy giving me a funny look as if to say 'what the hell you doing?'

I scrabbled for my socks, making sure they weren't inside out. For some reason it became absolutely essential that they were not.

"Oh, God." I was having a crisis of confidence with my skids. I'd managed to get them on without too much effort but the sequence of tying laces baffled me.

Lucy could see I was struggling.

"Let me. Ye lean or what?"

I bit back a fresh snigger. The shit I was about to get from my mum and dad would be unreal.

"We'll walk ye back home."

"Nah, it's ok."

Having Lucy and the living dead stroll up to our front door in that state would make matters infinitely worse.

"Rubes, ye can't even find ya left tit let alone ya way home."

In the end she and Casey escorted me as far as the golf course. Every step I took I could feel my feet flopping as if they were attached to my ankles by bands of elastic.

"Ye gonna be ok from here, doll?"

I nodded. I could see our house.

"Course."

Dad's van wasn't parked outside. With a bit of luck everybody would be in the pub and I could sneak inside and go straight to bed. God, I needed to lie down so badly. I opened my back pack and fished out the front door key.

"Take care then, honeybunch." She gave me a hug and a smooch on the lips.

I could hear them both laughing like a mob of seagulls as I trekked up the path to our front door – an uphill struggle all the way to our porch. Miraculously the key fitted in the lock and I managed to open the door, sure-fingered as a safe-cracker.

I let my back-pack drop by the bottom of the stairs and skited across the laminated floor in the direction of the kitchen.

"Wee-ee!"

I was absolutely gasping. My tongue was Velcroed to the roof of my mouth and my teeth were all furred up. The tap was running and my mouth positioned beneath the spout before Shona caught me.

"God, you're lucky Mum and Dad are out. Where the hell you been 'til now?"

I raised my face from the sink. Cold water spilled down my chin, soaking the front of my top, running down my neck and underneath my bra.

I just grinned at her. I couldn't help myself. She looked so serious. She leant in closer and grabbed me by the shoulder so hard it actually hurt.

"Hey, let go!"

"I don't believe this. You been on the booze?"

I tried to pull loose but she had a steel grip.

"You friggin' silly bitch – are you mental or what?"

76

"What d'you mean?"

"I can smell it on you."

"Smell what? I've not had any booze. What you on about?"

"Weed. I can smell it. An' look at your eyes. Been smokin' weed haven't you?"

How could she tell?

"No."

She shook me as if the truth would eventually spill out of me if she continued long enough.

"Ok ok. Leave me. We were only messin' about."

"Messing about? For God's sake. Messing with your life. You should know better."

I just laughed in her face.

"Look at the state of you. Shit, if Mum or Dad saw you like this they'd be thinking you were going into a hypo. They'd be stuffing you full of sugar. For God's sake Rube, use your pot noodle."

"I only had two or three puffs."

"You can't kid me. You're completely off your head. Look at you. You floated in here like some bloody hippy-chick."

I snorted another fresh laugh. I just had to.

"It's not funny. Risking your health for a couple of minutes of happy hippy dippy feelings. After all we've done for you."

That was like a cold slap with a wet flannel. The warm misty veils of sugary dreams temporarily parted. What did any of this have to do with her anyway? It was my life, my body. I can do what I want with it.

"Oh, get a life."

"Get? A? Life?"

"You've made your point, ok. You're worse than Mum."

77

"Can't you see what a stupid stupid thing you did?"

"S'pose."

I was becoming fed up with Shona's finger-up-her-own-bum attitude.

"Just go upstairs and get changed."

"What for?"

"Cos that top's soaked through. And it stinks of you know what. If Mum and Dad get wind of what you've been up to you'll be grounded for the rest of the summer."

"You gonna tell them then?"

"What do you think?"

"You probably will, knowin' you."

"Well I'm not. Besides, they'll want to know how I recognised the signs. Just shift yer arse."

She helped me tug off my trainers. Lucy had done a double knot and there was no way either of us had the patience to unfasten them.

"How come your socks are all soakin' wet?"

"No idea."

She followed me upstairs like some nanny putting a naughty child to bed.

"I can manage you know."

"Yes, sure. 'Course you can."

"How do you know what weed smells like anyway?"

"I see enough dope-heads in Leeds, Rube."

"I bet you've tried it an' all."

"Don't push your luck, lady."

"You have though, haven't you?"

"No way. Somebody offered me a drag once outside 'Phrenzy'. But the smell made my stomach heave."

Well I'd enjoyed it, even though I should have known better and felt a bit sick now. I propped myself against the door frame as the cloud base slid down below my ears again like a woolly hat a couple of sizes too big.

78

"Hey, are you still with us?"

"Just leave me alone."

"Not 'til you get out of them clothes and put somethin' dry on."

Cow. I fumbled with my belt buckle but couldn't make head or tail of the mechanics so I just peeled off my top and let it fall to the floor.

"Shona?" I sniggered.

"Yesss."

"Have you done it? You know..."

"I already told you. No way."

"No. I mean... you know? Shagged?"

That stopped her in her tracks.

"What the hell business is that of yours?"

"Just wondered, that's all."

Her face was a picture.

"Well, keep your nose out."

"Heeheehee. You have. I can tell."

"I'm warning you."

"'Cause you didn't say 'no' right away. Anyway, Leesha MacKenzie's done it an' she said it wasn't such a big deal."

"Does Mum know you hang around with trash like that?"

"So did you like it?"

"I said, that's enough. Mum and Dad'll be back any minute. I'll get your nightie and some clean underwear."

"'Cause I think I will when I eventually do it. I'm going to find a boyfriend this summer. Deffo."

"Ok. But first things first. I think you'd better get in the shower. Bring you back to your senses and wash away that ruddy smell. It's even in your hair."

"No way. I'm ok."

"No you're not. Come on. Let me give you a hand."

"I can manage for God's sake."

"Yes. I can see that."

"Shona! Leave me." She had already unclasped the belt on my shorts and unbuttoned the top. "You're just a secret lezzie."

"That's right."

She picked up my top off the floor as I slid my socks off.

"Come on. I said everything. I'll stick it all in the wash."

"An' you're a perv an' all."

"Ok. In that case."

"Gerroff."

The next thing she was attacking me and I ended up in a helpless heap on the floor. Shona tickling my ribs until I begged her to stop. Eventually she let me go and disappeared downstairs with my clothes. I dashed into the bathroom and got under the shower. She'd said she'd give me ten minutes max before switching the washing machine on.

I didn't need ten minutes.

Within five I was out, dried and dressed for bed.

Within ten I'd tested my blood and taken my injection for the night ahead, sneaked into the kitchen for a couple of wholemeal crackers and a smoothie and was under the duvet.

Within fifteen I was back at Lochend Park with Lucy and the guys. We all had our shoes off and were wiggling our toes in the water, giggling like a bunch of loons. Casey was sat right next to me, his left arm around my shoulder and his right hand inside my top. He was stroking my skin but really slow. I could feel his cold, claw-like fingers tracing the curve of each rib, kneading the thicker roll of flesh where I normally inject, his palm sliding across my belly then a finger trying to find a way inside the waistband of my pants.

"I'm Cody... low... pairs..."
The girl was standing there right in front of us upon the grey, rippling surface of the pond. Skinny and cold looking, dressed in a faded green cotton slip and pink woolly ankle socks. The sun was behind her, as was the silhouette of the trees and the flats beyond. Each window and gutter and branch and railing showing through her as if she was semi-transparent.

For a moment I struggled to stay balanced on the skin of water then I went under, gagging for breath and fighting to regain the surface. No plastic bag this time. No fingers at my throat. Just a slow, sinking sensation that I could do nothing about.

Then I woke with a huge intake of air. My room was still the same way I'd left it. The glass on the bedside cupboard half full of pink gunge. The plate – two broken crackers and a litter of crumbs evidence of an uncompleted supper. But my lungs ached as if I'd swum a full length of the baths without surfacing.

I sat up and unpeeled my nightgown from my skin. Phew. It was soaked through with sweat. And I could smell my body and all its poisonous secretions. This was another of those dreams. I just knew it.

It took me a while to come to my senses. And when I did. a fresh wave of panic threated to submerge me again. The image of this new girl was imprinted on my brain as if someone had drawn it there in ink. Someone called – Cody – who was waiting to die in Haarlem. No one else knew about her – just me, and Stefan.

81

CHAPTER 13

IT was the back of nine the second time I woke.

I'd put on a clean pair of pj's and dared to sneak into Shona's room with one of my pillows under my arm. 03:19 on my bedside clock. She was fast asleep and for once I don't think she noticed when I sandwiched myself under her duvet. I don't even think she registered the mattress sagging on my side of the bed. No comforting arm around my midriff, no tickle of warm breath on the back of my neck.

"WHEN the hell did you get here?"

She was sitting up with her back against the velvet-covered headboard buffing her fingernails. Wearing a bright yellow, baggy t-shirt I'd never seen before. "Dallas Cowboys" emblazoned across her chest in orange. I was flat on my back, rubbing away the sleep caked in the corner of each eye.

"Don't remember. I woke up in the middle of the night – some bad dream."

"Huh. You surprised?"

"What?"

"Doesn't matter."

I turned my back on her to face the window. I was so not in the mood for another lecture.

"I need my java. Shall I get you something, dope-head?"

I couldn't hold back the grin stretching wide across my face. "Just toast, please."

"Long as you don't get crumbs on my sheets."

"Won't."

I popped to the loo for a wee and to sort out the usual shit then climbed back into Shona's bed.

That dream. That girl.

It was too much like the first one I'd had nearly two months ago to be the after effects of the weed. First Levi, now Cody. It was definitely that Stefan thing again. Finding girls on the internet. Getting his filthy hands on them somehow. And probably killing them once he'd had his bit of fun.

SHONA plugged in her laptop while I nibbled away at my toast and marmalade: shredless of course. I hate the hard skin bits they put in it. Like bright orange toenail clippings.

"Shove over. It's like sharing a bed with a hippopotamus."

"What you doin'?"

"Just checking my e-mails. Keep your neb out."

I laughed. I could tell she had forgiven me for being such a pain in the bum.

I had been so pissed off with her last night for trying to tell me what to do, taking charge just because Mum and Dad were out. But I suppose she didn't have much choice. It could have been a disaster. If I'd passed out or something and everybody thought I was having a hypo – stuffing me with Lucozade or Mars bars because they thought I needed extra glucose – I'd have ended up with too much sugar in my blood and that could be even more serious than too little.

God, I hate this body sometimes. Everybody treating me like I'm some sort of china doll that's going to break as soon as they touch me. I thought back to what Midgey had said.

'Fine pair ay tits an' a nice wide arse.'

That was the real me.

Shona was still busy tapping away.

"You got any?"

"What?"

"Mail."

"Not that much. Just the usual Amazon junk."

I watched her from the corner of my eye. She'd logged in again but there was a new mail box on her screen now. She shrieked with laughter.

"What?"

"Nowt. Just a funny e-mail off a mate."

"Let's see."

"No way. I told you."

I lay on my back again and rested my eyes. "Sho?"

"What?"

"How come you've got two in-boxes for your mail?"

"Just shut up and take your dishes downstairs. I don't want you leaving them here."

I picked up my plate, her empty mug and a couple of dirty cereal dishes plonked on the window sill.

"HI, sweetheart. Have a good time yesterday?"

I kissed Mum and sort of nodded.

"Yeh. It was good."

I busied myself making two fresh coffees. One sugar for me, none for Shona.

"Don't go spilling coffee on the stair-carpet."

"Won't."

"I know you. And you're not both planning on spending the entire day in bed I hope."

WE weren't. It was Saturday and Shona was off out clubbing it with her mates later. Still, it was almost two when we finally emerged. She had spent most of the morning showing me all the clothes she'd bought while she'd been away. Dad would have gone mental if he'd seen half of the stuff she wore in Leeds.

"That's why I need so many part-time jobs," she laughed. "I'm so high-maintenance."

"Is that why you've got so many e-mail accounts as well? Must drive you mad answering them all."

"Not really. Makes life easier, actually."

I wasn't convinced.

"How?"

"It makes everything much more organised, Rubes. See. There's one for you and the rest of the family, as well as my mates back in Edinburgh. Then this one for all my pals in Leeds. And one for private stuff."

She showed me on her laptop

shonam@hotmail.com - showgirl@luvpets.com - syko@mispace.com

"And it's dead easy. I mean, you can open as many accounts as you like, and you don't even have to use your real name and address if you don't want to."

"Private stuff? Is S Y K O supposed to be Psycho?"

"Well, yeh. Psychology student, see. There's this guy I know. He's in his final year. Doin' the same course."

"Uhuh."

"And it's not what you think."

"Whatever."

"It's not."

"I'm not thinking anything, Sho."

"Well, it's not anyway. We're just really good mates, you know? And it is quite normal for a woman and a bloke to be friends without any of that."

"Yeh, I know."

While, of course, I didn't. I'd never thought of things like that. Besides, my mind was already in a whirl – and nothing to do with my new drug habit. I was pondering the possibilities. Possibilities I had never known existed until now.

85

CHAPTER 14

TUESDAY 4th of August, two days before my 16th birthday, Farran, my cousin, was found dead.

Uncle Andrew phoned Mum about half past eleven at night. We'd been watching a DVD – the one with Jennifer Aniston where she plays this woman who pretends to work in an office but is really a con-artist and she starts an affair with a man on a train and then when they're in this hotel room she gets raped by an intruder but the rapist is really her boyfriend and…

Mum's face. That sob she made. I'll probably never forget it for the rest of my life. I couldn't equate that level of grief, appearing out of nowhere, with anything that was a part of my life. Not even Struan dying in his cot. Though I was only six then and pretty much sheltered from it all.

She turned to me and Shona, tears streaming down her face and her lips twisted into a horrid shape. Not the shape those soft lips that had kissed me so many times were supposed to be.

"It's Farran."

And she shut her eyes and shook her head as if she was trying to get rid of the thought from her mind. Make it go away and have life return to how it had been before the phone rang.

Shona jumped up off the sofa and wrapped her arms around her. She looked back towards me then at the telly. Suddenly I was in charge of sound effects. I pressed 'mute' on the remote then decided I'd be better switching it off completely.

A nudge of Shona's head in the direction of the kitchen. Now I was in charge of refreshments. My heart was pounding as I waited for the kettle to boil. I was desperate to know what had happened yet dreading the worst possible news. Arrested again? An overdose? Or had that skanky boyfriend of hers done something to hurt her?

FARRAN had always been such a laugh, and a right tomboy. She'd said she was going to be a fireman when she left school. She was so fit – spent hours in the gym and even did a half marathon while she was in the Sixth form. Then she changed overnight. Left school before sitting her Highers and ran away from home within days.

I used to love it when she came and stayed with us. Sometimes when Shona was away she'd sleep in Shona's bedroom, but she also bunked up with me loads of times. I can remember one time when Shona had gone to Rock-Ness or something like that. We were getting ready for bed, both sharing the sink to brush our teeth, and suddenly instead of having a gargle or rinsing the water out of her mouth properly she kept it in there. Puffed out her cheeks and pressed her lips together and started trying to talk without the water spurting out of her mouth. It sounded hilarious. I ended up doing the same and we kept dashing into my bedroom then back out into the bathroom, mouths full of water and making silly noises 'til we had to spit it all into the washbasin. I've never laughed so much in my life.

AUNTY Grace hugged me for ages and thanked me for being so brave and coming to say goodbye. I couldn't hold back the tears. Shona kept tight hold of my hand during the service then Mum and Dad shepherded us towards our car so we could drive on to the graveyard. Nana Mac, Dad's mother, came with us. Nana Crozier from

Morningside followed the hearse with Aunty Grace and Uncle Andrew in a proper funeral car. It felt weird us all driving so slow down the by-pass.

It was much too lovely a summer's day to be dressed in black, watching a precious, nineteen year old girl's body get stuck inside a hole in the ground. At least her so-called boyfriend had the sense to keep away. She'd died of a heroin overdose. All thanks to him, no doubt. The vicar said something about everlasting peace during the service but what if he was wrong? Grown-ups don't know everything. Hell, I'd figured that out before leaving junior school.

There were about forty people in the cemetery. Not everybody in the church made the journey across town. I recognised most of them. Neighbours. Quite a few from the golf club – Uncle Andrew is like the President there. A few girls that had been in school with Farran. Aleesha's big brother, Kenzie. And Casey: Lucy's Casey. He was standing next to Kenzie, in a proper suit, shirt and tie but they both remained almost hidden out of sight beneath the trees.

We hung around the car park for a bit before heading off to the golf club for some food. People were going up to Mum and Dad to shake hands and give the occasional peck on the cheek. One woman gave me a smacker and Shona half-smiled as she took out her handkerchief to wipe away the lipstick smear left there.

"You doin' ok, Rubes?"

I nodded, still in a daze I guess. It was the first funeral I had ever attended. It was nothing like I had expected it to be. Most people seemed calm, almost resigned to what was happening. Like it was normal. But I couldn't help thinking about how Farran had died all on her own. She'd been dead for more than ten hours, according to Mum, before some guy working on the railway line found her. He said he thought she was sleeping rough. She looked so peaceful. I still wonder what her face would look like: a porcelain doll maybe.

Now I was wondering who would be next to die in our family. Perhaps one of my nanas. Which would be devastating, of course. But it could just as easily be someone younger – dead before their time. Perhaps me or even Shona. I wouldn't want to keep living if she were to go, I really wouldn't.

Two of the girls that had been in Shona's Pilates class came up to her. Group hug.

"Ruby?"

It was Casey, hanging round after most of the crowd had dispersed. I swear he had been waiting to catch me on my own.

"What can ah say, doll? She was a top lassie."

He gave me a hug and a kiss on the side of the head then turned and dashed away as if he suddenly had an urgent appointment to make.

Mum's radar misses nothing. "Mm. Who was that?"

"Oh, just some boy. Erm, he used to come to band practice."

"Aw, he seems nice." Clueless.

"You should have introduced us properly." Shona just as clueless.

I was too overcome by everything to respond coherently. Shona saw the look on my face and held onto me until I finally stopped crying. My tears did dry up eventually. My heart managed to slow its hip hop thudding and my muscles stopped twitching.

"Ok, hon?"

I tried to smile.

"Come on. Let's get you a cup of tea."

God, I hate life sometimes, you know?

MY 16th birthday has to be the worst birthday I ever remember having. Four days before the funeral. Nobody was in the mood for a party anyway, least of all me. And our five day holiday in the caravan at Dunbar for the week after had to be cancelled last minute. To make things worse I'm sure I was starting to suffer PMT – my belly felt like it had a half-inflated netball inside it.

Stacey was back home from Tenerife but she hadn't come near. Even after I texted her to tell her everything that had happened – and to let her know the big party was cancelled. She just sent a pathetic text back.

OK c u round x

Nothing else. I think deep down she was miffed. She never even bothered phoning me or sending a Sympathy card.

So the Saturday after the funeral I decided to hang around the house. Mum was weeding the borders under the window. Dad was giving the works van a wash and I offered to do the car for him. It felt fantastic using the jet-wash and spraying underneath the chassis: the noise and the sensation of all that power coming out of such a tiny nozzle. Shona had gone to stay with one of her friends in Newcastle and wasn't due back until sometime late Sunday or Monday morning. So I felt a bit of a Billy, but it was nice to be home and safe and to have Mum and Dad close at hand.

Dad had set up the barbecue round the back. He even suggested inviting one or two of the neighbours since it was such a lovely day but Mum gave him one of her looks.

"Not this weekend, John, eh?"

90

This was too nice. I almost felt guilty being so contented and relaxed after all that had gone on. I didn't deserve to feel so happy.

THE sun had really caught me. No wonder I expect. I'd been wearing just my new bikini top and skinny shorts since lunchtime. Even though my skin isn't exactly pale my shoulders were sore as well as the backs of both legs.

"I think I'll go up to my room for a lie down."

It wasn't long after nine but I was really knackered. Baked, if you know how that feels.

"Ok, sweetheart. Goodnight."

I was tired but I was also on a hunting mission. It wasn't until the night after Farran's funeral that I decided to open myself a second e-mail account like Shona. I'd entered my user name as Ruby Bradley and made up a fake address in Morningside. I'd even managed to include a proper Edinburgh post code that made it sound real.

dreamgirl@hipdancers.com

It had been easy to set up. Now it was time to return to that chat site and look out for Stefan. He wanted some private chat – well, bring it on.

Except that things didn't go to plan. Not quite. I hung around for half an hour but there was no sign of him. He was either out with his buddies, drinking Belgian beer and smoking spliffs, or he was busy getting rid of Cody's body.

In the end I couldn't keep my eyes open any longer. So I logged out, unplugged and drifted into another troubled sleep.

Of course, the dream this time started with Farran. Lying in that cold coffin with six foot of soil on top of her.

But the longer I stared into her pale, lifeless face, the more certain I became that it was Shona's face staring back at me. Her eyes flicked open then her broken lips tried to speak.

"Cody... low pairs... who Anita..."
None of her words made any sense. It was Cody of course; rising from the grave then standing in front of me. One of her pink socks was missing I could see. She fixed her sunken eyes onto mine and began to lift up the hem of her slip with her free hand. I could see her legs were caked with dirt and one of her knees was scabbed. Then as she raised her slip higher I saw the cuts. Three or four parallel slashes sliced into the flesh of her thighs like stripes. There was even fresh blood trickling from one.
I caught a flash of reflected light off something like a blade and...

I literally ended up leaping out of my bed, wide awake and scared out of my brain. I swear it felt as if the razor had cut into my own flesh, the dream was so real. My left leg stung and I was dreading finding blood and broken skin down there.

04:56. I switched on my bedroom light and sat back on the edge of the mattress. I had on my sloppy t-shirt which is about three sizes too big. I slowly pulled it up. There were two red grooves criss-crossing the inside of my right thigh. As clear as an 'X' written onto a sheet of paper. Not much blood. He hadn't cut deep enough. But it stung. I'd been branded with his mark. His kiss.

God, it was mental. It was like Stefan had seen me on-line and this was his way of sending out a warning. I wasn't the hunter after all. I was another girl he could kill as easy as that.

CHAPTER 15

SOMEHOW I managed to keep my legs covered up all day Sunday without arousing Mum's suspicions. I wore an old pair of tracky bottoms and told her I'd got sunburnt. She offered to rub cold cream on the backs of my legs for me but I told her to stop fussing for once.

I was more freaked out than ever about this latest dream. Imagining Stefan doing things to Cody and me being there. Not just watching what he did but experiencing everything as if it was happening to me as well. Cutting her flesh the way he had. Maybe doing other stuff – like raping her. Then killing her when he'd finished with her body. His tight fingers against her throat. And water all around me. Pulling me down into the dark depths until I joined Farran in her grave.

I didn't even venture out into the garden after lunch.

I spent most of the afternoon messing around with my Kindle – my birthday present off Mum and Dad. Looking what e-books I could get on-line for free. We had this English homework project for the holidays – read a classic novel by a Scottish author then write a report. Mum said I should try something by Sir Walter Scott but I know Mum's taste in reading. Slushy historical romances. No thanks. Dad suggested 'Dr Jekyll & Mr Hyde' because he'd seen the film. So I had a browse on-line, downloaded a copy and gave it a go. It was really hard going but the creepy setting reminded me of that old building where I'd seen Levi. And the first chapter where a child is attacked by some madman gave me the heebie-jeebies. I couldn't stop picturing it in my head.

AFTER tea I went upstairs out of everyone's way. Shona still wasn't back from Newcastle and I wanted to be on my jays anyway. I just sprawled on my bed listening to my iPod. Then I remembered that Shona had left her MP3 player in her room – full of new stuff she'd downloaded. Normally I never go into her room when she isn't here. But Mum had asked me to return that big swivel mirror that we're not supposed to take out of the bathroom. I knew Shona would be ok with me doing that for her.

Of course, I had a little nose while I was in there. Scooshed one or two of her sprays – I always love the way she smells. Clean and fresh. Checked the latest photos on her dressing table mirror – wondering which of the guys snuggled up tight against her was Harvey. They were all hot. That's when I spotted my *Chix17* magazine underneath her laptop. She'd gone and nabbed it without even asking. I'd been looking high and low for it because there was something in it about hair extensions I wanted to read. So much for respecting each other's private property.

I grabbed it and stamped back into my room.

I only skimmed the article in the end. Pretty pointless unless you had loads of funds to spare. I flicked through the rest of the pages, checked the dating adverts inside the back cover for a laugh then let it drop onto the floor. OMG I was sooooo friggggggin' booooooored.

I decided to put my iPod on again but first I had to hunt for my headphone cables that somehow always end up creeping their way under my bed. I couldn't reach them properly. Damn things. I rolled onto my side, stretched out my right arm, and that's when I saw it. What I'd scribbled down on the back cover of the magazine more than two months ago.

dukes@spazmoid.nl

He'd said Messenger was easy enough to set up. But it

took me a couple of goes because I'd not been paying much attention. And it kept asking me if I wanted to install other stuff as well. Well I hadn't got a clue about changing my 'default browser' – or installing a 'Bing bar' whatever that's supposed to be. But finally it came up – a little icon with my pink starburst inside it and my new name 'dreamgirl'. Then I typed in Stefan's e-mail address as one of my contacts and clicked onto it.

It was amazing. Straight away it said he was on-line and even said what he was doing!!! He was listening to a music track by someone called Basshunter.

I typed in my message

    *R   hello it's ruby here

and waited. He didn't take long to answer.

    $*   ruby? well hello.
           I didn't think I'd ever hear from you again.
           How r u?
    *R   ok - sorry I've been away so long
           my laptop crashd last time we were chatting
           I've got a new one for my birthday

That would explain why I'd disappeared so abruptly during our last session together.

    $*   I see -
           well that's ok
           and happy birthday
           ive been away myself for the last few weeks
           so it's good to hear from you
    *R   oh cool - where to?
    $*   hehehe - that's a funny thing you said

	because it was really cool where I went
	you'll never guess
*R	mmm - LA? or NewYork.
$*	no no - I mean really cool like ice cold cool
*R	oh I get it
	erm Iceland
$*	well, that's not a bad guess
	but try the other end of the globe
*R	?
$*	Antarctica
*R	no way
$*	well, very nearly - I was on a five week cruise
	out of Buenos Aires
	with my younger sister Dorothee
	and her husband
	he is an oceanographer
*R	wow
$*	it was winter down there
	so we didn't get very close to the Antarctic Circle
	but we saw some penguins and walruses
*R	OMG
	I would so love to see penguins where they live
$*	I have photos
	I shall send you one or two when I get time
	but anyway - what's new with you
*R	well I had my birthday
	still on holiday from school for 2 more weeks
	but it's been real boring because my friend
	- Stacey - has been acting real weird
$*	in what way
*R	well she has two other friends
	and all they talk about is boy stuff
	so now it's like she doesn't want
	to be bothered about me no more

```
$*    that's too bad
      don't you have any other friends
*R    Lucy - she's nearly17
      and got a proper boyfriend already
      and mum says she's a bad influence
$*    you mean she teaches you bad stuff
*R    sort of - just cause she's older
      she shows off - drinks alcohol
      - and she smokes weed
$*    ok
      that's not so good
      so tell me again
      how old you are ruby
```

Shit shit shit. I realised all of a sudden that I'd slipped up. That first time we chatted I'm sure I told him I was already 16. So now I should actually be 17, but of course he'd figured out I had lied. I wanted the bed to swallow me up.

```
$*    ruby
      it's ok if you are younger than you told me
      really
      I know sometimes people pretend to be
      someone else on here
      girls want boys to think they are older
      so that they appear more mature perhaps
      - get them to chat them up
      when they would not do so
      if they knew they were younger
*R    I spose
      yeh - you probably hate me now
      for telling a stupid lie
$*    sweet ruby
```

97

```
          of course I do not hate you
          - I understand completely
          but you must be careful you know
          if you are under 16
          this can be a dangerous place
          tell me truly how old you are
   *R     16 cross my heart
          im real sorry
   $*     ok I trust you
          and of course I forgive you
          it is not always easy to apologise to someone
          when you have made a mistake
          so anyway - you have now got Msngr
          and a webcam
          - perhaps you can let me see you sometime
```

What? How the hell did he know that? Shit, he'd be expecting me to strip off in front of him and all sorts of shady stuff.

```
   *R     webcam? how did u know
   $*     hehe
          there is a little symbol next to your name
          on my screen
          but that's ok
          let me send you 1 or 2 photos first and perhaps
          you can send me 1 back next time
   *R     ok
   $*     but ruby
          I have to go very soon
          my friends are taking me out for drinks
          but we can keep in touch
          we can e-mail each other
          leave messages if one of us is busy
```

I hope you have a good night ruby
take care until next time
*R   ok will do
and enjoy your night - bye
$*   bye

Then a few seconds later the message came up to say Stefan was offline.

MESSENGER. I love it.

It was a lot better than that pathetic Chatterteen garbage – so much more private and intimate. But, hell. My bloody webcam. It was built into the casing of my laptop so I couldn't exactly disconnect it. Shit shit shit. Why hadn't I thought of that before jumping back into the shark-infested ocean with both feet?

I needed time to think. Had he really been away all them weeks he said he had? Because if that was true, how could he have got his hands on Cody? I needed time to work everything out in my head.

Knock. Knock.

"I'm busy."

The very last thing I wanted right now.

"It's Shona."

Oh.

"Come in then."

I shut off my laptop pronto and leapt off the bed.

"You ok, retard?"

"Yeh. Why shouldn't I be?"

"Mum and Dad said you'd been acting a bit quiet. Time of the month is it?"

"No. Not really. Had too much sun, out in the garden all day yesterday in just ma cozzie."

"Yeh, I bet. Wasn't the weather unbelievable!"

"Mhmm."

"So anyway, ask me where I'm off to six days from now!"

"Why? What do you mean?"

"Me and Laura are going away for two weeks. And her mam and dad are paying. Guess where."

"God, I don't know. Spain or somewhere like that?"

"No no. It's much better than that. God, I'm so excited."

"So come on. Tell me?"

"The Big Apple, you know? New York New York. Yee-eek."

She squealed like a little kid. But who wouldn't? I screeched with her and we danced around my room before collapsing onto my bed totally out of breath.

"Oh my God, you lucky cow."

"Hey."

"Sorry. But O-migod, you are so lucky. Have you told Mum and Dad?"

"Course I have, you divv. They're totally ok with it – as long as I get back in one piece and study extra hard next year."

I couldn't help but feel happy for her. She'd only ever been abroad once, when we all went over to Belgium for that long weekend. That was about seven years ago. She probably deserves a proper holiday as much as anyone does. More than Stacey who gets to go away with her grandparents two or three times a year and isn't even grateful.

Then she gave me a hug. "Sleep with me tonight, Rubes, if you like. Then in the morning we can go on the internet and check out all the cool places to go sight-seeing."

"Ok."

I could put on my sloppy t-shirt which comes down below the knees. My secret would be safe.

POOR Shona. I know if I'd been in her shoes I wouldn't have slept a wink for the next six days. Too much to think about. We lay next to each other discussing all sorts of girly stuff until about half past midnight then she finally said she was going to put the light off.

"I really need my beauty sleep now, hon. Otherwise none of those American hunks will look twice at me."

I knew that wasn't true because Shona's lush. But we turned our backs to each other and the next thing I knew...

CHAPTER 16

I bin workin' real hard to save for new shoes. $125. Dat's like a whole weeks pay. An' by the time I pays the rent an' for grocery an' for Mrs Fernandez to look after Ramiro there ain't much left.

I axed Mr Granski for any overtime goin' and he said he do what he cud do. But still I only get to save perhaps ten or fifteen dollars a week.

An' dats how I come to be workin' so late thursaday night. I was tired to ma bones an' the streets were still wet from the rain all day long an' my shoes were leakin' thru ma thick stockings to ma feet an' I was cursin' under ma breath which I know is a sin.

An' may the lord strike me dead but when dat man axed me for some loose change I jus told him I had none. Even though I had forty cents left over from dat samwich I got for ma lunch. And he look me right in the eye den next thing my body's on fire an' my nerves are like twitchin' and I feel a blade held to ma throat an' he say he gonna slice ma face off if I even breathe too loud.

I thought he after ma purse.

But den when he pull me into shadows an' thru dat rusted door an' underneath all dem pipe-work I know he gonna rape me an' even kill me an' I starts prayin' inside ma head to sweet lord jesus.

Don't know how long I been down here but no one come lookin' for me. I tried to scream one time an' he beat me real bad. All the noise. Power drills an' stuff. No one gonna find me in a hurry. Mr Granski probly think Im bad news and get some otha girl on the tills. Mrs Fernandez. What she gonna do? Might decide to ring welfare but I don tink so. She know I short of cash and sometime Im workin' da streets if times are hard. Ma poor baby Rami. I do anythink for ma sweet little boy.

Ma soakin' wet shoes. Oh he took dem off me dat first night. Never seen dem again. The man took everthin' I own cept ma lil pink socks wot mama got me one time when winter so cold. An' ma green slip dat seen better days.

Of course, he seen my scar from when Rami got born. He liked to see dat he says. I swear he laugh when he say he wants to leave his mark on me too. I really tink he gonna kill me for sure. Him whisperin' he love me an' holdin' dat knife. Then once he see the blood he go way so I gets to dreamin' 'bout dat time I was in park with Jessaca and Rami in his buggy an' we seen dem girls and boys jus messin' by the water and how happy dey seem and how not a care in da whole wide world.

An' den I see dat one sweet young girl look at me like she know me.

An' I wake up and she still there and I try to tell her ma name. But he come back out of nowhere, ticklin' ma skin wid dat razor like he high on crack, Wantin' to have some more his fun. An' he cut me some more an' I swear he hear her cry out. His head turned like it got hit by a baseball bat an' his eyes searchin' for her.

An' she such a sweet young girl an' all I can do to save her is I grab him by da hair wid my one free hand and pull him back. He start to roar an' scream like a wild animal an' he punch me in the guts. Right down near ma scar. But I know right away dat six inches of blade is what I really feeled. An' ma legs give way an' I so tired and know I gotta sleep some more...

CHAPTER 17

CODY is inside that horrible room. It's the same one Levi was chained up inside. Damp brickwork with chunks of plaster falling off – and the choking smell of damp. She's crouched on the floor, looking more like a pile of bones wrapped in loose clothing than a human being.

There is just enough light to make out her face. What look like dried tears are braiding her cheeks in grey streaks and she has a cut lip with a bruise blossoming purple at the corner of her mouth.

I want to reach out to her somehow. Tell her I'm doing everything I can to find where Stefan has got her locked up. Her mouth moves as if she's muttering the same prayer over and over – trying to calm herself.

"Rami, o rami..."

I don't know if that's Dutch.

Then her head drops low and a hand appears out of nowhere. Or the shadow of a hand – definitely not flesh and bone. Fingers part the long, curling hair from her face then seem to trace the bone structure of her skull. She's no more than a doll, a china doll that will break with the least touch.

Slowly she climbs to her feet. Like a puppet that's had its strings pulled tight from above. Her free hand grasps the hem of that threadbare slip and pulls it up until her thigh is laid bare. A cross cut into her flesh – like a brand: stark black against the cold marble of her skin. The shadow hand appears again, blade open ready and flashing light like a steel fan. I know he's about to stitch another red streak across her leg, but as soon as the blade touches her flesh I feel its sting and it's like I can sense the hairs on the back of his neck regrouping. Soldiers primed for attack. Somehow he is aware that I'm watching him.

When he turns towards me there's no face visible. Just a hand shape drawing closer, the blade slicing the air like a conductor's baton. I suck in my breath, trying to make myself smaller, and then ... he's gone. Pulled away and spinning towards Cody until they merge into one single body and there's a searing pain in my belly and I convulse in agony and scream out.

Have you ever woken up to the echo of a scream? I don't mean the scream itself. Because that had already gone. Died in the mouth, or in the heart and lungs. But there was a scream, and this time it was mine. My gasping throat was dry and it felt scraped raw all the way down into my heaving chest.

A spotlight comes on and I'm cowering in the corner of the room, expecting Stefan to finish me off. One hand squeezes my shoulders, trying to hold me down as my frantic fingers probe inside my t-shirt, testing the skin along my thighs, searching for signs of fresh blood.

Then I see Shona's face poised above mine, trying to shake me awake.

"God, Ruby. You're freakin' me out. What's the matter with you?"

I couldn't form words.

"Ruby, say something. What's wrong?"

My fingers were covering every inch. Exploring the warm, damp flesh beneath the waistband of my knickers. When I pulled my hand from beneath the duvet I expected to find my fingers smeared red. But no. The blade had not left its mark this time. It was Cody who had suffered: given her life to save mine. My face crinkled up like a sun-dried peach. I couldn't speak – couldn't hold back the tears as I regained my bearings.

105

"Sweetheart. You're ok. Come on." Someone's fingers stroked my hair. Shadow fingers.

I turned onto my side and buried my face in the pillow. The duvet slid off me and I could feel Shona's touch calming me down.

"Hell, girl. You're soaking wet."

I tried to fold my arms across my front but she was having none of it. I felt the bed tilt then heard her open the drawer in her dressing table.

"Put this on."

She had that orange and yellow t-shirt in one hand.

"Come on."

I sat up and let her strip me. My armpits were soggy. Even the sheet and pillow beneath were damp.

"Hang on."

She got a hand towel to dry me off as best she could.

"Here you are. Let me spray my smellies on you instead of that lilac shit you keep using. You're such an old biddy sometimes."

Nana Crozier always gets me deodorant that smells of lilac. I like it.

Then she helped me struggle into her top. Her cool hands pulling it down past my midriff. Tugging it over my thighs as I tried to shuffle my bum to make it easier for her. Down as far as my knees. Finally she straightened the duvet again.

"I'll be back in a jiffy."

I assumed she had to go to the loo. But no. She came back in with my insulin kit.

"What you doin'?"

"I think we should check your blood, hon."

"What? No. It's ok."

"I don't think so. You were burning up like you had a fever or something."

I didn't have the energy to argue with her. I just held out my hand and let her prick my finger with a new lancet. I watched it all happening to someone else's body as she released a bubble of blood then smeared it onto the testing strip.

"You feeling any better?"

I nodded, numb with shock and embarrassment.

"7.2. Is it supposed to be that high?"

"Mhmm," I nodded again. "It's always higher at night. I've had my jab so it'll come down bit by bit."

She tidied everything away while I lay there sucking at my finger where she'd jabbed it. Shona had only ever done this once before. A couple of years ago. She probably saved my life that time. She'd found me sitting all floppy on the kitchen floor. There'd only been the two of us in the house and she couldn't even get through to anybody on their mobiles. Mum was away at the hospital visiting Nana Mac and Dad was working up the coast, well out of range.

Fortunately Mum and Dad had shown her what to do in case there was ever an emergency. How to take a blood sample and get a reading. It had been high. Well over 10. She knew she had to use my Novopen. Check there was enough insulin still inside it. Roll up my top and pinch an inch then stick the point against my skin. Click it so that it injected into the tissue just below the fat rather than directly into the muscle.

She told me later that she'd been shaking almost too much to keep it steady. Actually starting to cry as she drew blood from my finger then was forced to stab me in the side. Hurting her own little sister but realising it could be a matter of life or death. It had been that close.

Tonight there was no such panic.

107

She climbed back into bed and plumped up her pillows.

"Another dream was it?"

I'd calmed down a bit. I managed to swallow the rock lodged in my throat.

"Yeh."

"Bad one? It must have been."

"Yeh."

It went quiet then she asked the question I'd been expecting.

"I saw them cuts on your leg. So what's that all about?"

"Eh?"

"Rubes. You been cutting yourself or something?"

"Course not. I must have scraped it yesterday in the garden."

"Bullshit."

I clammed up.

"Look, I'm worried, ok? Aren't I allowed?"

"Worried? What about?"

"You self-harming, of course. When did all that start?"

"Don't be daft."

"I'm serious. D'you want to tell me, or would you rather tell Mum?"

I couldn't deny it without going into all that stupid dream stuff with everybody again.

"Ok."

"Ok what?"

"I was just messin', really."

"Messing?"

"Just wanted to see what it felt like, see if…"

"Tell me you are joking."

"Kerry Thompson in dance class used to do it all the time."

"And so?"

"I just wanted to try it. See what she got out of it."

"Oh, that's ok then. Panic over. No need to tell Mum and Dad for now – until you decide to try something else, see what that feels like."

"Oh, please Sho. Don't tell them."

"What's next on the agenda? You've already tried weed. A bit of self-harm. Are you going to sniff some glue, take a couple of roofies, snort a gram or two of coke? Or, I know. What about a little heroin? Do what Farran did. See how that feels."

Fucking bitch. That was such a mean thing to say. She had no idea what I was going through. No one did. Let's face it. Who could I confide in now? And to accuse me of wanting to end up like Farran. It was almost as if she was glad Farran had overdosed. That would be a great lesson for me – don't do any drugs or you'll end up dead like your cousin.

I cried myself to sleep. I didn't even notice her turn the bedside light off. She didn't snuggle up close to me or anything. Didn't slap my butt like she normally does when she gets out of bed in the morning and I'm still fast asleep, snoring right next to her.

I was expecting her and Mum to put in an appearance as soon as they realised I was awake. Give me the third degree. But no. Shona was obviously downstairs having her breakfast but had said nothing.

I padded off into my bedroom for my dressing gown. I desperately needed a shower but that would have to wait. I just checked my bod one more time to make sure there were no new cuts or bruises then I tidied round. Parked my laptop on top of my desk. Coiled up my iPod headphone cables. Straightened the duvet and turned the pillows over. Picked up my mobile and headed downstairs.

One new message (Unknown).

I paused on the stairs. Flipped it open and checked my in-box.

If u ever wanna chat bout farran text me, k c x

Uh? Who the hell was K C?

CHAPTER 18

REUBEN Garcia of the 24th Precinct had been shuffling the photographs on his desk for most of the afternoon. A plastic cup of plastic coffee squatted within reach but it was the furthest thing from his mind. He was haunted by the look of resignation in the dead eyes staring back at him from the photographs.

A tap on the door woke him from his reverie.

"Hi Reub. Sorry it took so long."

His partner Karl Iversen shuffled in, removing his raincoat and trying his best not to shower everywhere with drips.

"Weather's turning to shit out there."

"So I see. What d'you manage to find out?"

Iversen sat down and removed his note book – purely for show. Most of the facts were lodged firmly inside his head.

"Female. 5 foot 4. Latino. Age somewhere between 16 and 22 years old. Found about six miles south of the George Washington Bridge on the foreshore. This guy goes beach-casting and finds her washed up on the rocks. Pretty much the same set-up as that Levi kid."

"No ID?"

"Nothing. Cheap underwear. No jacket or trousers. Dumped exactly the same way."

"Mhmm."

"There's other similarities. Cut marks on the body. Plastic bag over the head. Contusions on the right-hand wrist suggesting she was tied up recently. Some kind of metal cuffs or chain – possibly a dog lead."

"Some of these cuts look different."

Garcia fanned three photographs and spun them so Iversen could take a look. Three close-ups of the victim's upper thighs.

"Well, it's the same kind of 'X' mark like we found on the first vic. Not deep enough to cause significant loss of blood. He's just had a little more fun with this one maybe. Branding her – marking his territory. Who knows?"

"What about the wound to her stomach?"

"That's relatively new. Presumably done just before he smothered her."

Garcia reached for a cigar then thought better of it.

"What's your gut feeling about this, Karl?"

"Has to be the same one who killed the other kid. Signs of sexual assault. Bruising down there rather than lacerations. This one's got a cut lip. Possibly she was less cooperative. He obviously enjoys using his fists."

"And a blade. Forensics come up with anything useful yet?"

"Not really. The river hasn't left them a great deal to go on. Traces of oil and concrete dust on the fibres of her slip, as if she was laid down on a garage floor or… Well, I dunno."

"Motor oil?"

"Hydraulic oil. Same as you find around the docks, used for fishing boats, construction sites, warehouses, engineering shops, agricultural machinery."

"Ok ok. So we don't know shit until we get an ID. What are the uniforms doing?"

"A couple of squad cars are leafleting the stores, diners, news-stands and cafes between here and Central Park. It's likely this one was locked up in the same place as the other kid."

"She's older."

"For sure. Harper reckons this one's had a baby some time ago. Scar from a C-section on her abdomen."

"So how come nobody's called in reporting her disappearance? Must be some husband or boyfriend missing her, or a kid at home waiting for Mama to relieve the baby-sitter."

"Dunno. She could be a single mom. The baby might not even be around any more. We're just gonna have to wait again."

"Yeh. Wait, and keep hoping some other girl don't get snatched. I've got a bad feeling about this guy."

CHAPTER 19

MUM didn't take long to comment on my bloodshot eyes.

"Shona's gone and told me all about last night. You didn't sleep too well again."

"I'm all right now."

Big sister was sitting at the breakfast bar sipping her coffee and pretending to ignore me but she still had her say.

"She woke up in a right state. I thought she'd had a friggin' heart attack."

I didn't dare challenge her.

"So what happened?"

"I had a bad dream, that's all."

Mum ran her fingers through my hair before resting a hand against my forehead. Her face was etched with concern. "Your sugar levels ok?"

Same old same old.

"Yeh. Why wouldn't they be?"

"Well, you know how I can't help worrying."

Shona shuffled her stool away from the bar and tried to help me out. "We checked them. When she woke up. Half past two this morning."

"Why didn't you call me or your dad?"

Shona shrugged. "No need. They were normal when I checked. No point waking the whole bloody neighbourhood just because…"

"There's nothing bothering you, is there?"

"What like?"

Mum wouldn't let it lie. She never does.

"Well you tell me. You worried about something?"

"Course not."

"'Cause you were awful quiet yesterday."

114

"No, I'm fine. Honest. Too much sun probably."

"You sure? You would tell me, wouldn't you?"

I turned my back on her. End of conversation.

"Got any sliced bread? I want toast."

"Use what's in the freezer."

I filled the kettle and studied the way it boiled as Mum finally took the hint and went upstairs to get ready for work. Then I stood behind Shona and wrapped both arms around her neck.

"Thanks."

"For what?"

"Not telling Mum. Looking after me last night."

She shook her head.

"Sorry for being such a pain."

"It's ok. You're not a pain."

"Ta."

"But don't think you're off the hook. It's 'cause I love you, not 'cause I've forgiven you for being such a... such a doolie."

She stood up, glared at me then traipsed upstairs.

I chewed my toast in silence. I'd only just noticed the rain spitting against the kitchen window. Great. So much for a day lazing on the sun-lounger round the back again.

"What are you up to today?"

Mum back: dressed, handbag and keys at the ready.

"Don't think I'm going to bother going out. Might finish my English homework."

"Oh, that scary book yer dad told you about. Well I hope that's not what's giving you nightmares. You need to give that brain of yours a rest."

As if. I kissed her goodbye.

The only scary thing about Dr J and Mr H was the idea of someone having a personality split in two. One normal

115

and one mad. That could be Stefan. It could even be me come to think of it. I was actually beginning to imagine I might be going crazy. Those dreams. The bruise on my side. The cuts on my leg. What if I'd done all those things to myself but couldn't remember?

THERE were two e-mails inside my 'dreamgirl' in-box. Both from lover boy, obviously, since nobody else had this new address. He'd sent them last night – presumably when he got back from the pub.

One just said

'Goodnight, Ruby. Sweet dreams.'

Was he having a friggin' laugh or what?

The second one said

'Oh I forgot, check out these pix.'

Six attachments. It took me about a minute to figure out how to open them. First I sneaked across the landing to check where Shona was. The last thing I wanted was her walking in on me as I ogled Stefan's mug shots. I could hear her gabbing away on her mobile. Lots of squeals and New York talk. Like radical or what?

008 July17.jpg : a man wearing a bulky blue parka with a fur-lined hood and orange waterproof trousers. He was standing with his back to a set of white railings on board a ship and behind him I could see dark blue water, a black headland striped with bands of ice or snow. He also wore ski goggles and was staring straight into the camera giving the thumbs up sign. I could hardly make out his face. I was expecting someone like David Beckham with a neat little beard but he looked more like our Art teacher Mr. Allman. His face was bright red and quite chubby. He

116

definitely wasn't a hunk. And he could have been thirty-three or even forty-three behind all that face fungus.

019 July 21.jpg / 020 July 21.jpg : snaps of two titchy penguins – waddling along a sandy beach it looked like – waving their flippers. The shadow of the person who took the photograph lay like a fallen tree across both pictures.

003 July 24.jpg : the head of what looked like a seal, or possibly a walrus, poking out of the waves. A bit blurred. Not exactly David Attenborough.

043 July 26.jpg / 048 July 26.jpg : two sunsets. A gorgeous red sky with gold-edged clouds and with what looked like icebergs on the horizon.

None of this added up. If he had really been away when he said he was and taken those pictures on those dates how could he possibly have grabbed Cody? Unless, of course, my dreams were some kind of flashback to stuff that had happened ages ago – before Stefan went off on his holidays. But they all seemed so real – not like live TV but as if I was actually there in the same building when it was happening.

I clicked onto 'Google Earth' and zoomed in on the Netherlands. That place with the long name where he had grown up. I knew I'd written it down somewhere, probably in my diary with all my other private ramblings. But I couldn't be bothered getting off the bed to dig it out from the bottom of my undies drawer.

I could remember it started with an apostrophe S then

a dash then 'Hero' or 'Herto'. It took me a couple of minutes to find what looked like the right place.

's-Hertogenbosch

I felt like some supreme god surveying the Earth from on high. There were green parks and football pitches and tennis courts. There was a lake with a river or a canal and loads of boats moored on it. It could have been a larger version of Lochend Park before I realised the lake was right next door to a container terminal. Fancy having one of those in the middle of such beautiful countryside.

I went into Street View and zoomed along a twisty road through a clump of trees, past houses with shutters outside their windows and little canopies. Funny little canal boats, bikes tied up next to cast-iron post boxes, black plastic dust-bins out on the road ready for collection.

It all looked so normal.

Then I zoomed out and flew north.

Haarlem

I did the same again. Swooped down for a peek then hovered higher up again, like an eagle searching for its prey. Come on, Stefan. Where are you hiding? Haarlem was more built-up – with a big airport on one side and the open sea on the other. Lots of red rooftops.

Everywhere looked so flat and green. I found a tiny little house all on its own with a lawn and borders filled with flowers like ours and a set of frilly orange canopies above the windows. Another just down the road had a little square hedge about a foot high surrounding their front garden and there were lanterns on top of their gate posts. I love being nosy.

But it was getting me nowhere. This wasn't the kind of place where young girls get snatched off the streets and murdered. It just didn't fit.

I logged out.

I stood for ages at the window looking down at the washout of a day.

Finally I pulled my mobile out of my trousers pocket and read that anonymous text again.

If u ever wanna chat bout farran text me, k c x

It was time to reply.

Hi k c. Sorry do I know u?

The reply took about a minute. Bzz bzz – bzz bzz.
One new message (Unknown)

Ruby its casey. Lucys casey. Thought we cld meet up afta colege 4 a chat if u like. x

CHAPTER 20

"**CODY** Lopez. 21 years old. Till-operator at the Juanita Grocery off West 107th. The owner, a Mr. Gradzinski, recognised her photo soon as one of the uniforms showed it round the store. The other girls confirmed it."

Iversen seemed to have found his second wind – following every loose strand the investigation uncovered as if it would lead them to the perpetrator. Garcia admired his enthusiasm but was more cautious. There was a lot of groundwork still to cover. He'd seen it all before. So many blind alleys that led you further away from the truth rather than closer.

"What's he say about her?"

"Not a lot. Says she'd put in for extra overtime then didn't even bother showing up – not even for her wages."

"And he doesn't think to tell anyone?"

"Figured she'd got herself a better job. Said he'd have fired her if she ever came back."

"A true saint."

"Yeh."

Garcia shook his head.

"Has he got her address, or is that asking too much?"

"Well, it took some getting. It's one of the cheap apartments overlooking Saint Nick's. Driscoll and Bergami called round to take a look. All locked up. No signs of a break-in or anything suspicious. Neighbours say there's been no sign of her for days. No sound of the baby cryin'. Reckons she leaves it with someone across the street. A Mrs. Fernandez."

"They been round to check her out?"

Iversen's eyes suddenly held a fresh spark of enthusiasm.

"No. Wanted to know whether we'd rather call on her.

Find out why she decides to say nothin' to anybody when she's left holdin' someone else's baby for more than three weeks."

THE woman who answered the door had the wide-eyed look of someone expecting bad news to come buzzing her bell any time soon. She looked whipped into resignation.

"Mrs. Fernandez?"

"Si."

"This is Detective Iversen, ma'am. And Detective Garcia. We're here to talk about Miss Lopez?"

"Si."

"Cody Lopez? We understand she brings her baby boy here for you to mind while she's at work."

Her face dropped.

"Could we come in?"

"Of course, of course."

They followed a pair of feet, swollen and clamped into a pair of threadbare slippers, along a narrow passageway into the dark kitchen. Smells of refried beans and burnt grease hung over everything like exhaust fumes.

"Rami... Ramiro. He has his sleep. He is such a good boy."

There were tears in her eyes but her face looked as if the grief etched upon it had been there for some time. A fortnight or more. As soon as she realised the child's mother would never be coming to collect him again.

Garcia took over – accustomed to sharing bad news.

"Mrs Fernandez. We're sorry to have to tell you but Cody's body was found yesterday morning. We believe she was murdered."

A stifled sob. She'd done all her crying a long time ago. "She's a good girl really. I know she always say her prayers."

"Do you remember when you last saw Miss Lopez?"

"Si. Three weeks ago. Jueves. A Thursday. She says she has to work more time at the store. Asked special to work extra."

"And she never came back."

"No. But I keep him real safe. I look after Rami like as if he my niño. He not any trouble."

"I'm sure you do look after him."

Iversen's gaze paused in its survey of the tiny kitchen and refocussed on the old woman's face. "So did Cody ever leave him here overnight before?"

She glanced at this young man in the smart suit as if he'd asked a trick question.

"Few, one or two time. She say maybe she has to work afternoon and night all together sometime, maybe five or six time. It is no problem to me."

Iversen persisted. "But three whole weeks? Did you not think something was wrong?"

"Si... maybe."

"But you didn't tell anybody."

"No. I want no trouble. I am sorry. She is... Cody such a pretty girl. Men find her muy benita. I know sometimes she go with men."

"Which men? You mean with strangers?"

"Cody a good girl. But sometimes when she bring Rami here she dress in tight skirt and all make-up and put on a lot of perfume."

Iversen turned and grinned at his partner.

"She was hustling?"

Garcia's eyes dropped as he whispered a prayer.

"I ask no question. She a good girl deep down, I know it in my heart."

122

CHAPTER 21

I was waiting under the bus shelter outside the 'Caffeine-ery' around the corner from the Art College. Casey had said he'd meet me here after three o'clock as soon as his class finished.

I'd been hanging around nearly fifteen minutes, tingling with anticipation. I'd taken an extra-long shower and done what I could with my hair. In the end I tied it back with a scrunchie and hoped for the best. I'd asked Shona if I could try a couple of scooshes of her 'Magni-chic' body spray, and I put on my favourite peach-flavour lip gloss and neon green eye-liner. Not too much because I still wasn't sure what he was expecting. I also had on my favourite jeans, that cerise top with the low neck and my pink fleece. And my back-pack of course. 'Casual chick' or whatever they call it. At least I looked a bit more like a student than some sad schoolgirl. Sometimes I look so out-of-place.

I finally spotted him with a gang of four other lads; hoping they weren't going to be sticking around. I hadn't gone to all this trouble to look sophisticated for a bunch of no-good neds.

No worries. They headed off towards the shops and Casey came up to me. Looking really happy to see me.

"Glad you could make it. Fancy a coffee?"

The place was buzzing with shoppers, probably because of the rain and the time of day. We each grabbed a medium latté at the counter then he led me upstairs where there was a bigger seating area. We ended up perched on a couple of doll's house chairs either side of a flimsy-looking corner table. The kind that look as if they're going to collapse as soon as you sit on them – and designed to squash as many customers into as little space as possible.

He'd had a big folder under his arm and he propped it against the table leg then took a slurp from his cup. It left a thin moustache of cream on his top lip.

"Had no idea you were in college."

"Ah s'pose Lucy's no said anything. It's just a summer course but I'm thinkin' about enrollin' full-time the end of September."

"Cool."

He sounded more intelligent than I'd been expecting. Of course, I'd never spoken to him properly before now but he seemed quite nice. Quite dishy even.

"Aw, well. Mr Allman says I was wastin' ma time no takin' it further."

Another synchronised slurp.

"So how you keepin'? No the best way to spend your school hols losin' Farran the way you did."

The penny dropped with a thud. We were here to talk about Farran, that was all. This wasn't a 'date'. Huh! As if.

"No. I'm ok really. But it was sad. A big shock, for her mum and dad especially."

"You was good pals, I ken."

"Yeh."

"She always used to say."

"What? Did you know her then?"

Stupid question, Rubes. Seeing as he'd been at Farran's funeral and had suggested meeting up to chat about her.

"Aye. We used to go to the gym together. When she was still at school. Her an' Kenzie an' me."

"Oh, right."

"Her an' Kenzie were… well, they were seein' each other."

"Honest? God, I had no idea."

"For three or four months, aye."

"Right."

"Before she… before she left home."

I didn't want to think too much about the reasons why Farran suddenly decided to leave home. It was like a big family secret. I'm fairly sure Mum and Dad know. Possibly even Shona. It had to be something really bad she'd done, but I couldn't see it being anything to do with Kenzie. Just because they were dating, perhaps even sleeping together. I mean this is the twenty-first century. Loads of white girls go out with black boys round here.

"Aunty Grace was really angry that Farran dropped out of school like she did, and then I never saw her again after that."

"No. I didn't either, much. Saw her hangin' round town with Hooky a couple of times. Didn't get to speak to her though."

Hooky. Skanky boyfriend and druggie.

"She was a right bonny lass. Had a wicked sense of humour."

"Yeh. I know."

I told him about the times she came to sleep over. How she'd do all her exercises each morning and show me the basic moves. That time we had a pillow fight and she trashed Shona's 'Snow White' bedside lamp. Putting shaving foam inside Dad's slippers on April Fools.

"So have you got any idea why she ran away from home?"

He gave the tiniest of nods. "Mhmm. Next time, aye?"

"Ok."

There was going to be a next time!

The café had gradually emptied. I hadn't noticed the time. There were only about half a dozen couples left up here. 'Couples'. I decided that was going to be my

125

favourite word for a while. 'Couples'. I love it. 'Couples' like us making their cups of coffee last as long as possible so they can sit opposite each other and blether while the rest of the world passes them by. It seemed so natural us being there together.

"My sister's going to New York next week."

"No shit? To work?"

"No no. Just on holiday. With a girl friend from college."

"Lucky lassie."

"Mhmm."

"Shona, right? Ah sort of remember her from when I was still at Pentland. She wasn't long in the Sixth when I left."

"She's in university now. In Leeds."

"Doin' what?"

"Psychology."

"Oh, wow."

He slid back his chair and picked up his folder. That was it then. End of our non-date.

"So, you going to be an artist then?"

"Looks like it. Graphic Design prob'ly."

"Got any of your pictures with you in that?"

"Some, aye."

"Can I have a deek?"

An embarrassed grin.

"Please? Just a little peep?"

"What? Now? In here?"

"Where else?"

"Dinnae ken."

"So come on. Can I?"

He grinned.

"We'll go to the LR. Won't be so many in there 'cause term hasn't started yet."

126

"LR?"

"The L-Room they call it. Where most of the students chill out between lectures."

"Inside the college?"

"Where else?"

"So am I allowed?"

"Course you are. You're my guest are you no?"

IT was huge. With two coffee-making machines and a photocopier and a big laser printer. But there were sofas and bean bags and cheap chrome coffee tables everywhere as well. Most of the tables had empty pop cans or paper cups marking the passage of numerous bodies.

A girl with long blonde dreadlocks and a pierced eyebrow was perched beside one table working her laptop. And the biggest sofa under one of the windows was taken up by a guy and a girl deep in frantic conversation. I'm not sure whether they were breaking up or just madly in love with each other.

"Over here, Rubes."

He led me to a soft, sagging couch in a horrible creamy plastic with holes where the stuffing poked through. As soon as I sat down I was sure it would swallow me up because the springs had collapsed. Then he slumped alongside me and hooked a table with his foot to drag it closer.

"Some of it's not that good, an' there's some work in progress. So don't be too harsh."

He unclipped two of the elastic straps securing the corners, opened the folder out then unfolded the cardboard flaps holding the papers neatly inside. It was like I'd been allowed into his secret world. Enchanting. Scary. Intimate. This wasn't the stuff he showed just anybody, I could tell.

The face of a girl filled the left two-thirds of the first

127

sheet. The rest of the page was almost bare. But the weird thing was her skin. Half of her face was crinkled and creased like antique leather, or the bed of a dried-up lake. It sounds horrible but she was beautiful, and the texture of her skin didn't make her look ugly at all. There were words written across the whole page in tidy printed capital letters. The printing was dark on the right-hand side of the page which was blank, but a light grey or cream where it crossed her face.

WELLA - L'OREAL - GARNIER -
NEUTROGENA - ESTEE LAUDER

All names of make-up and stuff. Beauty products.

"It's meant to be a statement about beauty," he explained. "How lassies waste money on cosmetics an' tryin' to look pretty..."

"It's fantastic."

"Different I suppose. I was wantin' to show that beauty isn't, well, isn't skin deep. Even though all the magazines tell lassies they need to buy everything they advertise to look bonny."

"Oh."

I could feel my face beginning to turn red. He couldn't have failed to notice my lip gloss and sickly green eyeshadow.

"It's ok. Ah ken what ye're like, ye wee mares. Ah spend enough time with Miss Lucy, remember."

I grinned then my smile faded as I thought of Lucy for the first time that afternoon.

"But if you realised how that stuff gets made. Honest. 'Cause the old man used to work on the dockside an' he says how fishin' boats sometimes used to catch sharks."

"Real sharks?"

128

"Oh aye. Small ones, like. Not killer ones you see on TV. Anyway, they take out their livers an' sell them to places that make lipstick an' skin cream an' stuff."

"No way."

"Aye, right enough. But the stench, God. He says you never smelt anythin' so mingin'."

"Yeuch."

"Most lassies don't even need to put on that crap anyway. I mean, look at youse. Hell, you're a total Daisy."

Gulp blush gulp.

"I was always drawin' cartoons when I was a bairn. Dexter, Taz, Powerpuff Girls. But I only started thinkin' about takin' it more serious, I suppose, after finishin' at Pentland."

He took out the next batch from his folder. These were of Lucy. I knew straight away it was her. The first one took my breath away. Reminded me of the way I'd felt about her the very first time I had ever seen her at dance class, and in the changing rooms afterwards.

Standing naked in a room next to a small window. The light on her skin was like something out of a dream. He'd drawn her from one side and her left arm was held across her chest with her fist pressed against her lips as if she was kissing it. You couldn't see her boobs or anything you weren't supposed to. But he'd drawn her from real life. Her flat stomach with that neatly knotted belly button and the darker patch of fine hair below. Her long, straight legs, her muscular thighs. He'd even drawn those nodges of muscle like knots of flesh under the skin above her hips. Her bare feet with her crooked big toes and dark nail varnish. Her long hair tied up into a top knot.

"God, this is so beautiful."

I almost wanted to cry it was so touching to see my

129

friend look like this. A very private moment that he had captured and made magical with just a pencil and a few crayons. I almost felt like an intruder in someone's bedroom.

"It's one of my favourites. But you'd best no tell her you've seen it or she'll murder me."

"'S ok. I won't. I absolutely love it."

There was another one. Just a portrait this time. More like a cartoon really but you couldn't mistake her cheeky face: that sparkle in her eyes, her dimples.

Then another. Just her face. Asleep perhaps, eyes closed. But he'd done it almost exactly the same way as he'd drawn that first picture of the other girl. One half of her face looked like it was covered in leaves. Dead leaves you get on the ground in autumn: each one etched onto her face until it looked almost like a jigsaw. She was still pretty but there was something sinister about this. As if she had no idea he had drawn her.

And there were words printed across the page again. Each capital letter written with exquisite care – fading from cream across her face to dark red at the margins.

SLUT - BITCH - WHORE - SLAG - COW

And there was other stuff that was even worse.

I was stunned. He turned it over as soon as he caught my reaction.

"Sorry, Rubes. It's no what you're thinkin'. Honest."

"God. How do you know what I'm thinking? It's sick."

"It was just me messin' about. But it's no what it looks like."

"No?"

"I'm no writing those words about her. It's hard to

130

explain. It's just that sometimes I think I love Luce more than she loves me, you ken?"

"So?"

"So that was myself bein' angry. Angry with myself, no with her."

"Didn't look like it."

"I'm no very good at... at sayin' what's inside my head. What's goin' round inside my brain. But I can draw. So that was me drawin' all the bad things I could possibly feel about her. Gettin' them out of my system. Doesn't make much sense I suppose."

"Can I see it again?"

"No, doll. Leave it."

"Please. It's ok, I won't tell her. But can I have another look?"

I studied it for ages. Couldn't take my eyes off it. The face was beautiful, like he'd captured a sleeping angel. Or even a dead one. Like Levi might have looked perhaps. Or Cody. Or even Farran. The words were nothing. The F word and the C word. I'd heard them all at school anyway. At junior school come to think of it. I knew that the person who had drawn this face loved her without a doubt.

"Could you draw me?"

"What?"

"Draw me. Just my face I mean. Something like this or that first one you showed me."

"What? All screwed up?"

"Well, yeh. 'Cause I'm really screwed up, you know."

It was nearly half past five.

"Could do, ah suppose. You free the morrow, in the afto then? Early?"

"Can be."

"Same place? The bus stop?"

"Yeh. What time?"

131

"About quarter past one. An' text us if you can't be there, or if you change your mind."

There was no chance of that.

I stood waiting for my bus. Watching him walk down towards Matalan as far as the lights then turning right. I was still floating.

CHAPTER 22

MUM'S car was on the drive when I got home but she must have popped next door to visit Mrs Dawson because the house was empty. Shona had been busy organizing everyone and had left a note on the fridge as usual.

MUM - C U ALL TOMORROW NITE - RUBY SAYS
SHE'S DUE IN ABOUT SIX
DAD - UNCLE ANDREW PHONED - WILL RING
BACK

I was about twenty minutes later than planned but no sweat. I wanted to send Casey a text just to say thanks but what if he was with Lucy? It was quite likely. She'd want to know who was texting him. It could get very complicated very quickly so I decided it was best not to. Yawn.

There was lasagne cooking in the oven. I opened the fridge and began to prepare the salad. Shona usually does thoughtful things like that without being asked. But I suppose being sixteen and the only daughter at home most of the time now I should start to make an effort.

Mum came in just as I finished slicing some mushrooms.

She swayed her head and rolled her eyes, acting as if she had come over all dizzy.

"Am I seeing things? Wow. What's got into you all of a sudden?"

"Nothing. Just trying to make myself useful that's all."

She gave me a hug then put on her oven gloves and checked the lasagne.

"Another ten minutes."

I was wondering how much more lettuce to shred.

"Is Dad going to be home for tea?"

"He said he'd be back about a quarter to seven. Uncle Andrew's phoned to arrange drinks at the golf club later."

First time they'd been out together since Farran's funeral. Funny how soon things return to normal. The space she'd once occupied already filled in. It was like she had never been here.

"Mum."

"Fetch the plates. And there's coleslaw in the fridge if you want."

"No ta. Er, Mum."

"Sit yourself down and I'll dish out."

I began to help myself to salad.

"You know why Farran ran away from home, don't you?"

Her face turned pale for an instant before recovering her composure.

"It's ancient history, love. Her and her mam fell out after she decided to leave school without finishing her Highers. Somebody put a lot of silly ideas into her head. That's all."

"Oh."

"Is that what's been worrying you? Look. You're missing her, I know. You always used to have such a grand time together. Your dad and I were only saying the other night."

"What?"

"Well, how quiet things have been this summer holiday. We haven't seen Stacey around here for ages. Things still ok with you two?"

"Not really. Stacey'd rather be with her trashy mates. But I'm not bothered. I was out this afternoon with another of my friends anyway so I'm cool about that."

"Oh, who?"

Where was the harm? I still had this fuzzy feeling behind my rib cage just thinking about him. I had to let it out.

"You don't know him."

"A boy? Oh. So where did you go?"

"Just for a coffee and he showed me round the college where he's a student. He's doing Art and he's really talented."

"College? How old is he then?"

"Oh. About nineteen I think. He left school the summer before Shona."

"Right. And you don't think he's a little old for you?"

Eh?

"Mum? Too old? For what? He's only a mate."

"Sorry I asked. I don't want you getting hurt, that's all. What's his name?"

"It's Kevin."

I suddenly remembered that's what the K stood for. Kevin Cameron.

"He was the one in Farran's funeral. The one you were asking about. We had a long chat about her 'cause they used to be good mates. He says he remembers Shona as well. He's going to be a Graphics Designer."

Mum could tell I was excited about things but she asked no more questions. If we'd talked about Farran it was possible he'd mentioned why she'd run away from home. She left me basking in the glow of finally having a guy in my life as we ate our teas in silence.

THE other man in my life was waiting upstairs for me.

He was already on-line. I clicked on his name and waited.

*R   hi Stefan

135

A couple of minutes went by. Perhaps his laptop was on but he'd left the room to dispose of another girl's body. Sorry. Only joking, and in bad taste.

$*   ruby
     how are u
     I was just thinking of you
*R   oh
     nice things I hope
$*   did you get my pics ok??
*R   oh yeh
     I loved them - especially the two little penguins
$*   they are so cute
*R   so what have u been up to
$*   oh a few chores
     is that the right word?
*R   hehe
     what - like laundry and dusting?
$*   that's it exactly
     lots of laundry
     and tomorrow maybe I iron
*R   poor thing
$*   so you have had a good day
     yes?
*R   really good yeh
     went out with a friend
     had a coffee and a long talk
$*   well that's good
     you did not go shopping
     hehe
*R   no
$*   right
*R   I forgot to tell u
     something important last night

136

$*   really?
*R   about a bad thing that happened over the holidays
     bad news in our family
     I probably wouldnt be telling just anybody
     stuff like this
$*   ruby
     u don't have to tell me anything you don't want to
     but I'll always be here if you want to talk
     about anything

Hmm.

$*   I'm a good listener
     and I don't judge people
     or try to make them change
*R   ok
     my cousin died
$*   how sad
     I'm so sorry ruby
*R   yeh
     my cousin and she was only 19
     and she was a really good friend of mine as well
$*   that's so sad
     can I ask how she died?
     you don't need to tell me if you'd rather not
*R   well it's a long story
     she left home - ran away from home I mean
     and she got in trouble with the police
     taking drugs and stuff
     and they think she died of a drugs overdose
$*   I don't know what to say
     except I feel sorry for her as much as you
     and her family
*R   thanx

$*   no need to thank me
     you are still upset
     I'm sorry - my words are not much help
*R   its still nice of you to say that
$*   we have same problem here in Netherlands
     with teenagers dying from drugs
     even though we have a more open attitude
     many still prefer to experiment with hard drugs
*R   she was on heroin
$*   what was her name
*R   Farran
$*   that is a pretty name
     is it Scottish
*R   don't know really
     she was a lot of fun
$*   ruby
     you must never forget that
     as long as you remember Farran
     and the fun she gave you
     she will never be completely gone

I'm a stupid mare sometimes. I suddenly started crying and had to go looking for a tissue.

$*   ruby
     are yu ok?
     let me know before you log off

I was having second thoughts about Stefan being a cold-blooded killer. He seemed to have a soft centre.

*R   sorry
     yeh m ok now
     just got a bit weepy

138

$* hey it's ok
    are you in bed?
*R not yet
$* you sound as if you need a cuddle
    an arm around you
*R well
$* it would be nice if I was there with you
    but perhaps I should let you rest
    and we should say goodnight
*R no it's ok
    I'm feeling upset that's all
    just need someone - you know
$* I'll wait
    tell me when you are undressed and in bed
*R uh?
$* you need to snuggle under your blanket
    trust me - you'll start to feel better

This was beginning to get weird. But it was late, after eleven. So I put on that yellow t-shirt Shona had lent me and climbed under the sheets.

*R ok
    I'm snuggled down now
$* good
    is your light on
*R why?
$* just so I can picture you in my mind
    unless you want to put on your web-cam
*R not really
    don't know how anyway
$* you just click on that little icon
    see it next to your name?
    with the blue circle around it

139

```
            but you don't have to if you don't like to
    *R      not sure
    $*      it is no big deal
            lets just talk
            so what are you doing tomorrow
            any plans?
```

   I balanced my laptop at the edge of the mattress and just turned on my bedside lamp. I was buried under the duvet anyway. He'd only see my face and I wasn't that fussed whether he fancied me or not.
   Click.
   Suddenly I could see myself in a little box looking out at the screen. OMG. I looked like a walrus or something peering out of a snow-hole.

```
    $*      hehe
            hey there you are
    *R      I know
            just wondered what it wld be like
    $*      so you are a very pretty girl
            like I knew you would be
    *R      thnx
    $*      so what are you planning to do tomorrow
    *R      in the afternoon
            I'm meeting my friend again in town
    $*      the same one
    *R      yeh
    $*      and what is your friend's name
    *R      casey
    $*      is she pretty like you
    *R      hehe
    $*      did I say something funny
    *R      it's a boy
```

	Lucy one of my friends
	its her b/f
	boyfriend
$*	wow
	does she know you two are meeting up
*R	yeh - its ok
	there's nothing shady going on
$*	shady?
*R	we just talked
	he used to be friends with Farran
$*	oh I see
	it is good to have someone else to talk with
	about your cousin
	I am happy you are not alone
*R	thanx
$*	so ruby
	let me have a proper look at you
	sit up so I can see more of your face
	because all I see are your eyebrows and
	the top of your head

I shifted myself and suddenly my laptop slid onto the floor. Oops. I retrieved it and made room for it on my bedside table then angled the screen towards my pillow so I was facing it again.

*R	sorry
$*	hehe that's ok -
	tilt your screen a little higher
	then I can see you better

It took a couple of manoeuvres but finally I was sitting on top of my bed talking to some guy in the Netherlands who was watching my every move. It was harmless

141

enough. It didn't even feel like it was really happening –
that he could actually see me all the way over in Haarlem
or wherever he was. It was all pretend.

```
$*    I like your nightshirt
*R    its Shona's really
      my sisters
$*    its really neat
      Dallas Cowboys
*R    hehe
$*    you have a nice body
*R    oh I don't know
      my butt is a bit big
$*    hehe
      your butt looks cute
*R    and I have stretch marks
$*    stretch marks???
*R    yeh
$*    sweet ruby
      you do not have stretch marks
      what do you mean?
*R    where the elastic of my pants
      and my bra straps
      leave marks
$*    hehe
      you are so funny
```

It was no laughing matter. Mum and Nana keep going
on about their stretch marks all the time.

```
$*    show me what you mean
*R    what???? no way
$*    its ok
      I have sisters
```

and have had lots of girlfriends
so I have seen everything you have got
I'm sure
but trust me they are not stretch marks

There was no way I was letting this creep take a close-up look at me. I know exactly what stretch marks are. Stacey has got the same and she says the only way to avoid them is to use loads of moisturising cream or go commando.

Except, of course, he insisted on telling me. How his older sister got them when she was pregnant. Your belly gets bigger and bigger like a balloon, month by month, then suddenly – whoosh. It made sense. I felt a complete neek.

*R	you probably think Im stupid
$*	of course not
*R	no?
$*	never - girls worry too much
	about looks
	and you are very beautiful
	do you know that
	I like your long legs
	and your smile is astonishing
*R	thanx
$*	I think I am getting like that boy
	the one you danced with??
*R	what do you mean>
	which boy?
$*	you said was turned on
	is that what you said?
	remember?
*R	I am turning you on?

$*   of course
      you are almost naked
      and on your bed
      and its like I'm there with you
      almost touching you

Shit. This was like some friggin' nightmare. He couldn't seem to string more than two sentences together without bringing up S-E-X. I was debating whether or not to log off and go to sleep. I was shot. And yet, I had such power over him at times. Imagine a 16 year-old girl having complete control over a grown man. It was awesome.

*R   don't know wot 2 say
$*   you are such a pretty one Ruby
      it would be so good if you took your
      nightshirt off for me
*R   Huh? I don't think so
      I mean are you mad?
$*   that's ok
      I was only teasing you
*R   wotever
$*   forget I said that
      but I can't take my eyes off you
*R   mhmm
$*   you must send me a photo of you
      do you have one?
*R   maybe
      I can find one
$*   in your new swimsuit
*R   no way
      just my face
$*   that's ok
      that is more than enough

144

*R   scuse I need a wee

I had been trying to hold it in but I couldn't wait any longer. I leapt off the bed and dashed to the loo. I could feel this pulse throbbing inside my head and in my neck. Like I was crossing a tight-rope high up above everything: knowing that every step could be fatal. Balance was critical, yet if I were to slip I'd bounce back, like off a trampoline.

I shuffled back onto the bed, giving him an eye-full of butt. Then I sat peering at myself through my little window. Was he still there? Breath on hold, desperate to discover what my next move might be? I could imagine the look that would cross his face if I were to strip off. Ruby Red Riding Hood meets the Big Bad Wolf.

    *R   Stefan
           Im back
           what wld you really like me to do
    $*   hehe
           I could not tell you
    *R   its ok
           I don't mind
           as long as its not something gross
    $*   TAKE EVERYTHING OFF
    *R   OMG
           what???
    $*   sorry didn't mean
           to press the caps lock
           and you can do it under your bed sheet
    *R   ? wot for
    $*   just so I can imagine you
           naked - you know
           with just a sheet over you
           and pretend I'm in the same room

I slid under the sheet and fumbled for the hem of my t-shirt. This was mental. Then I slid lower down and pulled it up over my head. It felt weird. Finally I sat up, making sure the bed sheet covered everything from the shoulders down while I continued typing. Totally mad.

*R   happy now?
$*   hehe
       now your underpants
*R   ? don't peep then

I lay back, stuck both thumbs in the waistband, and slid them over my feet. I nearly had a heart attack when I turned to face my laptop again and accidentally moved the blanket uncovering my bare butt. But the webcam was aimed somewhere above my head. I sat up and held up my undies so he could see I'd really taken them off.

$*   now you are naked ruby
*R   yeh
$*   does it feel good?
*R   spose so
$*   it would be so good if I was there with you
       no?
*R   no way
$*   so you are happy to lie in bed naked and all alone
*R   mm
$*   mm?
*R   yes - of course
$*   don't I get a quick little peep
*R   peep? of wot?
$*   before you go to sleep
       a little goodnight peep
*R   wot dyou mean

146

$*   well
       you take off the sheet perhaps
       for one or two seconds
*R   as if
$*   you say yes?
*R   no way
$*   it is no big deal
*R   it is to me
$*   of course
       you are shy and I understand
       and you are young still

I thought back to that drawing of Lucy that Casey had done. Her standing naked in the same room as him as if it was the most natural thing in the world. She obviously trusted him with her life.

*R   you will probably laugh
$*   I promise not to
       never
       and you prefer not to
       so I understand
*R   hmm
$*   it is time to go to sleep anyway
       I will dream of you tonight
       and imagine what I cannot see

I let the sheet slip down three or four inches, conscious my boobs were now partly exposed. Then I clambered onto my knees, watching the sheet fall away revealing everything I had.

$*   XXXXXXXXXXXX
Stefan is off-line.

He was gone. As if I had pulled out his life-support plug myself.

I wasn't even sure if those X's were kisses or if he'd pressed on the X button accidentally before logging off.

I had a long lie in. I needed it because it took me ages to get off to sleep. My body felt as if it was still spinning somewhere in cyber-space between my laptop and his. My skin felt tingly and hot and… well, there's other stuff that I'm not about to go into. I couldn't believe everything that had happened yesterday. After such a shitty start to the holiday I'd gone out with my best friend's boyfriend for a coffee, promised to meet him again and flashed everything I've got to some perv on the internet.

It was gone ten by the time I surfaced to make myself some toast and a coffee. But instead of getting dressed I decided to take out my private diary and do some catching up. It had been a couple of weeks since I'd written anything important. Not one word about poor Farran.

IT'S funny. Me and Casey are so alike. I don't talk to Mum about all my hang-ups. Not even to Shona – except about stuff like periods and make-up and trying to control my weight. She is a girl after all. But things like what I think about my life – how I really feel about it – no. It all goes in here instead. I don't draw stuff like Casey. I scribble everything down in my private blog. Streams of words – almost as bad as that Chatterteen crap. But of course, it's for my eyes only so nobody will ever be able to dig this up on 'Google' – no prying eyes – no need for an user ID or password.

I had a flip through it. I'd filled up so many pages during the last couple of years. Most of it was paranoid teenage garbage. Embarrassing to look back on.

Dear God, do I deserve to have diabetes?
Yes.
Will you ever find a way to cure me?
No.

I suppose because I sometimes say the 'F' word it's entirely my own fault I'm cursed. But I do wonder why God doesn't forgive people for saying it. It's only a word after all. It must be a full-time job if he has to listen to everybody - and surely he's got more important stuff to think about.

I love me madly. I hate me madly.

How come Shona is always so perfect? I mean, her body and the way she looks. And me, I'm so gross. Now there's wiry little hairs sprouting everywhere. And there's no way I'm ever waxing down there.
And she always smells so nice - while I whiff sometimes.
Do boys' bodies smell as much as girls'? I can smell myself all the time. I think I'm becoming obsessed with it. Especially when I'm in bed. It's not that nasty a smell, but Shona reckons it can drive boys wild. Pheromones or something.
It's supposed to attract mates. I reckon perfume was invented to cover it up. Otherwise boys would be jumping on us all the time, trying to have sex in the street the same as dogs.

I'm a cracked little doll and no one can put me back together again. Life really sucks. Can you hear me God? Life Sucks. Get it sorted.

I couldn't even remember writing half of this garbage. But I needed to record all this new stuff while it was fresh in my mind. Those amazing pictures Casey'd drawn. And my evening with Stefan. If God ever gets round to reading this shit he'll be wondering where he went wrong when he created Ruby MacGregor

FUNNILY enough I felt even better about things as the day progressed. I couldn't stop grinning on the bus ride into the city centre.

While writing everything down I'd realised that Ruby MacGregor isn't just one girl after all. That's why it's been so difficult trying to figure out who I'm supposed to be. I'm a pie chart divided into four segments at least.

Girl One is the poor chick with diabetes – who has to be in full control of her life to stay healthy.

Girl Two is the quite nerdy kid in school – I can so live with that because Lucy's just as brainy.

Girl Three is the sweet little girl Mummy and Daddy love so much – the little girl who never grows up – no funny business in bed at night – no sexy thoughts.

And Girl Four is this teenage sex machine who wishes Stefan really had been there in bed with her last night and who fancies Casey sooooo much.

Shona always says we're all wired up differently inside our heads. I realised I could be all these different girls without having to worry about which was the real me. I wasn't just Dr J and Mr H. Shit, I was Miss A, B, C and D.

150

CHAPTER 23

CASEY was at the bus shelter waiting for the four of us. I wanted to fall into his arms and have him kiss me in front of everybody. But he just stuck his arm around my waist and we headed towards the college. Not even a cuddle, but this was ok for starters.

"AH'M no sure I should say."

I had been pestering him to tell me all he knew about Farran and why she'd run off the way she had. It's hard to sit in silence while someone is concentrating on drawing you. There were about eight other students in the L-room but none paid us any attention. Three or four of them were playing on Game Boys or PlayStations, one was reading a newspaper and the others were just sitting drinking coffee, listening to their iPods.

"But you did promise."

"Ah ken, but sometimes a promise is better being broken. Ah only said that to make sure you'd come back today."

He had a strange way of making me feel that perhaps he fancied me without saying so right out.

"So why do you hang round with those two neds?"

"Midgey and Jaker?" He laughed. "Somebody has to look out for them. It's one of my good deeds. An' anyway, I grew up with Midgey. Did you ken his dad's an alkie an' probably in need of a new liver?"

"No."

The image of a shark's liver crossed my mind for a second.

"Aye. Been a boozer all his life. His ma's got no time for either of them."

"Am I one of your good deeds as well?"

"No way MacRae." He grinned like he was keeping some big secret all to himself.

"What?"

"Nowt. Just try an' keep your head still while I do this."

It was nice, being there and not having to act all sophisticated like I normally do around boys. Wondering what they're thinking about me. Do they see me as a needy little kid who's desperate to appear attractive? Or some saddo prepared to behave like a slag just to get noticed and escape being a virgin forever?

"Have you told Lucy you're here with me?"

He shook his head.

"No. There's nowt to tell. Why? Have you said anything?"

"No. There's nowt to tell."

We both laughed. His mouth was quite sexy and his eyes crinkled up really nice when he smiled.

"Ah thought you was best mates."

"We are, but…"

"Ah just thought lassies told their bezzie mates everything."

I shook my head. "Not really." I picked my words carefully, "I mean, she's never told me whether you and her have slept together or not."

Not my best line. It went very quiet and I swear he was rushing to get the sketch finished so he could be on his way. I knew I'd blown it. My heart was already breaking into millions of little pieces. How thick can you get?

"Sorry. I'm being a cow. I don't know why I said such a stupid thing."

His mouth was clamped shut.

This was getting uncomfortable. We'd been talking

152

like old mates and suddenly I was afraid of even breathing too loud in case it set him off or something.

"It was Kenzie and 'er mam."

I took a deep breath, making a note to say a thank you prayer to God or whoever is up there before going to sleep tonight.

"What? Her mam didn't like her seeing him? 'Cause he's like a Muslim or something?"

He shook his head and laughed. "Oh no. Nothing like that. Her ma an' Kenzie were in each other's pockets, you ken?"

"What do you mean?"

"Well, Farran came home early one afternoon straight from school. She was meanin' to go to the gym but her leg was givin' her gyp so she changed her mind. They never heard her come in the house. She saw them together."

I couldn't help making a face. "What? You mean, they were having sex or something? Kenzie and her mum?"

"No quite. But they were all over each other."

"No way."

"Perhaps I shouldn't be talkin' to you about this. But Farran told us everything. She came straight to the gym in a right state. Ended up splatterin' her muesli all over the toilets. They didn't even realise she'd been in the house."

"Erm, so what did she see exactly?"

"Kenzie had his shirt off an' 'er mam had her arms wrapped around him. On their sofa. Farran says she near boked right there in the hallway."

"God, I can't get my head round this."

"I ken, doll. It's hard to believe."

I didn't know what else to say.

"You're sorry you asked me now, are you no?"

"Not sure."

He held up his drawing for me to have a look.

153

"It's nowhere near finished. But I've got the shape of your noggin' – your big gob an' that long neb of yours."

It was good even in its crude form. I knew that anybody who saw it would realise who it was – if they already knew me, obviously.

"So, what you going to do now?"

"Well, I'll prob'ly copy it onto a sheet of art paper an' start off with some pencil work, then build the skin tones up…"

"No. I mean now. You going straight home?"

"Don't have to yet. I'm no meetin' Lucy 'til back of seven when she finishes work. Why?"

"Just asking. Thought we could talk a bit more, I don't know."

"What about?"

That was the sixty million dollar question. I had no idea what to talk about.

"You still serious about us drawin' you like that picture of Lucy?"

For a split second I imagined posing naked for him like she had. But I knew what he meant.

"With them words. Yeh. An' one side of my face all sort of transformed like it's not really skin."

"I could do that. An' I been thinkin' – maybe have half your face turned into rock or crystals you ken?"

"Crystals?"

"Well aye. Rubies, what else?"

"Oh, 'course. Yeh. that might be cool."

"But I'm not sure what words I could write down."

"'S ok. I already thought of that."

I showed him my medical identification bracelet then spent the next hour or so telling him all about my diabetes. Glucose, blood testing, urine testing, insulin injections, ketones, hypoglycaemia, hyperglycaemia, the works. I'm not sure what I was expecting after all that. A quick excuse to get away I suppose: a sympathy kiss for the sick retard and then a swift exit. But he didn't budge.

"You really are some piece of work."

"Huh? What do you mean?"

"Well. Ye hold yourself together pretty well for someone in your condition. I'd never have guessed."

Hmm?

"Is that a compliment?"

"Course it is, you muffin. I'm totally in awe of how you're managin'. How you look after your body an' don't let anythin' get in the way of livin'. God I'm a dick."

"What? Why?"

"Well. Gettin' ye to smoke weed with us. Christ, I'd never have done that. An' Lucy needs her arse kickin' 'cause she kens all this already, I'm assumin'."

"Most of it. Yeh."

"Well. I'm sorry. It was bad enough thinkin' about what I'd done, then havin' yer cousin dyin' from doin' drugs."

"That's ok. Mam and Dad don't know. Just Shona."

"Och. So you told her then."

"She was there when I got home. I was still off me head."

"I'm surprised ye came anywhere near me after that."

"It's all right. And I'm glad I did now 'cause you're nothin' like I thought you were."

"Oh, yeh. An' what's that supposed to mean?"

"I just thought you were another nugget. A typical schemie."

"Thanks for that."

"So when's my picture going to be finished?"

"Oh, depends."

"On what?"

"Well, I might need to see youse again. You ken? Keep remindin' myself of what you look like in the flesh."

"Really."

"Oh, definitely. My memory's not so good, see. So just to be sure. Perhaps one more time, or two, or maybe even three."

"Cool."

"Is that ok? I mean, ye don't mind?"

"No. I don't mind at all."

CHAPTER 24

STACEY must have sent her text while I was on the bus ride home. But my phone was in my jacket pocket and I never noticed. I was too churned up inside. My heart was skipping like one of them stones skimmed across the surface of the pond in Lochend Park. And I couldn't stop studying everybody's face on the bus, wondering whether they realised what was going through my mind. It was embarrassing, romantic slush.

Daydreaming. I do it all the time.

Then the bus got stuck at a set of traffic lights for ages and I could feel the engine throbbing through the seat. And there was a smell. Like a stuffy room or dirty bedsheets. Then I felt a sharp stinging sensation right inside my nose and... when I looked down my jeans had a patch of blood where the zip is and it began spreading down the insides of both thighs. I nearly screamed.

OMG. Thank goodness there was nobody sitting next to me. I grabbed my bag from between my feet and tried to use it to cover my embarrassment. But then I realised the blood would get smeared all over my bag. We all have accidents but this was a disaster area. I tried to tug my jacket a little lower but it was no use. A dark patch began to form on one of the pockets as well – like an oil stain. And rips appeared under each knee. What the hell was happening?

Then, just when I was on the point of totally freaking out, my seat gave a lurch as the bus started to pull away from the lights and... my jeans were perfectly fine again. Not a single speck of blood anywhere in sight. No oil. Nothing. The smell seemed to have cleared away too. Just the usual stench of diesel fumes, and some orange peel someone had left in bits under the seat.

I couldn't make sense of it. I thought perhaps I'd had some kind of brain seizure but I felt perfectly fine. Except for one other tiny niggle – some nagging memory that I couldn't quite put my finger on, but I was too worked up to think straight.

IT wasn't until I got home and took my mobile out of my pocket that I noticed one missed message.

Hi Roob - soz not bn in touch. U up 2 much? Fancy goin out 2moz? S xx

I had promised to meet Casey Thursday afternoon so Wednesday was fine. It was Lucy's half day. He had already arranged to go with her to the arcade.

Hi S - not much. Yeh 2moz grt. U comin here or we meet up? Roobs xx

About an hour later she replied.

1200 end of my rd ok?

Yeh. C u then. xx

Cool ciao xx

Ciao. God, she's such a poser. But it would be fun to catch up. She could tell me all about her holidays. Show off her tan. Tell me about the latest cool guy she'd given a blow job to – as if.

IT was a hell of a change in seven days. From being Billy-no-mates I was suddenly in demand.

158

"What are you looking so distracted about? You look like you're in another world."

Mum doesn't miss much.

Well it felt like I had crossed over into another dimension for a couple of minutes this afternoon. But I was back home now.

"Oh, nothing? I'm goin' out with Stacey tomorrow."

"Well that's nice. I was beginning to think you two had fallen out."

"No. We're cool."

Yeh. We were cool.

CHAPTER 25

THE first breakthrough came with a code 10-53D.

"Looks like our guy's driving an ambulance?"

Garcia couldn't imagine anything more bizarre.

"Involved in a traffic violation sometime around three o'clock yesterday afternoon. Corner of Amsterdam and West 106th. An ambulance pulling out of the Fire Lane gets rear-ended by a C-Class Merc. The ambulance driver jumps out waving a blade, hammering on the windshield then screaming how he's going to kill whoever's inside. Total fruitcake. Looks like he's about to succeed only there's an RMP heading the other way sees it all. They pull up and as soon as they hit the siren our man disappears like his ass is on fire."

Garcia's lips curled in anticipation.

"Not your regular paramedic then."

"No. First thing they thought was a car-jacking. But looks like the guy was on his own."

"So why do we think this driver's our perp?"

Garcia couldn't see the link.

"He was driving an old Ford Traumahawk. Clearly no longer in commission so he must have got it from some used car dealer. I've got someone at the DMV checking up on the licence plate but it's unlikely to be registered knowing our luck. Anyway, the insides had been ripped out. Our man using it as a bolt hole. There was a sleeping bag, various bits of clothing as well as the usual junk – dirty hypos, spoons burnt black with all sorts of filth and…"

"And what, Karl? Spit it out. You've got me chewing my nails here."

"There was dried blood on the floor. Just in the one corner, like someone had haemorrhaged out. And an item

160

of women's underwear. That was stained in blood as well. That's what made them call it in."

"Can we get a match?"

"Not yet. But I'm guessing it could be the kid's. You saw all that blood on her pants."

"Anything else to tie it to our case?"

"Forensics are combing for fibres. There's too many prints to make sense of much. And the prints on the steering wheel have given us nothing to go on."

The air seemed to sizzle as the two detectives weighed up the information and made new connections.

"That's good work, Karl."

Iversen nodded eagerly, his nostrils flaring as if he could already scent their prey.

"Can't wait to get my hands on him if he's the one."

"What about a description?"

"Not much. The suit driving the Merc was no help. Wet his pants by all accounts. The attending officers reckoned this mobo looked like your typical skel: Caucasian male, about five four, collar-length hair, dark, straight, face as drawn and wide-eyed as your average junkie. Wearing a check lumber jacket and track suit bottoms. Could be carrying a back-pack as well. Not sure. They say it all happened so quick. Pure chance they were passing by at the time."

"But he's well gone."

"Disappeared into the crowd. By the time they realised what they had he was dust. Could be anywhere by now."

That's what Garcia was afraid of. Their suspect was out on the streets without a safe place to hide. A lone wolf. Desperate maybe. Reduced to surviving on his wits. There was no telling what he might do next.

161

CHAPTER 26

THERE had been a tremendous thunderstorm just after tea and although it did little to settle my nerves it seemed to clear the air. Shona was back home but was busy downstairs ironing all her clothes before the Big Apple. I could hear her and Mum having a quiet chat in the kitchen. The words 'some boy' suspended in the middle of their conversation was enough for me to realise who it was they were talking about.

I so wanted to send Casey a text but knew it was better not to. We had arranged to meet up on Thursday. What else was there to say?

I couldn't get off to sleep though. Replaying the entire afternoon in my head. Not just that horror movie moment on the number 25 bus, There were other more pressing matters rattling around inside my brainbox. Had I really gone and said that stupid thing about Casey and Lucy having sex? Could I still remember exactly every word he'd said to me? Or was there something important I'd missed. For example, what did he really mean when he said that I was some piece of work? It was like trying to figure out a load of maths problems inside my head. It made my brain hurt.

And that bombshell about Aunty Grace and Kenzie. No wonder Farran did a runner. And no wonder Aunty Grace always used to look so guilty. God, poor Uncle Andrew. He must know all about it. And he's a lovely man. Mind you, he is a lot older than Mum's sister and he can be hard work. He's golf mad like Dad, but he also likes crosswords and playing Scrabble. Sometimes having a conversation with him is a bit like playing Scrabble. As if he's weighing up every word before saying anything to see how many points he can score.

I was wondering whether or not I should tell Shona that I knew everything. Ask her what Mum thought about the whole situation. But not tonight. I just wanted to lie in bed and pretend Casey was lying next to me. He is so melt-your-pants hot. We weren't doing anything really. But he was there next to me whenever I wanted to reach out and hold his hand.

Gush.

STACEY was dressed in a really skimpy vest top and a pair of ultra-tight shorts that came down to her knees but showed every single bump and bulge. If they'd been pink I'd have had to look twice to make sure she wasn't in the scud. But no. They were a kind of purply-blue. No VPL in sight. And her top was black with white zig-zags. She looked lush – but a total slag.

As soon as she saw me she gave a shriek and ran up to me, both arms wide apart to receive a hug. It was like we hadn't seen each other for twenty years.

"Hiiaah! Oh-migod. I haven't seen you all holiday."

A kiss on either cheek. She's so sophisticated.

"I know."

"I mean I've been so occupied. Ten days in Tenerife. La-la-laave the place but it took another week to get over it. Jet lag, you know. And the temperature difference. We were in the 90's the whole time. And then we stayed at Leslie's for like four days. Partying. One Beverly Knight after anutha'. Takeaways and tequilas 24/7. And I've still got so much networking to do. So how's you?"

"I'm, erm…"

"Never mind that now. We gonna hit the shops?"

When we'd been in junior school we were never out of each other's homes. In the summer holidays we only spent time apart when she went off with her mam and dad to stay with her grandparents. She even came with us twice to the caravan. But then I quickly realised Dunbar couldn't compete with Greece or the Costa Brava.

We took the bus into town and had a look around the mall. 'Miss Tammy' – 'Primark' – 'Monsoon' – 'Lloyds Pharmacy'. I had just over fifteen quid that was supposed to last me the rest of the holiday so I wasn't going to be spending much. I ended up getting the same body spray as Shona and two packs of sanitary pads in a two-for-one offer.

Stacey was staring at me as if I'd bought a pregnancy testing kit or something equally gross.

"What in a herry's handbag are those for? Don't tell me you actually need all them? You are so yesterday."

"What d'you mean?"

"Didn't I say? Mum put me on the pill. For my birthday."

"Uh?"

"Well, she says better safe than sorry. Just for my holidays, of course. But I take them all the time now. It's so much more practical."

She got herself some cranberry-flavoured lip gloss and I nearly bought myself the same. But I remembered what Casey had said about shark livers. Then we popped into 'Next' and Stacey found a pair of black hipsters that I reckon were at least two sizes too small. But she's forever taking stuff back and exchanging it. I couldn't be bothered.

"So. Un café, senorita? That's 'coffee', Rubes. In Spanish."

I would never have figured that out for myself.

"Yeh, ok. Why not?"

"My treat."

Something bleeped and she slid her bag from her

164

shoulders. Then she took out her phone, peered at the display and began tapping away as if I'd disappeared.

"You don't have to."

I took out my purse as she continued to prod the screen and we joined the queue.

"No Rubes. Put that away. I feel like I've been neglecting you."

Sometimes Stacey behaves like such a fashionista. The girl behind the counter smiled at her politely as she put her phone away and decided what to order. Treating her like some celebrity even though she's a certified airhead. In the end she splurged on a medium latté for me and a large cappuccino and a chocolate muffin for herself. Then as soon as we found a table she began to fill me in on her hot summer.

Bronzing herself under the tropical sun every day. Going topless to get an overall tan – like I would believe that even though I reckon she's got tanorexia. Then she went on about the bars in the hotel. All-inclusive, whatever that's supposed to be. Drinking Margaritas and Breezers and Mo-jee-tos. I'd always thought they were called Mo-hee-tos, but what do I know? I don't speak Spanish.

"Oh, God Rubes. I'm so sorry going on about booze an' stuff. I mean, you must be devoed. You can't even have one teeny Smirnoff Ice can you? I don't know how you stand it. I'd want to top myself, really. Take an overdose or something."

An overdose. That was such a sensitive thought given the way Farran had died.

Then she quickly moved on to the guys. The hotel was a regular stud farm by the sound of it. Chico who worked in the cocktail bar. He was so ripped. And he said he would have no choice but to marry her if she stayed much longer. Manuel who spent all his free time on the beach.

The smallest pair of trunks ever with most of his merchandise on permanent display. Mario and Luca who kept following her around like a couple of lapdogs.

"They kept arguin' whose turn it was for the sun block."

"Why? Were they gay or something?"

"Noooo, you stupid mare. They were taking turns to rub it on ma bod."

"Oh. I bet their hands were everywhere then."

She gave a smirk. "Oh, yeh. An' I mean, everywhere. North and South. Each of them would kill to have me all to themselves. I just know it. It was so funny. Guys are so shallow, you know. So superficial."

"So did you pull anyone? I mean…"

"Well I'm on the pill, Rubes. Have I got to spell it out?"

"Which one?"

Her phone gave another bleep but she continued chattering away as she dug it out and studied the tiny screen.

"I pulled them all. I mean it was a holiday so what else are you supposed to do? They're so different from the guys round here who are all so meh."

She had no idea about me and Casey, obviously.

"Anyway. What about you? Tell me everything. You been havin' more of them weird dreams?"

I shook my head.

"Nah," meaning yeh. It's so easy to lie to someone as self-centred as Stacey.

She stopped mid-text and fired a smirk in my direction. "What about chatting to that perv on the internet?"

I didn't really want to let on, but what the hell? "A couple of times, yeh."

"Oh, right. An' why would you wanna do that? I mean, I thought you reckoned he was some freak. Or even a serial killer."

"No. Not any more. He sent me a couple of photos."

Suddenly I'd got her full attention, I could tell because she'd stopped pecking at her iPhone for all of ten seconds.

"No way! You have to show them to me. I mean, were they pictures of his dick or what? Don't say he sent you porn."

"No, Stace. Just normal ones. Him on holiday. And penguins."

"That is so pervy. So have you sent him any of you yet?"

"Noooh. But he's seen me on my webcam."

"Never. Did you put on a show?"

I laughed.

"I just teased him one night. Gave him a quick boob flash."

"Ohmigod. You are such a tramp. Did I tell you about what me and Les and Trudes did one night? Oh. It was so wicked. We found this guy in Florida who wanted to watch us dancing on cam, in just our underwear."

"God, how bogus."

She snorted with laughter at my reaction, as if she was enjoying being such a slut.

"I know. We danced tight circles round each other like a bunch of lezzies. And he gave us marks out of 10."

"Huh?"

"And guess who got 9½. Moi."

"Honest?" I gasped, unable to hide my disgust.

"For sure. He said I had a gorgeous butt. Said I would go down a treat in the States."

"Oh, I forgot to tell you about Shona. She's off to New York on holiday."

167

"Really? Anyway, then he dared us to... you know."

"To what?"

"Touch ourselves."

"That is so gross."

I couldn't imagine doing anything of the sort. Ever. I sucked the dregs of froth from the bottom of my cup as she finished her texting. Then she put her phone away and gave me a pitying look.

"Rubes, we were only doing it for a laugh. God, you are so up-tight."

"So are you saying you actually did it in front of him? Eeeewwh!"

"Of course not. It was only pretend. It was hilarious."

Not.

"And he kept sayin' if we didn't stop soon he'd explode."

Hell. All I could think about was what I'd done for Stefan the other night. Was he perhaps expecting me to do the same stuff as Stacey? More than likely. I felt sick.

CHAPTER 27

"**FANCY** a dander for a change?"

It was another sunny day, so why not?

"Where to?"

He took me into Leithend Park as far as the boating lake then we sat on one of the benches and watched the world float past. The sun was glorious – hardly a cloud in the sky. I was wearing my new lemon top. I nearly went and put on my spangly denim shorts but in the end I wore my low rise, faded jeans. I know my bum looks better in them because they're shaped just right. I'd also borrowed one of Shona's baseball caps. I looked like an American tourist – or a student on their gap year.

"Nice here."

Brilliant opening line, Rubes. Write that one down in your journal for future reference 'cause it could probably come in useful next time you're on the pull.

"Aye. Bonnier than Lochend."

"Is that where you went yesterday."

"Aye. Once we got back from the shops. Had a couple of bevvies. An' Leesha came as well."

"Oh. So are her and Jaker back together?"

"No way. He gave her the elbow months ago."

That was something Aleesha had conveniently forgotten to mention to anyone. Or, at least to me.

I bit back a snigger. "Really. Oh. I thought…"

"What?"

"Well, I thought they were getting serious."

"Don't make me laugh. He's sniffin' round that Kelly Brennan now. Her that used to work with Luce's mam."

In the bargain stores round the corner from the flats.

"Right."

"Says he can't wait forever to… well, you ken."

"You mean sleep with her?"

"What else? An' Leesha won't let any laddie get inside her pants 'cause if her dad found out he'd probably kebab their goolies."

I was laughing out loud now, but still trying to come to terms with what he was telling me.

"And you're sure?"

"Course I'm sure. Kenzie follows her round like he's her minder. Her family bein' Muslim an' all that. Lassies are meant to wait until they're married an' even then their parents have to agree first."

"God, and I thought she'd been at it with Jaker for ages."

"Where the hell d'you get this stuff from?" He stared at me like I'd done something stupid. As if!

"Well, Leesha says she'd already done it an' it was so-so. And Lucy won't let on about you and her. I mean… if you have or not."

"Oh…"

"Soz. It's none of my business." The ground was about to swallow me up again – except it didn't.

"We only slept together the once, if you must know. Just before the school holidays started."

"I'm a nosy cow."

"That's ok. I'm surprised she hadn't posted the news all over Facebook."

"She wouldn't do that."

"Ah'm no so sure. It just felt like, well. It was like she wanted to tick me off her list of things to do then move onto the next thing."

"That sounds so shady."

"Well that's what it seemed like. Once we'd done it she acted as if she'd gone right off me for a couple of

170

days. It was like: get ears pierced – tick, get a tattoo – tick, see JLS live – tick, get shagged – tick."

We said no more about the matter and just watched a couple of kids chucking a Frisbee. The weather was far too nice to be doing anything as strenuous. I shut my eyes and let the warm sun melt away all my cares.

"Fancy a cannie?"

"Eh? Oh, no thanks. I can't drink."

"No. I meant a Coke, or a Diet Coke if you'd rather. I'll get us a couple of chilled ones from that ice cream van if he's got any."

I watched him join the queue. My wee manny. Was he mine now or wasn't he? Then I noticed two young women at the water's edge, one pushing a baby buggy back and forth. A little boy in a blue romper suit. The mother, if that's who she was, used one hand to hood her eyes as she looked over towards where I sat. She seemed familiar but I couldn't place her. Then she gave me a little wave and I recognised the gesture.

It was Cody. Without a doubt. But how could she be here, alive again and wandering around Edinburgh?

"There you go."

Casey handed me the can but it was as if he'd handed me a hand grenade. I was still staring at her as she dissolved into the crowds.

"It's ok. I haven't given it a shake. Not tryin' to get you sprayed in cola."

"That's ok."

Where had she gone? I tried to pick out her yellow, stripey top and bare midriff from the mass of bodies but there was no sign of her. A guy on a skateboard slalomed between a pair of Pentland Second-formers acting like silly schoolgirls. A fat man stood by while his dog peed against a lamp post. And there they were disappearing into

171

the distance. Cody pushing the baby buggy accompanied by another much younger woman – torn jeans cinched around her narrow waist by a wide, white belt. Dark hair in a top knot. Wearing a faded green sweat shirt that looked so out of place in this heat.

The same cheap, white plastic belt from that time on the bus. It had been threaded through the loops of my blood-covered jeans for all of thirty seconds. Levi's jeans, obviously. But it didn't make sense. The two of them walking round Leithend Park in broad daylight. Unless they were trying to pass on some kind of warning to me. Or were they telling me they were leaving for good? Walking out of my life together? Cody waving goodbye? Was this dream business over at last?

"You ok? You look miles away."

"No. Thought I saw somebody, that's all."

Casey was sitting next to me again – his leg touching mine.

God. This was supposed to be a fun day out. Come on, Rubes. Snap out of it.

Pfftsssss.

I lifted the can to my lips and began to chug down the fizzing cold liquid burning through my throat and filling me with gas and sugar and all sorts of e numbers. I love it.

"D'you wanna go and sit down over there in the shade?"

He led me across the grass towards a stand of trees. Then he sat on the ground and brushed away the lawn clippings and twigs to make a clean place for me to settle next to him. Time seemed to stand still. I know that's a feeble thing to say, but it did. It was like the rest of the world was shut behind a screen. We were surrounded by silence and the warm air scented like honey and freshly-mown grass.

I felt his hand take hold of mine and my heart did a flutter. He kept exploring each finger as if discovering something new. Then he raised my hand to his face to breathe in the soft scent of my skin and fingernails. I was in paradise. Like there was a magnetic force bonding our bodies together and sending sparks between each single one of our molecules. Slowly he shuffled his bum forwards then lay down on his back and gestured for me to do the same.

"Shut your eyes."

"What?"

I had no idea what I was meant to do next. Did he expect me to climb on top of him or something?

"Ah'm tellin' you to relax, Rube. Enjoy the sun."

He gripped my hand again in his and gave it a squeeze.

"Don't you wish that some days could just go on an' on?"

I nodded.

"Oh, yeh. Definitely."

"You comfy there?"

"'S ok."

It was like lying on Nana Mac's cobbled back yard but I wasn't going to tell him that. I squinted at the sky and watched a single puff of white cloud like a little island floating across from left to right. It felt as if the whole of the planet had turned upside down and that we were stuck to its surface gazing down instead of up. Staring into endless space that went down and down into nothingness and forever.

"Is it ok if we sit up? I can put my arm around your shoulder."

My back was beginning to ache.

173

"Course it is, hen."

He raised himself and I sat up alongside him then slid my right arm behind his neck. God. Was I being too forward? I let my fingers rub against his cheek then his sideburns then I traced the shape of his ear. He started giggling.

"What you doin' now, lassie?"

"Just messin. You don't mind do you?"

"Course not. So you had many boyfriends then?"

"Not really. No, just…"

"Just the one?"

"Well sort of. We had a dance. And a bit of a snog." I started smiling at the absurdity of the memory. Me telling Casey about a snog as if it was such a big deal when him and Lucy had already had sex.

"Cool."

"I'm still a bit scared, I suppose."

"What of?"

"Well, finding my way round boys. You know. Tryin' to figure stuff out."

"You're not doin' too bad for a newbie."

The grin I kept in reserve for special occasions came out of cold storage.

"Ah'm the same, you ken? Most girls, ach. I haven't got a clue what they're expectin'. They says they just wanna be friends, an' then get miffed when you don't try it on with them. Or they're only after the one thing, an' after it's done they blow hot an' cold."

"Most girls? Why? You had loads of girlfriends then?"

"No, I have no. Just Lucy…"

"Huh. I don't think so, mister."

He laughed, turned to face me and put one hand either side of my waist before beginning to squeeze.

"What's that supposed to mean, you wee muffin?"

174

"Ok ok. Sorry. I take it back."

Then our faces came closer together and our lips met and he kissed me, and he kissed me, and he kissed me.

I could taste him on my mouth for the rest of the day. My lips were numb from snogging. As well as the bones in my back where I'd lain down again as he continued to kiss me like what seemed forever. My tongue had been inside his mouth most of the time searching for the secret entrance into his heart or lungs perhaps. And his tongue – it did everything a tongue was designed to do I suppose. I was hypnotized. His hands could have gone anywhere he wanted to put them but he just held onto my face, as if he was afraid it might break loose and float off into the sky. Afraid I might change my mind and tell him to pack it in.

No way. I wanted to do it until it went dark and the stars came out.

Too soon he eased off, gazing down at me with a huge grin on his face.

"Happy?"

"Mmm."

He sat up again, opened his legs and patted the ground between them. "Park your wee bum in here,"

Did he want me facing him? No. He took my waist like one of them ballet dancers and lowered me to the ground so that my butt was pressed tight between his thighs. This was probably the best part of the afternoon. He wrapped his arms around my middle, squeezing me not too tight, and nuzzled the back of my neck and my hair and my ears. And we talked.

He told me everything about him and Lucy. How he was beginning to realise she wasn't looking for a proper relationship. Just someone to show off to her mates. How he didn't feel the same way about her now they'd had sex either – probably because she'd given it up too easily. And the way she'd acted when he took her to 'Phrenzy' one night. Dancing with every guy she could find, trying to make him jealous. How he went off and got bladdered all on his own.

I told him a bit about Stacey. What a real cow she was turning into.

"Stacey McLeod. Och, I ken that one. She's out on the pull every Friday an' Saturday. Her an' the other two mingers."

I laughed. That would be Leslie Miller and Trudy King. I'd seen some of the photos Stacey had posted on her profile page – post-club. The three of them looking sweaty and cruddy: mascary and caked in make-up, wearing shapeless black box skirts that showed off their flabby thighs.

"Corn-fed heifers, Kenzie calls 'em. Fattened up and waitin' for a shag then the next thing you ken they're droppin' bairns left, right 'n' centre."

"You don't fancy them then?"

"Are you jestin'?"

"I thought they were supposed to be sexy."

"Haha. No way, babe. You wanna ken what's real sexy? Shall I tell you? "

I assumed he was going to say massive boobs or a tight butt or like a lap dancer or something. I could just picture Stacey lap dancing on her webcam if any boy asked her to.

"It's doin' this, doll. Holding you like this. No pressure. None of that showin' off shite to your pals. This is probably the sexiest thing ever."

And, oh God. Even thinking about it when I finally lay in bed that night with the memory of that entire afternoon bathed in a kind of golden light and the heat of the summer ticking away bit by bit like a bomb about to go off. I was ready to explode.

Boom!

CHAPTER 28

FRIDAY was panic stations. There was just this one long weekend left before we started back at school. I had to finish my French vocab lists as well as my English project by Tuesday. I'd also promised Shona I'd go with her around the shops so she could get a few last minute bits before packing. And I'd promised Casey I'd try and see him if I could.

But in the end I couldn't. I sent him a text just after 10:00 when I knew Lucy would be at work. I said sorry about a dozen times and told him I was free all day Saturday, Sunday or Monday if that would be ok. I also told him how much I'd enjoyed our afternoon at the park. I couldn't believe I was turning down a hot date with the boy of my dreams but I couldn't really put the rest of my life on hold.

The entire day was a blur. Shona was totally focussed on NYC. Mum was focussed on getting everybody through the day with the minimum of stress and fitting in her weekly shop at the same time. I was stressed out thinking about Casey. He'd already texted me back to say he'd have to spend all Saturday with Lucy because she was wanting to share as much time as she could with him before school started. I thought I'd be ok about that – but it was difficult.

THINGS didn't settle down until later that night. I was shattered. Physically and mentally.

Shona looked just as whacked – hoisting herself off the sofa and giving a long, long stretch. "Comin' upstairs, Rubes?"

"What? Are you two off to bed already?" Mum asked.

"No. Just want to finish packing then spend my last few

hours this side of the Atlantic with my favourite sister."

Shona had been giving her wardrobe a clear-out. Making way for the new outfits she was going to buy on Fifth Avenue. There was a pile of her rejects stacked on the chair in her room.

"Take your pick, hon. It's you or the charity bag."

I took the lot. I'm not proud. Besides, Mum and Dad are always broke so the only way I can keep up with the likes of Stacey MacLeod is by recycling. Most of Shona's hand-me-downs were like new anyway. There were tops and a couple of micro skirts she'd never even worn. Some t-shirts had faded from too many washes but they were still good enough as nightshirts.

"You wanna double up with me again tonight?"

"If you like."

I might have guessed that she was fishing for information.

"So, what's going on?"

"What do you mean?"

"I mean boy-ologically."

"Nothing. Just had a bit of a hectic week, that's all."

"Yeh, I bet."

I tried to change the subject.

"Did I tell you Stacey's on the contraceptive pill?"

"No way."

"So she reckons. Said her mum put her on it."

Shona grinned. "What a slut. I hope you're not getting any bright ideas."

"Noooo!"

"So who's the guy?"

I tried again.

"Stacey's guy?"

"No, you divv. Yours. Mum's told me. It's written all over your face anyway."

179

I gave up and told her everything I dared.

Shona said she remembered Casey from school but he'd not made much of an impression – good or bad. Fortunately she knew nothing of his history with Lucy.

"So you're officially an item then?"

"Sort of."

"Well, how many times you been out?"

"Three times – since Monday…"

"Omigod, Rubes. You are such a tart."

"But it's complicated."

"Huh, that's guys for you. Tell me about it."

But how do you explain that you're meeting up with your bezzie mate's boyfriend on the sly and letting him snog the face off you?

"What I mean is, he's already with somebody else."

"Somebody else? Sugar! So, I mean, what the hell are you doing even thinking about…?"

"We really get on. He's sweet and he's funny. And he's hot. And I think he really likes me which…"

"Which means nothing, hon. He's just after a bit on the side. Like most of the neds around here."

"That's not fair. He's not like that."

"Huh."

I told her about his drawings. College. The afternoon in the park. The cuddling and the stuff he said about it being so sexy.

"He sounds a right smoothy, I'll give him that."

"But he's not. I mean, he's just normal."

"Ok. He may be everything you say he is, but don't go building your hopes up."

"I'm not."

But of course, I was.

Then somehow we got onto heavier stuff. Shona letting slip how she'd had to take the morning-after pill a

180

couple of weeks after starting uni. Headline news or what? A guy she had latched onto in a club in Wakefield making a complete fool of her.

"Was that Harvey?"

"How do you know about him?" From the look she gave me I could tell he was supposed to be some big secret.

"You must have mentioned him in one of your e-mails."

"Oh, well. No. It wasn't Harvey. Just some low-life scumbag who was only after one thing."

"An' you give it him?"

Smirk.

"You could say that. On a friggin' plate."

"Sorry. So who's this Harvey?"

"Och, he's a real sweetheart. I mean, we're best mates an'… well, it's an open sort of relationship. As soon as he finishes his course next summer that'll probably be it. But I'm not too fussed."

"You must really like him."

"God, oh yes. He's such a dish. And he's funny and smart, and like he's got this vulnerable side as well. He totally understands women. I even thought he must have been gay to start with."

She snorted with laughter.

"But he isn't."

"Definitely not."

"So have you and him?"

"God's sake, Rube. Give us a break. I mean, girls don't tell, you know? Once you've done it you don't brag about it and stuff like that any more. It's, well… it's so immature."

That sounded about right if Aleesha and Lucy were anything to go by.

181

"And you really don't mind that you're going to be on your own again soon as he leaves uni?"

"Mhmm. I'll get over it. Find some other hot guy. Anyway, life isn't supposed to be a fairy story. People don't generally live happily ever after. It's hard enough getting lucky for a couple of years at a time. That's all I'm looking for out of this relationship. Making sure I get what I can while it's available. Don't stick all your hopes and dreams inside the tomorrow bank, Rubes, and expect to be able to cash in your cheque when you're ready a few years later. Life doesn't work that way."

My eyes suddenly sparked with tears. Farran used to go on about stuff like that all the time. Living life to the full. I wiped my face on my pillow so Shona wouldn't notice how upset I'd become. I was wondering if that's what Farran had been trying to do when she decided to drop out of school and leave home. It seemed unlikely. And it certainly wasn't the way Mum and Dad would have wanted me or Shona to behave – living for today and forgetting about the future. But it made me think. Any one of us could drop dead at any moment without experiencing everything life has to offer.

CHAPTER 29

THE second breakthrough followed a series of setbacks. The blood samples were inconclusive. Type A matched Levi Washington as well as three million others in the Metropolitan District alone. And Garcia had been warned the DNA profile could take another two or three weeks at least. The holiday season was probably to blame for the latest backlog. Or a fresh wave of cost cutting. Political priorities a long way from what he considered professional policing. As for identifying the driver, the vehicle was registered to some hippy landscape designer from Little Italy. But he'd already reported it missing more than six months ago. The trail was long cold.

Then Garcia took a call from the front desk.

"There's a gentleman here asking for you by name. Says he wants to confess to a homicide."

He was in his mid-fifties, clean-shaven and relatively well dressed. But the odour of sour whisky poisoned his breath and his face was pock-marked and pale as putty.

"What you gonna confess to today, Herbie?"

There were cranks owning up to murders on a daily basis when the temperature on the city streets hit the 80's. Herbie Walker was a regular visitor downtown. Craving notoriety. Willing to admit to any crime as long as it allowed him a few minutes of attention and a free cup of NYPD coffee.

"This guy you're lookin' for. The one who killed that young girl they found by the Hudson. It was me."

"Really?"

"Yeh, Mr Garcia. Don't know what came over me. I just seen her there and the nex' thing I know she was dead."

"You knifed her?"

183

"That's right. Knifed her an' dumped her in the river."

"Where exactly did this happen?"

The guy's gaze switched to the fluorescent light above the desk for an instant.

"It was close by. I seen her at the back of one of the stores where she was doin' tricks."

Much of the detail had been kept from the press but somehow they'd got wind of Cody's seedy sideline. Garcia was desperate to bring this pointless interview to an end and get back to doing something constructive.

"So you decide to slit her throat an' dump her 'longside the Parkway, right under our noses?"

"Yeh. That's right, Mr Garcia. You knew that all along, didn't ya? So you got me. I deserve to be punished."

Iversen arrived just as Herbie was being escorted back onto the street with another warning for wasting police time.

"Forgive me father, for I have sinned," he whispered to his partner.

Garcia made to grab him as they took the stairs to the squadroom together.

"You could say that. Confession might be good for his soul. But I'm tellin' you, it's not doing me any favours. It's like we're taking two steps back for every single step forwards."

"Not necessarily. I got some good news at last."

Garcia stopped in his tracks and turned.

"So what gives?"

"The underwear they found in the back of the guy's LV. A turquoise brassiere. The Washingtons identified it as their daughter's about an hour ago. We didn't let on where it was found, and we managed to keep them from seeing the worst of the blood."

"That's good work."

"Also I sent one of the squad cars round again to see that store owner where our little hooker worked."

Garcia shook his head.

"I already told you, Karl. The fact that she worked the streets to make ends meet don't mean..."

"Ok. I get it."

"She's somebody's daughter, somebody's momma. Got as much right to our respect as anyone. And she didn't deserve to end up dead like that no matter what she was doin'."

Iversen smirked.

"Anyway. They found a mustard-coloured smock stuffed under the driver's seat. The store owner confirmed it's the same type as what the girls at the store wear. Everything ties this vehicle to Cody and Levi. So our guy's the one. Yeh? We got him by the balls, Reub."

"Almost. All we gotta do now is find where the hell he's holed up."

"I've got a couple of guys checking out CCTV cameras west of Central Park but he could be underground for all we know."

Garcia nodded. "Yeh. Underground with all the other rats that infest the city. This job gets to be more like pest control every friggin' day."

CHAPTER 30

ONE e-mail all week. And from the last person I wanted to hear from.

> **Hi Ruby, how's my dreamgirl?**
> **I wanted to say a big thank you for Monday night.**
> **You are an extraordinary young lady, you know. I**
> **hope you don't have any regrets for having a little**
> **harmless fun.**
> **Stefan xxx**

I wanted to wipe him from my memory – erase everything I had done off my hard drive but of course I couldn't. I was desperately trying to figure out how much of me he'd seen. He would have got an eyeful of my boobs when I dumped the top-sheet. But what about my private bits? I was hoping it had all happened too quickly for him to see much. God, why am I such a dweeb?

I was bored senseless. Dad had taken Shona down to Newcastle early this morning to meet up with Laura at the airport. From there, believe it or not, they were flying to Amsterdam – then changing flights for one to the USA. She would be in the Netherlands by now probably.

Casey was with Lucy. Her smooching and rubbing herself against him like a bitch on heat. He has no feelings for me. Not really. Bleh. But that's ok because if he did I'd be stressed out thinking about him every second of the day. And I wasn't. I was stuck here all on my jays with nothing better to do than get in touch with a creep.

He was on-line. And as soon as he noticed I was there
he said hi.

$*   so there you are, ruby
           how are u tonight
*R   fed up
$*   what - you had too much to eat
           then you should lie down perhaps
*R   no - I mean fed up
           like depressed with my life
$*   that is not good
           why are you so sad
*R   lots of reasons
           and I wish I hadn't

I didn't even know what to call what I'd done.

$*   hadn't what?
           you are in trouble?
*R   no
           but I told Stacey what I did
           what we did on monday night
$*   Why did you tell her? That's not very smart
           What has she said?
*R   Nothing
           She laughed and said it was gross
$*   Ok Just remember not to talk about this to
           anyone else.
           It's a taboo. I hope that's the right word.
           So your friend doesn't accept that,
           just don't talk about it with her.
           So why did you decide to show me your body?
           You are really pretty,
           but it's very intimate and private!

And remember, I'm much older than you.
Do you understand
I could get in trouble
maybe in your country
because you are not yet 18
and if this was happening for real?

OMG. He'd never written so much before. Ever. Was he mad at me? Or just scared for his own skin if Mum and Dad found out? And what did he mean about it not happening for real? It had been real enough to freak me out for most of the week.

*R   I'm scared that I made you cross -
     I would never do anything to get anybody in
     trouble cause it was my fault anyway -
     flashing my body off like some slag
$*   is slag
     not a very nice word I think
*R   well no
     it's like a stripper
     or a laptop dancer
$*   sweet ruby
     you are not a slag
     you are a sweet young girl
     who wanted to make me happy so
     you didn't make me cross.
     I wont get in trouble, don't worry.
     It wasn't your fault,
     I promise you, I teased you
     and you teased me.
     That is ok if no one gets hurt.
*R   ok
     thanx

          Stacey would keep a secret anyway
          cos I know loads of shady stuff about her -
          stuff she does on her webcam
    $*   ok
          so relax and tell me about your week
          it is not so bad as that surely

I told him a little about Casey – just the bare bones.
His pictures and how he was doing a drawing of me. And
I told him about Shona going off on holiday.

    $*   Schiphol airport in Amsterdam
          is very close to my flat
          the planes keep me awake all night
          hehe
    *R   I'm goin to miss her
          cos we start back in school
          next Tuesday
          then I won't see her much
          because she goes back to uni
    $*   she is how old
          19?
    *R   yeh
          probably more your type
    $*   ah well
          I think you are also my type
    *R   am just a kid
          So although you had fun Monday night
          I'm probably not that special
    $*   to me you will always be special
    *R   sorry
          I'm just feeling tired
          - and confused about stuff
    $*   what stuff

*R   stuff between boys and girls
       sometimes I feel a freak
$*   what I saw Monday night
       is not a freak
*R   OMG
       I'm blushing just thinking about it
$*   lets not talk about that
       if it makes you embarrassed
*R   and what were all the xxx's
       were they kisses
       or did you press x by mistake
$*   hehe
       they were goodnight kisses
*R   right
$*   because you gave me a wonderful memory
       to take with me to bed
       you understand?
*R   sort of
$*   ok
       so you understand how
       a man sometimes has feelings
       the same way girls have feelings for boys
       - physical feelings
*R   mhmm
$*   there is not so much difference
       between a man and woman's body
       the way sexy thoughts
       make physical changes happen -
       a girl also gets turned on
       right?

I wanted to climb under the duvet and curl up into a little ball and pretend I was back in Casey's lap with his arms wrapped around me again instead of listening to

Stefan's boring crap. He was beginning to sound like Dad giving me advice about puberty. Boooooring. But of course, he was also looking for a re-run of Monday night's peepshow. So I made an excuse to log off before things got totally out of hand.

I closed my eyes and tried to form a dream of me and Casey together forever. The touch of his skin and the rough weave of hair on his arms and the taste and feel of his tongue. Trying to remember what it felt like with my bottom pressed against his crotch. Wondering whether or not he'd been turned on. Even trying to imagine what we might do the next time we were alone together. Would he squeeze my bum cheeks the way he'd squeezed Lucy's that time?

I got my wish inside my dream and it ended up being another really hot one. But there was no way I could share the details with Lucy or she'd have torn my eyes out. Dreams? I'm still wondering how we come up with them – one minute I'm in the arms of my lover, the next I'm watching another poor girl who's waiting to die.

DREAMGIRL

GIRL THREE

CHAPTER 31

THE girl in the picture was not who I had been expecting. It was Ruby MacGregor as I'd never seen her before. He'd got the bone structure and hairline exactly right. The same soft eyes and stubby nose. The same dark eyebrows, lips a little too thin, mouth a little too wide. But there was also an internal glow that somehow he had captured transforming my face into a work of art. That's what this was. I'm not beautiful however you twist that word around to make it fit – but this picture was. Simple. Honest. And stunning.

"Oh my God, it's fantastic. I can hardly catch my breath."

"It's you, is it no?"

I nodded. Yet I was still amazed that's who it was.

"But ah'm no so sure about this one."

The first had been a straightforward portrait. The kind you expect to see when you go round art galleries and museums. But the second was totally different – what I'd asked him to draw. Mostly black and white again, but not as lifelike. The face was almost an exact copy but he'd shoved it to the left side of the page, and about a third of it was no longer my face any more. My hair was swept to one side so it uncovered that portion and instead of skin and flesh on show there was a cluster of tiny red crystals. It looked as if they were growing out of my head. Sounds gross but it was quite cool.

And on the other side of the page the whole background was painted a rich, dark red to match my name. He'd also included most of the words I'd told him.

DIABETES - HYPOGLAECAEMIA - GLUCOSE - KETONES - INSULIN

"I had to look one or two of them up on the internet to make sure I'd spelt them right," he laughed. "So, you freaked out or what?"

"No. It's..."

"Air-brushing," he added as my fingers traced the lettering.

The words were like banners of silver emblazoned across the page. Not printed in solid lettering like in his other two pictures but sprayed on in a very fine, metallic mist. You could read them when the light hit the words just right but they also looked as if they were about to fade into the red mist behind.

"It's just awesome. I mean, everything about it."

"You think so?"

"Absolutely, I mean. I never thought it would be as fantastic as this."

We both stared at it for ages as if hypnotized. A few people walking past our table seemed to slow down in order to sneak a quick glance before moving on but I didn't care if they saw it was me or not. I was so overwhelmed at his talent.

"It must have took you ages."

"Well there were a few late nights. But I don't mind puttin' the hours in when it's special. I really got into it."

He tugged another two sheaves of paper from his folder. One was that sketchy outline, the very first picture he'd drawn of me.

"You might as well take this if you want it. It's just the rough draft ah drew last week."

He rolled it up carefully and passed it over.

The sheet beneath was covered in tiny detailed pencil drawings of what I realised was me again. My eyes floating in nothingness. My mouth – open, closed, smiling, scrunched up. One of my hands. Each finger

195

perfectly sketched. There were even three pictures of me standing up – face-on, in-profile and from behind. He'd got my curves about right.

"When did you do these? I mean, I never posed for them."

"It's all in here." He pointed to his head.

They were so good. But it felt weird seeing them here. Like a CCTV camera had taken pictures of me without me knowing and suddenly I was live on 'STV News' or something. Weird that he'd carried images of me inside his head accurately enough to come up with these. The way my hair fell to my shoulders. The way my waist bulged a bit under that top. My tight butt in my favourite jeans.

I was touched.

Then he checked his watch and the spell was broken.

"Ach. Ah promised Lucy I'd meet her about four. Ah'm sorry."

The world stopped turning. As if someone had flipped a switch. So this was the brush-off I'd been half expecting. A cup of coffee and some cast-off sketch he'd scribbled. That's what he was leaving me with. He'd been humouring me and now it was all over.

"Oh. That's ok."

It so was not ok. I was shrivelling up inside and I could feel my face flushing red. There were even tears on standby but I was determined not to let him see me cry.

I fumbled for my slouch bag off the back of the chair. Stabbed the roll of paper into it like a sword piercing my heart.

"You don't need to go yet."

"Better had."

The chair scraping against the cold tiles like fingernails tearing fresh gouges into my flesh. Shona had

196

warned me not to get too attached, but I can be such a needy bitch sometimes.

"Rubes, ah'm real sorry."

"It's ok. Really. I... I understand."

"No. Ah mean, I'm sorry about ruining our plans for the day. But I'll make it up to you the morrow if you let me."

I came up for air. Was he throwing me a life belt after kicking me off the diving board into the deep end?

"Er, ok I suppose." I couldn't decide whether to cry anyway or start laughing.

"Can ah text you laters?"

"Course. I've got a dental check-up in town at ten then I'm free after. All day 'til about five."

"Great. Lucy's off away with her ma an'..."

"I don't want to know."

He nodded. Message understood.

I leant forward to kiss him. He placed his hand behind my head and steadied me as I drew life from his lips. Then I sighed with relief and walked out.

MY jaw was actually aching from clenching my teeth together so tightly. I was trying to hold the taste of his mouth intact inside my own until I got home. I even managed to keep my gob shut for most of the rest of the afternoon until it was feeding time.

Mum tiptoed around me. I knew she knew that there was something going on but for once she didn't feel a need to interfere. I mean, one minute I was convinced he had dumped me and I was leaden-hearted with despair and the next we were back together and my feet had a spring to them. But where it was heading I wasn't sure. I was happy on one level but so mixed up on another.

Casey had taken the memory of my body home with

197

him and sat up for hours in his room drawing these exquisite pictures. I felt honoured. And yet I'd gone and flashed my naked bod at some loser on the internet just to give him a quick thrill and to make myself feel... what? Sexy? No way. Grown-up? Not even that. Special I suppose. Stefan had actually told me I'd given him a wonderful memory so I should feel flattered. But I felt cheap. I couldn't help wondering what he had done with what I'd shown him. Created something magical like Casey or kept it like a forbidden secret in the back of his dirty mind?

God. I was cracking up.

I went upstairs and dug out my journal. I needed to write down these thoughts before they drove me mental. Writing stuff is always easier than talking about it, even to Shona: my own personal agony aunt. I can't even bear to think about some of the bits I wrote in here now, but at the time they helped me sort my life out I suppose.

I wish I could be in a coma and live the rest of my life in a dream existence. Edinburgh's own version of Sleeping Beauty. The real world sucks.

Nearly two years ago. I was such a drama queen in those days.

I watched Lucy in dance class again last night. <3 I can't take my eyes off her. She is so fit and the way she moves her gorgeous gorgeous butt. I think I'm becoming a lesbian.

May last year. That latest crush lasted about as long as my nail varnish. And yet I still fancy her, sort of. But I'm definitely not gay. I think. I probably love her sooooo

198

much because I want to be just like her. I can be so weird at times.

May 5th - Struan would have been 10 today. My wee little brother. Where is he now, I wonder? Is he living in some other dimension - a happy 10 year-old boy who doesn't even know I exist? I wish I'd got to know him. I never did but I miss him so much.

Creepy or what?

BOY ONE : Luke Moffat : 8/10

2 dances 1 long snog. Felt his thing pressed against me when we stood next to each other queuing for drinks. OMG.

What a joke. Boy One, as if there was going to be a long line of hotties queuing up to taste my cherry lipstick. Luke Moffat. He'd never said a word to me since that night. I ceased to exist. No idea what I did wrong. He couldn't even bear to look at me whenever we passed each other in the corridor. I so don't need him. He's left school now anyway. Stacey reckons he's started work in his dad's builders' yard. Labouring. Loser.

THIRTY-SIX hours from now I'll be starting another year at school. I hate going back after the holiday. But this time will be even worse because Lucy and Aleesha are both going to be in the Lower Sixth. Lucy might even be made into a prefect. She won't want some pathetic Fifth-former cramping her style. And Stacey's moving in different circles now she's trashed her exams so we'll probably only get to see each other at lunch time or if and when she can be bothered to walk home with me. I can survive on my own anyway – and Mum says this is the year when studies have to come top in my list of priorities.

Boooooring or what.

Shona had given me nearly a full jar of body wax. She said it smelt off but it should still work. I had some serious repair work to do before going back to Pentland. My legs were Itchy and Scratchy and my armpits needed strimming, my eyebrows were too thick, and my hair could do with a double shampoo. I was having it restyled next Sunday but I still decided it would be best to let it dry on its own instead of using the drier because I didn't want split ends. I must have still been under the shower when Stacey phoned and left a voicemail.

"Hey girlfren. Call me soon as."

She sounded excited about something.

I felt like a brand new person when I finally finished my routine. A brand new woman even. I wrapped a clean bath towel around my head, put on my green silk pj's and fluffy dressing gown and got comfortable. Ready for a good, long, girl-to-girl chat.

"Hiya. You ok?"

"Sure am, honeeee. An' how 'bout you?"

"Just got out of the shower."

"Ooh. All nice and buffed up ready for Tuesday?"

"Well, sort of. You an' all?"

"Will be after tomorrow. Mum's taking me to the hairdressers and we've booked a session at that new nail salon. Next to 'Café-chino'."

Casey and I had met there for coffees this afternoon. If only she knew.

"Sounds great."

200

"You bet. Can't wait to get back to school. There's so much news and goss to catch up with."

"I s'pose."

"So anyway, honeeee. What's the dealio with you and Casey?"

CHAPTER 32

THE dream was as menacing as the other nightmares I'd had – but this time there was no girl. Just a space awaiting the next victim perhaps.

An empty cellar, narrow windows high up beneath the low ceiling, grimy and cobwebbed and barely letting in any light from the outside world. Just a watered down yellow haze. Brick walls with fallen-off plaster, a set of metal shelving down one side, a black, plastic bucket, some cardboard cartons and the chain.

The chain was bolted to the wall with a loop attached. Like a dog collar. But no signs of the dog. Just puddles of what might have been dog wee but looked more like tar or oil. Like under Dad's van when it had that leak. And there were spots of rust on the dirty concrete as well. Or maybe patches of dried blood. Blood seemed more likely because this was a torture chamber.

There was a smell as well. A dream with a smell like the seaside at Dunbar after the tide has gone out and the brown husks of sea kelp begin to bake in the sun or when there are crab shells washed up on the rocks and those stagnant, salt-encrusted pools where the water has turned a mossy green. But worst of all was the noise. Constant. Like the generator on Dad's jet wash but with the volume turned up to +20 so that my fillings hurt and my head throbbed.

Yet even above this racket I still heard the door opening. I knew it was the same door with the screech of metal against the frame and the scrape and the slam that followed. It had to be Stefan. His shadow falling across the floor like in those penguin photographs, thrown down like his coat after a hard day's labour. Honey I'm home.

No features I could make out. The drag of feet across

bare concrete. His moving shadow taunting me as it stepped over a pair of discarded trainers, a plastic bucket, a rolled-up, moth-eaten blanket, some empty burger trays, and one pink, woollen stocking. Then a hand shape, fingers fumbling for the chain and tugging it tight. Testing its strength and then...
Nothing.

The pitch black night and absolute silence was more disturbing than the nightmare images I'd been expecting. It was the silence that woke me. But I was calm for once. I'd not even broken into a sweat. Cool and calm. Frozen in place actually; terrified that if I moved or made a sudden sound he would hear me. The man. Stefan, or whoever he was, getting this chamber of horrors ready for his next victim.

And there was this horrible sensation of doom hanging over me like a mosquito net, trapping all the primitive fears underneath and keeping out the real world. The safe world. I could only think one thought. I was his next victim. Somehow, I don't know how, I would be girl number three.

I almost overslept. Mum had given me a shout just after eight before leaving for work, and the next thing I knew it was five to nine. I literally jumped out of bed, had a wee, a wash and a jab, brushed my teeth, got dressed then dashed out of the house for the bus. No time for breakfast. No sugar intake. Shit. But if I was late for the dentist she would as likely as not find a tooth that needed filling. Just to be awkward.

Casey had arranged to meet me at quarter past ten round the corner from the surgery. He hadn't said what his plans were for the day but I was hoping I could fit in the time to eat something as soon as poss. I even thought we might go back home, have breakfast together then perhaps listen to some music. Or watch a DVD. Or maybe fool around.

"**HIYA**. You ok?"

"Yeh, sure."

"Your peggies alright?"

"Ha ha. Yeh, thanks."

He looked a bit quiet.

"Been waiting long?"

"No. That's ok."

It could be me picking up weird vibes but he seemed out of sorts.

"So, do you mind if we went back home first?"

"What? To your house?"

"It's ok. Mum's at work til half five. But I need to have my breakfast. I didn't have time earlier and if I don't get something to eat soon, well – my sugar levels are getting low."

"Och, aye. Of course. If it's ok to come to your gaff."

"Well, totally. I can make you toast if you like 'cos that's my speciality."

"Ok."

We sat next to each other on the bus. No one got on that I knew. Not that I was bothered, but Stacey had already seen us kissing. Putting two and two together to make five. I'd explained we had just bumped into each other and had a coffee but she kept insisting she wouldn't breathe a word if there was more to it. I could trust her.

"It's ok, hon. I won't tell. Honest."

I said nothing else. But of course, she still went and told Lucy.

I was working my way through a bowl of Weetabix and waiting for the kettle to boil while Casey watched the toast. It was so weird. So grown-up bringing a guy back

204

home. Especially as we were here on our own. There was definitely a sense of something in the air, and it wasn't just the smell of toast.

As we sat down to eat Casey looked straight at me and I knew I had been right. Something was wrong.

"Ah suppose I'd better tell ye. 'Cause you're gonna find out sooner or later anyway."

"What?"

"Me and Lucy. We split up."

"God no."

He told me the whole story. Yesterday as soon as they met she told him he was dumped. Didn't even give him a chance to argue. She had the whole speech prepared – about her mum saying how she had to study harder now if she wanted to go to uni. It didn't leave time for a relationship as well.

Casey suggested they could still see each other at weekends and that's when she turned on him.

"See each other? What's the point when you're already seein' someone else? Don't try an' deny it 'cause somebody saw you an' your wee skaggy slut this afternoon in town. All touchy feely over your coffees. Showin' her the pictures you've drawn of her."

He had no idea how she knew about us. She wouldn't say. But of course, it had to be Stacey. Who else? She'd stuck her claws in long before phoning me last night. What a cow.

"I said it wasn't how it looked. That it was another student in the same class helpin' us with an Art project."

"Right."

"An' she went radge. Said she knew it were you."

Shit. I let my eyes drop to my cereal bowl. I didn't want to reveal what was going through my mind. I was really gutted that Lucy had found out about us this way.

205

Dreading what she would say or do next time she saw me. But I was also thrilled that it was all out in the open and that it seemed he hadn't put up much of a fight. That he was choosing me instead of Lucy.

Then it hit me. We were about to cross a line, if he intended for us to keep seeing each other. My life would change. There was no way I could compete with Lucy. She's so street smart. So funky and clever and unpredictable. And so sexy. Her body. I mean, she's like some slinky jungle cat and I'm just a little hamster. If Casey was serious about us getting together I would have to up my game. I was going to be in a relationship. And it scared the shit out of me.

Literally.

I had to excuse myself and dash to the loo. God. How embarrassing. I was praying he wouldn't want to use the bathroom for a while because, phew. I scooshed loads of air freshener but that wasn't any help.

I rinsed my face and checked that my breath didn't smell while I was at it.

"You've gone and got changed?"

I'd popped into my bedroom to tidy things up in case he wanted a look, and I'd changed out of my school trousers and cerise top. I didn't want to look like one of those desperate housewives.

"Well, yeh. You don't mind, do you?"

He grinned. "Cool top."

It was an old one Shona had given me.

2 KOOL 4 SKOOL

So right for the occasion, don't you think? It was like a shimmery orange with black printing and was quite a tight fit. I'd also put on one of her hand-me-down skirts. Not the shortest of the short but still a micro. Short enough to show off my waxed legs and fading tan. My knees were more like blancmange than jelly but I thanked all the gods in the universe that I'd given my bod the once over yesterday.

"So what d'you fancy doing? I mean, shall we stay in?"

"Dunno Aye. We can do. My heads a bit done in after last night. I didn't get much sleep. So aye, we could sit here an' just hang around if you like. Just do nowt."

"Nowt?"

"Well, you ken what I mean. Just chill."

"Great. I'll fetch some CDs then we can sit in the front room."

I didn't know what to choose. Something sophisticated. Amy Winehouse. Rihanna.

He said he liked the same music as me. I set the volume fairly low so we could carry on talking. I was desperate to hear him say it. And I had to leave it to him to say because if I blurted it out I would sound like some anxious, lovesick kid.

"Shall I get us another coffee first?"

"Ok. But don't be too long."

He'd left his jacket on the back of one of the kitchen chairs and taken his shoes off in the hall. He was sat on my sofa in just a 'Biffy Clyro' t-shirt and a pair of nut-huggers. I so wanted to go in there and rip them right off him.

I decided to take my mules off and leave them in the kitchen because they whiff a bit even though my feet are clean. I was at home so why shouldn't I be comfy? Anybody would do the same.

I put our mugs on the coffee table then settled onto the couch next to him and lay back against the cushions.

"You know, I'm really sorry Lucy found out about us. I mean the way she found out."

Testing the water. Hoping he'd come out and say it.

"That's ok."

"I mean, we're top mates and I do feel a bit shady. She's gonna go mental."

"Perhaps."

Perhaps what? It had been a bad idea meeting that second time? And the third? Perhaps we should never have carried on as if we were anything other than friends? Was he going to say we were best finishing it even before it got started? Give him a chance to try and make up again with Lucy? That wasn't what I wanted, but...

"Well, she's gonna have a right go at you. But it was me she got humpty with. Ah should feel guilty seein' you behind her back, but I don't. An' now we're finished it's like a huge weight off my shoulders. It means we can, us two, can carry on seein' each other properly. If that's ok with you. If you want to."

"Oh yeh. I really do..."

And the most amazing three hours of my life began before I even managed to finish my sentence. It was scary and also so scrumptious. On a pie chart probably 30% scary 70% scrumptious.

We started by kissing. My hands inside his t-shirt. His hands around my waist under my top. His shirt thrown onto the lounge floor and my lips against his bare chest tasting his warm skin. His hands sliding up and down my legs almost under my skirt. More kissing. His fingers weaving through my hair. My lips under his chin and across his throat. His hands under my top, exploring my spine and my ribcage. My bra gone when he asked me if I minded him undoing it. His cool hands massaging my back. Under my top. His mouth chewing at my ear lobes then gnawing at my neck. My toes curling up in ecstasy. Kissing again. His right hand pressed against one of my boobs. Under my top. Tongues and lips growing numb and a finger sliding across my tummy then under the waist band of my panties and...

"Woah."

... we stopped for breath. And it was so good to gaze into his face and see that he was ok with stopping when we did. He was totally relaxed with that. He kissed me on the forehead.

"Ruby."

"Hmm? What?"

"Nowt. Ah just like sayin' your name. I wanted to say it."

I lay back and he grasped my legs and pulled them up so my feet were in his lap. I could feel him there but he didn't seem at all bothered. He started to stroke them really tenderly like mum had done the night I got my bruise.

And that's when I told him everything else.

Every sordid detail. The dreams right from that very first one. The sudden pain between my legs and that freak saying he loved me. The punch in the kidneys. Cody at Lochend Park and the cuts on my thigh. Freaking out at the swimming pool. I decided not to mention that weird moment on the bus – or seeing Levi and Cody together at the park. If they were gone, they were gone for good. But I told him about Haarlem and Stefan. Everything I'd done on my webcam.

"God, you're bloody mental."

"I know. Sorry."

"No. Ah mean, I'm just amazed you've told me all this. All this private stuff I mean. Have you told anybody else?"

"Not really. Stacey knows a bit, but not everything. I don't want everybody thinking I'm going mad."

"Huh. So why'd you tell me?"

"'Cause you're so sorted. An' I trust you, an' I don't want to keep any secrets from you. You're not cross with me, are you?"

"Wow. 'Course I'm not."

"So d'you think I'm mad?"

My bum was getting numb and I was conscious that as I squirmed about one of my feet was pressed down hard in between his legs. I was flashing a load of knicker as well but I assumed he wouldn't mind that.

"No mad. Sounds like you've got a hell of an imagination though. Maybe you've been watchin' too many late-night horrors."

"Well I haven't, but no matter. I just hope you don't mind if I turn out to be some kind of psycho freak."

"Course no. Ah think you're the sexiest psycho freak I've ever met."

And we kissed a bit more. But it was mostly a case of finding something useful to do with our mouths now that we didn't need to talk for a while.

"Do you mind that we didn't?"

He caressed my cheek. We were standing in our porch, getting ready for him to leave.

"Didn't what?"

"I mean, haven't. That we haven't had like sex, or even started any really heavy stuff."

"Hey. This is where ah can say 'Aye, I do mind, an' I never want to see you again because you're nothing but a tease.'"

My God. My eyes welled up with tears just thinking about that. It actually felt as if the sun had shrunk into nothingness and I was about to be sucked up with it into a black hole.

"Or I can say 'No. Ah don't mind at all 'cause I get to take things real slow. Ah get to find out more about how your mind works, how your amazin' body feels. Get to discover how bonny you are a wee bit at a time. Go at your pace so you're comfortable, an'...'"

I swallowed my fear. Shuddering heart slowing to a steady throb. "So."

"Ah'm saying 'No'. Ah don't mind. I want this to last. The longer we wait the better 'cause we get to make the best of every moment. Ah mean, d'you ken how special you are?"

And the dam burst. I wept like a silly mare as he gave me a hug. My heart was still churning as he paused at the gate to wave back. And I was no better when Mum got home from work. Like a wrung out flannel – floppy and damp and freaked out and blissed out. Paradise getting closer at every step. Except there was school tomorrow and I knew that there were going to be a few speed bumps along the way.

CHAPTER 33

"**HERE** she comes now, friggin' lowlife skag."

"You feckin' sore. You got some nerve showin' your face round 'ere."

Lucy and Aleesha waiting for me outside the school gates. I'd been expecting a reaction even though Casey had promised to phone Lucy again to explain it was him who'd started the whole thing. He was going to tell her about his text and about Farran. Me getting upset then one thing leading to another. It's weird – if Farran hadn't died we wouldn't have got together in the first place.

My instinct was to run for cover or try to pretend they weren't even there but I'm not made that way. The only way past this was to pass through.

"I know you hate me and you prob'ly think I'm sly goin' behind your back. But it didn't happen like that, honest. It wasn't planned or anythin'. Wasn't tryin' to steal him from you, Luce. I hope you know me better than that."

She looked like a rather bored cat that's just noticed a helpless mouse it can tear to shreds, for the fun of it.

"Hey, I don't know you, bitch. I don't know you at all."

"How c'n you even stand there 'n' talk such shite? You faggin' slag."

Aleesha the born-again virgin, second-in-command. Like a little echo off to one side. Making the occasional snide, sniping comment while her pal paused to reload. I totally ignored her.

"I mean nothing's even happened, if that's what's bothering you. And he did love you, you know."

"Whatchu mean nuffink's happened? You seein' each other aren't ya?"

"What I mean is we haven't… haven't done anything. You know? Haven't screwed."

She started coming towards me. "You feckin' cow. Is that s'posed to make me feel better?"

"I was just…"

The next thing I knew she had me by the hair and was trying to pull my scalp off in one piece. "You just don't gerrit, do ya?"

"Ow."

"Casey hasn't shagged you. Not yet. Prob'ly 'cause he thinks you're a bit more than jus'… jus' some easy piece of ass."

"Let me go then."

She swung me around until I was facing the school gates and I could tell she was trying to force me onto my knees. There was already a crowd surrounding us. Vultures with their mobiles flashing away, anxious to record the event for posterity.

I managed to remain upright and turned back to face her again even though my hair by now had tightened into a knot. I wrapped my arms around her shoulders in an attempt to reduce any leverage she had. If I kept on my feet there was less chance of my getting a kicking.

"Ok. You made your bloody point. Now jus' let go."

But she wasn't quite done. She hawked a mouth full of phlegm, spat in my face and shoved me away like a bag of trash that she had no further use for.

"Ye're a sick, sick slut an' a dirty bitch an' I hope ye both burn in hell. I hope ye die like yir bag-head of a cousin."

My feet hit the kerb edge and I fell flat on my backside onto the pavement.

"Right, now then, ladies. What's going on here?"

Mr Vernon. The R. I. teacher.

213

"Shouldn't you be heading for registration?"

I hadn't even heard the bell. I clambered to my feet, wiping away the grit embedded in my palms then using my sleeve to wipe away the spit running down my cheek.

"What just happened?"

"I tripped over, sir."

"Well it didn't look that way to me."

I brushed the dust off the back of my trousers, grabbed my back-pack and headed through the main gates. I had no intentions of snitching on Lucy as that would only make matters worse. She'd had her moment of glory in front of all her mates. I could feel sorry for myself because of what she'd said but it was only words. I had Casey now and he was all I needed.

THERE was a postcard from Shona when I got home.

To Mum, Dad and Li'l Sis

Howdee Y'all - New York is awesome.

I just lurve the yellow cabs and the general vibe.

Breakfast lasts all day - the portions are ginormous.

Central Park - wow, so huge.

Miss you all terribly (not!).

C U Soon, mwamwa, Shonaaaaagh!

She was mental.

She'd picked one with a picture of the Statue of Liberty on the front and drawn a pair of shades on its face.

I needed to text Casey to let him know I'd survived my ordeal with Lucy. But first I had to go upstairs, get changed and try to give my trousers a bit of a clean. A length of stitching below the pocket had torn but hopefully Mum wouldn't notice before putting it in the wash.

Eventually, after I'd had my tea, I texted him and told him everything: how much I was missing him and how much I'd enjoyed yesterday. We had agreed not to see each other until the weekend, what with school and not wanting things to get too heavy too soon. So we just carried on sending silly little texts backwards and forwards until I finally said I had my homework to finish. Something about prisms for Physics. I didn't really get any of it but I never do get Physics.

Bedtime I decided to spend a half hour on my laptop. There were a couple of e-mails to reply to. One from Nana Mac hoping school was ok. And one from Shona that she had sent from an internet café on Amsterdam Avenue, New York!

> **Girl, you would so love this place. Fifth Avenue and Madison Avenue and the Guggenheim Museum and Central Park. It's like being in a movie. Gawd, I luuurve Amereeca.**
> **Catchu laters.**
> **xxx**
> **Sh - u no who.**

Stefan had also left me a message late last night. Just to wish me all the best for my new school term. What a friggin' joke. I still couldn't make out whether he was just some kind of cuddly teddy bear or a creepy psycho who was trying to get me to trust him so he could pounce. I sent him a quick reply saying thanks and that we would chat soon – maybe Wednesday night.

IN the end it wasn't until Thursday night that I had a chance to get around to it. Wednesday turned out to be another pig of a day. Stacey and the two ugly sisters came

215

up to me during morning break and Stacey started acting all concerned.

"Lucy been givin' you a hard time, doll?"

"As if you care."

Her eyes swivelled in their sockets like a pair of mismatched marbles. "Well I was only askin'. No need to throw a benny 'cause I'm tryin' to be civil."

"Huh. If you're that bovvered why did you go and tell Lucy you'd seen me and Casey together in the first place? It was none of your business."

"Who says I did?"

"It's obvious. Just the kind of mean trick you'd pull to get one over on me."

"Ooh, listen to Miss Conviviality. Well you're just a fuckin' gadgie. Get one over on you? What could you possibly have that I might want?"

"You tell me. A little self-respect to start with? A proper, real-life boyfriend instead of some fantasy one? Or, ooh I know. A hymen?"

"Yeh, well everybody knows what a stuck-up little bitch you are. An' as soon as he realises he's datin' Mother Teresa an' finds out how frigid you really are he'll drop you like a sack o' shit."

"And everybody knows youse three are just a bunch of corn-fed heifers, fattening up ready for a shaggin' before ye start droppin' bairns everywhere."

The look on their faces was priceless. I was quite proud of what I'd said because she had no answer. They stood there with faces like smacked arses.

But Stacey still managed to get in one last dig before turning on her heels. "Ok, loser. Have it your own way. You an' Casey were made for each other, obviously. But ask yer wee manny who it was that got yer dead cousin started on drugs."

CHAPTER 34

10:15 Thursday night, ready for bed, I still hadn't dared mention to Casey what Stacey had said. I knew he smoked weed of course. Maybe he took pills like Ecstasy or whatever. He said he'd seen Farran with Hooky after she ran away from home so maybe they'd kept in touch. But God, he wasn't the one who started her on heroin surely? I needed something to take my mind off such a horrible thought.

*R	hi there
$*	hello to you
	how is school
*R	I hate it
$*	oh now
	I thought you enjoyed studies
*R	not anymore
	well, schools ok
	but I hate the girls there
$*	I see
*R	fallen out with
	Lucy and Stacey
$*	what is fallen out with?
*R	fight/argue/not friends
$*	oh dear
	so you are angry I guess
*R	spose
$*	feeling in the dump
*R	hehe yeh
	that's exactly where I am
$*	no matter
	you have school tomorrow also?
*R	yeh
	just came on for a few mins

	to say a quick hello
$*	well that's nice of you
*R	I got a postcard from my Shona
	so that cheered me up a bit
$*	good
	she is having fun in America
*R	sounds like it
$*	a picture postcard?
*R	oh yeh
	Statue of Liberty#
$*	aha
	a famous landmark
	did you ever see an old film
	Planet of the Apes
*R	don't think so
	why
$*	well it's about a spaceman
	who discovers a new planet
	controlled by apes
	But right at the end of the film
	on the seashore he finds
	the head of the Statue of Liberty
	buried in the sand
*R	so?
$*	well - it isn't a new planet at all
	he's in new york
	a long time in the future -
	the planet is the earth
	and apes have taken over from men
*R	wow
	I get it
$*	and did you know
	New York used to be called
	New Amsterdam

God, I was being given some crummy history lesson now and all I'd wanted was to say goodnight.

```
*R    not really
$*    yes many Dutch people
      settled in America
      near to where is now New York
      there was even a place close by
      Nieuw Haarlem
```

And all of a sudden something the size of an asteroid must have gone bump into our house because my bedroom floor turned into a trampoline and my whole body gave a lurch.

```
*R    what?
$*    it's called Harlem now
      but it's also quite famous you know
*R    ?
$*    basketball?
      the Harlem Globetrotters?
```

I made my excuses and crawled under the duvet. Everything I accepted as fact was suddenly turned upside down. Casey had quite possibly been supplying Farran with drugs – and Harlem was in America not the Netherlands. How could I have got it all so wrong?

Levi and Cody. They did sound American: like cheerleaders or someone out of 'High School Musical'. If that was the case it meant Stefan wasn't as much of a creep as I thought he was. But it still didn't explain why I'd been having dreams about strange girls way out on the other side of the Atlantic. Then one final thought slid into place. One thought that kept me awake for most of the night.

Shona.

CHAPTER 35

FRIDAY night I was still stressed out. Casey told me he was out with his mates so not to text, and I had Statistics homework that I couldn't get to grips with. I also had this nagging feeling that now Shona was in New York – perhaps even Harlem – she could be in danger.

I'd sent her an e-mail telling her how creeped out I was about her and Laura being in such a big bad city all by themselves. But she hadn't answered it yet. I felt a bit embarrassed really making such a fuss but the trouble with e-mails is that you can't unsend them. So sooner or later she'd be asking me why I was being such a nelly. I'd say I was just missing her – and tell her to be careful.

*R	it's only me
$*	how are you tonight
*R	bit better than last night
	the weekend starts here
$*	hehe
	so you had a bad first week
*R	yes
	and I've got homework
	that doesn't make any sense
$*	what is it
	you are struggling with
*R	oh Statistics - modes, medians and means
$*	wow - well my maths is not so hot
*R	that's ok
$*	I would try to make you happy
	because you also make me happy
*R	ok
$*	when you let me watch you

```
*R    right
$*    on webcam
*R    mmm
$*    would you do it again sometime
      perhaps?
      it doesn't need to be tonight
*R    no I'm tired anyway
$*    I understand
*R    perhaps 2morrow
$*    ok
      send me an e mail first
      and I will be sure to make no other plans
*R    ok
      goodnight then
$*    goodnight ruby
      xxx
*R    xxx
```

God, talk about being obsessed? He wasn't going to let it go. He had a grip like a Rottweiler. And he was only after one thing. Another flash of Ruby flesh. Yeugh.

05:15 Saturday morning I received a text from Lucy. The buzzing woke me up and the first thing I thought was that she was going to start sending me abusive messages all the time from now on. Late at night, early in the morning. Cyber-bullying. We'd had a talk about it in school last year.

But quarter past five in the morning? She was taking the piss. I nearly deleted her message without reading it because I knew we had nothing more to say to each other. But then I thought what the hell, if she wants to have a go I'll have a go back. It just seemed a bit off her trying to wind me up at such a ridiculous time of day. And on a weekend.

I clicked on her message.

Rube. KCz in trouble. Give me a bell when u get this. Luce x

All sorts of things started flashing through my head. Why would she bother telling me something like this unless it was true? Something serious like an accident? Maybe he was in hospital even. But how come he'd got in touch with Lucy instead of me? I was desperate to phone her yet I was dreading what the text might mean.

I sat on the edge of my bed, wrapped the sheet around my shoulders and tapped in her number.

"Hello?"

"Ruby. Oh, thank God. Listen, Casey's been lifted."

OMG. Well at least he wasn't hurt.

"What happened?"

"Kenzie's here. He's been here since about two o'clock this morning. Something kicked off outside 'Phrenzy' last night. Casey's still in the police station."

Out clubbing? He'd not mentioned where he and his mates were going. So the first thing I was thinking was drugs. Perhaps Stacey was right and he was supplying drugs in town. Perhaps he was caught dealing. Or got involved in a fight.

"Was he in a rammy then?"

"Well, there's all sortsa rumours flying round. But it's that Stacey MacLeod."

"Stacey?"

"Yeh. They're saying Casey's raped her."

222

CHAPTER 36

THERE was no way of me getting back off to sleep. Too many thoughts were skewering their way through my head. Had Casey actually gone and done what Lucy was saying? The very thought made me question everything I knew about him.

All I could see was Stacey's she-devil grin staring right at me. Her wicked eyes boring into the very core of my body. She'd managed to get back at me in the way she knew would hurt most. I couldn't fight for Casey's reputation. I could only weep until my eyes became rimmed red raw and my cheeks glistened like the sluttiest make-up ever.

But I also realised I had to confront the world sooner or later and if I went downstairs with a washroom face Mum would cotton on that there was something seriously wrong. If she ever found out the details it would be me and Casey finished. In fact it would be me and boys finished until I turned twenty one. And even then she'd probably insist on an arranged marriage between me and someone like that neeky Peter Fogarty up our road. He collects stamps, parts his hair on the wrong side and goes to church with his mam and dad every Sunday. I would so rather die.

I had to get round to Lucy's as soon as I could. But seven o'clock on a Saturday morning was pushing it. Unheard of in this lifetime. So I took my time having a shower, carrying out my normal routine and getting dressed as if I was going to the gym. Something I'd only ever done twice in the last year.

Dad hadn't even left for work.

"Good grief. Have you peed the bed?"

"Very funny. Not."

"Well we don't normally see you this side of nine o'clock on a weekend."

"I'm just going to the Leisuree. Me and Stacey."

That was the best excuse I could come up with. I hate telling lies, mainly because I always get caught out sooner or later.

"Well, if you're needing a lift you'd better get a move on."

"No, it's ok. I need some carbs and fluid first. I said I'd walk round to hers for about eight."

"Oky-doky. Just don't overdo it your first time."

As if.

LUCY'S mum answered the door and let me in. Their front room smelt of sweaty feet and joss sticks. And I don't have a hyper-sensitive nose. It just did. There was a quarter bottle of vodka on the coffee table and half a dozen crushed Red Bull cannies. Lucy was lying on the couch under a duvet – and at the other end of it I could see the top of Kenzie's head. He was fast asleep but Lucy looked like she hadn't slept at all. She looked torn.

"Wanna brew, darlin'?"

I said a tea please: milk with one sugar.

Lucy shuffled into a sitting position. She was still in her nightie – barefoot and with her hair more messed up than I can ever remember seeing it.

"This is awful, Luce."

She looked at me long enough to make me feel uncomfortable. "Yeh. I can't stop thinking about it."

"Me too. I mean, it doesn't make sense. Casey and Stacey? He can't even stand her."

"That's what I said. She's either makin' it all up or..."

"I wouldn't put it past her."

Lucy seemed surprised that I was suddenly dissing my best friend. "But why would she?"

"Well we had a set-to earlier in the week. I told her exactly what I thought of her and she didn't like it."

A smile like a whiplash crossed her face. "Huh, I bet. The fackin' snotty bitch. She can be such a wee clype."

"Exactly. She'll have made it all up out of spite."

"D'you think we should go round there?"

"You will no." Mrs Brown in the doorway with a mug in either hand. "Ye'll stop here, the pair ay youse, until ye both calm doon. If ye tackle her it's gonna make things look a lot worse for Kevin. Ye dinnae do anything, ye hear me? Naebody even knows what's supposed tae have happened yet. Come an' have yir drink."

We sat in subdued silence until Kenzie's bare arm appeared from under his end of the duvet.

"Look oot. Here's Sleeping Beauty. Ye ready for some breakfast then?"

"Gruh. Ooh, hi."

"Hi."

He knew me by sight I suppose but we'd never really had much to do with each other. He was four years older than Aleesha and had left Pentland the year before I started there.

"Breakfast? Some toast or Shreddies?"

"Er, no ta Mrs B. Just black coffee please."

Lucy reached out a hand and stroked his hair like a mother calming a child after a bad dream. "Ye feelin' any better now, hon?"

"Yeh, ta."

"He'd had a bit too much to drink last night."

"No I hudnae. It was just aw this business, ye ken?"

"So were you there with Casey when it happened?" I

225

ventured, desperate to know all the facts no matter how unsavoury.

"Nae, doll. Ah wis already inside wi Barcode an' Shabby. It was hoatchin' sae we couldn't see a thing. Then somebody says they'd just heard the stabz hud pulled up ootside. Thought they were gonna raid the place."

"So what are they saying happened?"

"Well, one ay the lassies who seen it reckoned Casey an' Jaker were in the queue waiting tae git in, larkin' aboot wi thit Stacey an' her entourage. Then suddenly Stacey's top's been ripped off an' Casey's lyin' oan top o'her on the kerb an' she's screamin' blue murder."

"Huh. That sounds mental."

"Ah ken."

The whole story seemed too far-fetched to even think about.

"She's got to be lying."

Lucy's mum sat on the arm of the couch and began to unpick the tangles in Lucy's hair. "If she is, the polis will find oot, hen. What time were this did ye say?"

"Och, it wis the back of eleven."

"So they could all ha' been steamin' by then – the lasses as well as Casey an' Jaker. Straight from the pub tae the club, lookin' for a laugh mibbe."

Lucy turned to face her mother and her eyes seemed to drill into her skull.

"Ah'm only sayin' pet. The dreenk kin make laddies go off their heeds. Ah've seen it wi ma ain eyes many a night."

"Casey's not like that."

"Ye seen um when he's hammered?"

No. I hadn't.

"Anyway, we're no daein' arselves any good sittin' roond here clackin' our jaws. We dinnae ken the facts sae

226

let's just wait a wee while."

Kenzie peeled off the duvet, got up to his feet and asked if he could take a shower. He only had on his boxers. My God, he was so buff. Aunty Grace, well. She's got good taste.

Lucy's mum cleared away the mugs and dragged the duvet back into Lucy's bedroom.

"Thanks for textin' me."

"Yeh, well. I done it for Casey not for you. An' anyway, I s'pose you'd do the same for me."

"Yeh, course."

It went quiet. I was beginning to wonder whether we could ever be mates again. She'd said a lot of horrible stuff yet I'd forgive her, of course I would. But I'd stolen her guy from her.

Fortunately Kenzie came back into the room – fully dressed and smelling of apple shampoo. Lucy got to her feet and gave him a really long hug now that he was all set to leave. Nothing new was going to happen in the immediate future so I said I'd better go home as well. He offered to walk me as far as our road. His family lives somewhere by Holy Corner and there's a bus goes to Bruntsfield Road from the top of Fingal Gardens.

He was a bit quiet. Didn't have a lot to say for most of the way.

"I seen you at the funeral."

"What?"

"Farran's. I saw you and Casey there."

"Och. Aye."

"She was my cousin."

"Aye. Leesha's prob'ly mentioned it."

Nothing more. There was no way I was going to bring up the Aunty Grace episode.

"I know why Farran left home. Casey told me

227

everything and it's ok. None of my business anyway. But ending up doing drugs…"

"Aye. She were a bonny lassie, and ah was a fackin' nobhead. It's all ma fault her an' her family fell out. But lettin' that toe-rag get his hooks into her. Ah still can't believe she'd do somethin' so stupid."

"Hooky."

"Aye."

"But she'd started doing drugs before they got together. Right?"

He stopped in his tracks. "Whatchu mean?"

"Well, some of the girls were sayin' like she'd been messin' about with weed an' other stuff for ages."

"You're jestin'. She was dead against anything like that. Used to give me an' Casey a hard time just for havin' the occasional spliff."

"Oh, right. I must have got my wires crossed."

"Deffo."

It went quiet for five minutes until he reached the bus stop.

"Ah told Luce ah'll give her a bell if ah hears anythin', kenlike?"

"Thanks."

"She'll probably ring you herself."

"Aye. I just wish I could phone Casey on his mobile. Find out if he's ok."

"Thair's nae chance o' that, darlin'. The polis won't want um talkin' tae anybody 'til they've finished interviewing um an' stuff."

"S'pose not."

"You ken he could go doon fir this? Even if he was jist messin' aboot with the lassie. She's still underage."

"What? But Stacey, I mean, she's a right sket. D'you know she's on the pill?"

228

"Well, she might well be, but she's still a bairn in the eyes of the law. Her an' the other plastics she hangs around with. Everybody kens they're jail-bait."

I nodded, desperate to reach home and bury myself up in my room away from all this crap. Stacey. I mean she's bragging to me about how she's shagged every barman in Tenerife, been dancing in her scanties for some perv over in Florida, out on the lash with her mates. Dressed like tarts the three of them, plastered in make-up and she's probably already necked three or four Bacardi Breezers at least. Then suddenly she's an angel. All innocent. If anybody was asking to be raped it was her, so she probably deserved it. If that's what happened.

But God, her and Casey? I still couldn't believe it.

CHAPTER 37

MAKE SURE YOU HAVE SOME LUNCH
BUT DON'T TOUCH SALMON QUICHE THAT'S
OUR TEA
HOME ABOUT 4.30

MUM'S note on the kitchen table. I grabbed a can of
Sprite and a banana and went straight upstairs. Then I got
changed into my pj's and climbed under the duvet. I was
dog tired, but not from being woken early. Tired from
Stacey's lies about Farran and Casey. Tired from the
poisonous rumours and tittle-tattle that were certain to be
all around the school by Monday morning. Tired from
worrying about Casey all on his own in some police cell.
My brain was in limbo, waiting to hear the worst.

I'd already lost someone precious to me this summer.
Been there, done that, got the mug and the t-shirt. But this
feeling was different to the way I had felt about Farran.
Casey was still alive. Yet it was like he was dead inside
my heart – he'd let me down so badly. I had to get through
this somehow. The only thing I could do was focus my
anger on Stacey. It was all her fault. She had probably
begged him to shag her out there in the street and he'd
been so pissed that he'd jumped on top of her without a
single thought for me. He was a man after all.

But he was my wee manny.

I got my laptop off the desk, propped it on my knees
on top of the duvet, switched it on then went on-line.

There was a short e-mail off Shona.

> **Hey, ma wee retard sistah. Scaredy cat or wot?**
> **Meow Meow to you too. I'm fine, really. Me and**
> **Laura are lapping it up here so don't worry your**

**whiskers. High fives and big kisses XXXXX
Sho**

She can be really funny when she wants to be. I decided to have another look at 'Google Earth'. See if I could spot her and Laura parading round New York like wide-eyed tourists.

'Harlem : New York, NY, USA'

Well, Stefan was right. There it was, right next to Manhattan. Central Park. Hudson River. Blocks and blocks of buildings exactly as I had imagined it would be right from that very first dream. This had to be where Levi and Cody had lived before they were murdered.

There were thousands and thousands of streets though. 1st Avenue. 3rd Avenue. 7th Avenue. Madison Avenue. God, Shona said she'd been there. Lennox Avenue. Amsterdam Avenue where that internet café was. And then all the other ones going left to right. W 96th Street. W 110th Street. W 125th Street. It was like a maze, and I hadn't got a clue where the entrance was let alone the exit. I didn't know where to start looking. Didn't know what it was I was looking for anyway. I might as well have taken a pin, stuck it in the screen and started there.

And wow. That silly thought actually made me smile. First time all day. Pinky. Pin cushion. Jabbing myself twice a day to stay alive. Jabbing a pin in a city thousands of miles away to find some crazy killer. How hilarious is that?

FINALLY I saw a name that stuck out. I'd heard of Doc Martens boots so I zoomed down onto 294 Doctor Martin Luther King Junior Boulevard and clicked onto one of the camera icons in Street View.

It was an exciting world of colour and commerce. Gloriously sunny – I could almost hear the drone of traffic and the hustle bustle of everybody going about their day on the street. I made a 360^0 circle.

FedExKinko's – Starbucks Express – atmos.

A blue and white bus M101/George 193 St.

A guy in a red shirt in a 4x4.

A couple standing in the shade of a red and yellow parasol.

CBT Paratransit – Access-A-Ride.

McDonalds – Bank Of America – Touro College.

Payless Shoesquare – any bag $10.00 – Champs Sports.

I clicked ahead to the next camera.

A huge multi-storey building with the American stars and stripes flag outside.

Dr Jays.

A lady in blue jeans, white vest and turquoise top sitting on the sidewalk in front of a small table beneath a blue patterned parasol selling – no idea. Bottles of perfume?

Black people everywhere. A gangsta rapper in white sneakers and a baseball cap on a road crossing. Two others in baggy shorts and headphones. High school students – white shirts and striped ties.

Click.

Studio Museum Harlem.

A bus stop : M60/M100/M101/Bx15.

An Asian girl in a faded blue housecoat and backpack talking on her mobile.

Click.

Jimmy Jazz – Burger King.

Gem Super Value Stores : Housewares – Stationery – Health & Beauty Aids.

Blockbuster Video – Fishers of Men II – Kaarta Imports – African Fabrics.

It was hopeless. I couldn't make any sense of it – presumably because I had no idea what I was searching for. It was a bit like that Chatterteens forum but with pictures instead of meaningless words.

I skipped a few blocks left to where there was a road cutting diagonally across the grid squares.

Saint Nicholas Avenue/West 120th Street.

No shops – just blocks of red and white buildings. Apartments? Brownstones.

Brownstones? What were Brownstones? Somehow I knew the word yet couldn't remember hearing it anywhere before.

203 Saint Nicholas Avenue.

A School Xing.

Lots of big fancy cars.

A black girl in white jogging trousers, white

233

hooded top and black back-pack riding her bike along the sidewalk.

Had she perhaps known Levi?

A police station. A big armoured Police jeep parked outside. And a huge poster on the wall like something out of 'Oceans Twelve' – 'We Are Here When You Need Us'.

I zoomed back out of Street View.

NYPD Police Station Precinct 28. Harlem.

There were loads of little photo squares you could click onto.

Harriet Tubman's statue at 122nd and St Nicholas – looking like the Queen of Hearts from Alice in Wonderland.

Brownstones at 122nd and Manhattan. So – at least I hadn't invented the word. Weird.

Morningside. It seemed strange that a part of New York had the same name as where Nana Crozier lived. A beautiful road with trees and parkland on one side and further along a huge, coloured poster.

PS/IS 180 - Home of the Jaguars - Where Excellence In Education Is Our Only Choice.

I knew the place. Knew it like the back of my hand.

The echoing voices in the corridors. Steam filling the changing rooms. Mr Spelt the Music teacher. Miss Dior and Mrs Egerton. Jay Diaz and Sammy Novak in my Special English class. Peanut butter and jelly sandwiches for lunch and Oreos. Basketball matches on a Friday night. Effie had been here with me loads of times.

I felt queasy, almost sea sick. Though I've only ever been sea sick once when Uncle Andrew took us out in his boat past the Black Rocks and it got a little choppy. I can remember that horrible churning inside my head as well as my guts.

This was some sort of school. Even though you couldn't tell that from the outside, I knew it for a fact. I just knew that this was Levi's neighbourhood. This was where she spent her days in pretty much the same way that I'm serving my sentence at Pentland Maximum Security Prison.

And close by was where she'd been captured, locked up, and eventually murdered.

CHAPTER 38

I must have fallen asleep after switching my laptop off because the next thing I knew it was after five and somebody was tapping at my bedroom door.

"Yeah?"

"Can I come in?"

Mum.

"Yeah."

"Oh, you're in bed, love. God. What a dreadful shock? How was Stacey when you went round?"

I must have looked as baffled as I felt. How the hell did Mum know? And what exactly did she know?

"Oh, yeh. Awful."

"Did you see her? I mean, was she home?"

Home? I was still half asleep, half cotton-woolled inside my dream world where Casey and Shona were walking through Harlem. Where exactly was Stacey? Was she back home or at the police station or hospital or what?

"I didn't go in."

"No. I suppose she's not in a fit state to see anybody. How's her mum taking it? I should perhaps phone her."

"God, no."

"Why ever not? They must be devastated."

"She is. I mean, they are 'cause when she told me…"

I'm useless at lying. Some kind of switch clicked on inside my head and I started crying and shaking. Mum obviously assumed I was upset because my so-called best friend had been assaulted.

"Hey, come here." She gave me a cuddle then told me to come down for my tea when I felt better.

I should have stopped in bed. Should have crawled back under the duvet and tried to find the way back into 'Google Dreamland' where the streets are safe and

everybody lives happily ever after. But instead I put on
my dressing gown, had a good wash and went downstairs.
They were waiting for me.

"HAVE your tea first then your dad and me want a word."
"What about?"
"Have your tea first. We'll talk after."
I could hear them muttering in the lounge. At least
they left me to eat in peace but everything tasted like shit
and I couldn't manage much more than a couple of
mouthfuls.

Dad came back into the kitchen as soon as he heard
me putting my dirty dishes in the sink. The look on his
face like a road sign – DANGER AHEAD.

"Did you know your mum's just phoned Stacey's
house? They say you haven't been near there today."

Mum chipping in, "Why did you lie to us? Where did
you really go off to this morning?"

I sat like one of the waxworks exhibits out of Madame
Tussaud's but Mum wouldn't let this lie.

"Stacey's mum's telling me that you and this Casey
lad are supposed to be, I don't know. Seeing each other?
Is that true? Eh? Come on. We're getting to the bottom of
this even if we sit here 'til midnight. There are no secrets
round this table, you know that."

"Oh, really? So what about Aunty Grace and Kenzie
then? That's a hell of a secret if you ask me."

Obviously adults are used to handling surprises. Mum
and Dad didn't so much as blink.

"Ruby, we need to know what's going on with you
and this boy. We're trying to help you; not make things
worse."

Help me? How the hell could they help me?
"I went round to Lucy's."

237

"Lucy Brown? At the flats? Why would you?"

"She's a mate, all right? Even though you don't much like her. Casey's – he's her boyfriend, an' she texted me 'cause she didn't know who else to talk to about it."

I fished out my phone from my dressing gown pocket and showed her Exhibit A. Message received Saturday August 29 – 05:13am.

Rube. KCz in trouble. Give me a bell when u get this. Luce x

"So why did you have to go and lie to us?"

"Dunno. 'Cause you wouldn't have let me go round there if I'd have told you."

"Love, if she's that much of a friend then we understand. Of course we would."

"Hmm."

"But, you know, getting involved with people like that. I mean, her mum's not exactly right in the head, and what's the story about this boyfriend? If what they're saying is true he deserves locking up."

Not right in the head? Well, I couldn't see Mum letting me spend the night on her sofa with a hot guy wearing just a pair of Calvin Kleins, so maybe they were right.

"But Casey isn't like that."

"Really? Do you know him? This boy?"

"Well, yeh. I've seen him with Lucy a couple of times. He's ok, honest."

"Not from the stories we've been hearing."

"It's Stacey. She's probably made most of it up. And anyway, even if it did happen she's only got herself to blame."

Dad drew in a gasp of breath. Finally I'd caused a tiny

238

ripple and got a reaction. "What's that supposed to mean?"

So I told them everything. Her being on the pill. Her escapades in Tenerife. The way she dresses. I even told them about her webcam antics – and how she and I had fallen out.

"So what you're saying is that it's perfectly all right for any young girl to get raped if she behaves... well, because she acts like a tart. Am I right?"

"Well, not exactly, but..."

"No buts." Dad gave me the works. I knew about most of it anyway so he was wasting his breath. "Ever wonder why girls like Stacey behave that way, or dress the way they do?"

I shrugged.

"Do you think she's happy the way she looks?"

"Don't know why you're asking me."

Mum took over the mike. "Well, a lot of girls that age have low self-esteem when they see all these super-models on TV or in magazines. They can end up doing all sorts of stupid stuff to become noticed, or to get attention."

Hmm. Tell me about it. I was probably as guilty as Stacey the way I'd been leading Stefan on.

"What about her friends? Do they act the same way?"

"Well, yeh. Trudy and Leslie always dress like total slags when they go out. That's why I don't like hanging round with Stacey so much now."

Mum gave Dad a puzzled look. Maybe their younger daughter wasn't such a doolie after all.

"She's probably trying to compete with them," he suggested.

"It's a teen eat teen world, trying to be the first girl to hook a boy," Mum added. She had obviously read all this crap in one of her women's magazines. "Then some lad sees them behaving like that and thinks it's his lucky day."

"Yeh, but Casey can't even stand Stacey."

"Listen, love, every boy's conditioned to fancy every girl given the right set of circumstances. They can't help it."

"Your mum's right. As soon as a lad sees a dolly bird his eyes will follow her like a dog let off the lead until she's out of sight. Even if he's got his arms wrapped round his sweetheart at the time. That's how boys' brains are wired."

"It's true, love."

I was rapidly losing this battle of wills. Two against one – and I knew that most of what they were saying was right.

"Ok. I know. Shona's told me all about it. Pheromones."

"Aye, well. That doesn't mean they can go chasing anybody they take a liking to and assault them just like that."

"So you really shouldn't go round saying things like that about Stacey or anybody else, should you?" Mum resting a reassuring hand on my shoulder. She wasn't disowning me just yet.

"I haven't been."

"No. Well, good," she gave me a gentle squeeze.

"I just wasn't thinking straight."

Mum decided it was time to fill the kettle but Dad wasn't done with me yet.

"The poor lassie hasn't long turned 15 has she?"

"So?"

"So even if she's told him he can, well, do stuff to her, he still needs locking up."

"What do you mean?"

"Because she's underage. How old is this lad?"

240

"Dunno. eighteen or nineteen."

Dad shook his head. "There you are. He's an adult, so he knows well enough. Even if she was the one who started it."

"But that's so unfair."

"It's not unfair love. Youngsters need protecting 'til they're old enough to make their own minds up. If Stacey did play a part in any of it, well that's a pity. A hard lesson for her to have to learn. But this Casey. He's a grown man. He should know better. No excuses."

OMG. I felt sick with worry and disgust and shame. I didn't stay downstairs much longer once the lecture was finished. I said I was sorry again, made myself a cocoa then went back upstairs. I just wanted to curl up under the duvet and sink into a coma. But first I knew I had a text to send. I'd never be able to sleep peacefully until I cleared my conscience.

Stace. I no we r not spose to be m8s any mo but im awful sorry bout wot hapnd. Thinkin of u, rube xxx

CHAPTER 39

WHEN I checked my glucose levels before finally settling down for the night I realised they were low. I needed refuelling. I'd had my breakfast earlier than usual, only had a snack at lunchtime and not eaten much tea. So I went back downstairs for some chocolate biscuits and a glass of my favourite grape juice.

Dad was out and Mum was in the front room with the lights off watching an old black and white film.

"You still hungry, pet?"

"Not really, but my blood's a bit low so I thought I'd better have a munch."

"How low?"

"5.4."

"God, love. Stop down here an hour with me. Make sure it's up again before you go to bed."

"I know. What you watching?"

"Some old weepy. I've seen it before but there's nothing else on except the football."

I lay next to her.

"I got an e-mail off Shona this morning."

"Oh, good. You should have said. Is she ok?"

"Yes. Lovin' it there."

Central Park and the smell of greenery and sun lotion. Amsterdam Avenue choked with cars sitting at the lights spewing out the poison of exhaust fumes. Scents of Chinese spices and barbecue sauce and stale beer.

A red hand on the road crossing.

Walk.

Don't Walk.

Blue scaffolding caging off the sidewalk. An Oriental woman in a blue housecoat yattering into her mobile and a speech bubble of Japanese or Chinese letters above her head.

'How is Yoma? Has the baby come yet? Tell her to stay strong.'

Brownstones. Carved stonework at the entry doors and little Juliet balconies and the sun baking the sidewalk.

Cold Beer & Sodas – Candies & Cigarettes – Hot & Cold Sandwiches – Coffee, Tea & Chocolate – Fresh Meat – Fruit & Veg – Frozen Food – Ice & Ice Cream – School Supplies

Suddenly Cody sprang to mind. She read that sign every day on her way into work. I knew it. Then another in some foreign language. The only word I could make out was 'Peligrosas'.

Manhattan Avenue.

Three grey, industrial-sized wheely bins round the back of the alley. The hum of fermenting garbage overpowering in the heat.

Tiny lights inside the grocery store. Cody at the till serving Shona and Laura as they stocked up on taco shells and salsa dip and beer and popcorn...

...and that stomach churning stench and my body doubled up as I heaved.

It was still dark but the TV was turned off. I could smell the sick and taste the acid at the back of my throat and I knew this was no dream.

I realised I was upstairs in my room and reached for my bedside light.

Click. It was utterly minging. I'd boked all over my duvet and down the front of my pyjama jacket. I got out of bed, praying the room would stop spinning long enough for me to make my way to the bathroom. I folded up my duvet in half to contain the mess then carried it outside my room. I'd not even noticed the time on my bedside clock. The bathroom light seemed ten times brighter than normal. I plonked the duvet inside the bath and turned the hot water tap full on, hoping to wash away the worst of the vomit. Gross. Then I took off my pj top. That was honking as well and I threw it into the bath.

"Ruby? Are you all right in there?"

Mum calling me from somewhere. I was filling a drinking glass with cold water so I could swill away the vile taste in my mouth.

"Not really."

She came in, with her black and pink, silk bath robe flapping behind her like butterfly wings; her hair in curlers.

"What's happened?"

"I don't know. I was sick and then I woke up. Sorry. I made a mess on my duvet."

"It's not your fault, sweetheart. Do you want me to help you get cleaned up?"

She filled the wash basin with hot water, dunked the face flannel then swabbed my face and neck and chest.

"I'll get you a clean t-shirt while you dry off."

I felt ashamed, as if I'd gone and wet the bed or something. And yet I hadn't been able to help myself. I'd not even felt ill beforehand or stuffed myself on something I shouldn't have. It came totally out of the blue.

"Use Shona's bed. I put clean sheets on it Monday morning. I'll make yours up tomorrow. You're not still feeling sick are you?"

"No. I wasn't even feeling sick before. I just sort of remember smelling popcorn."

"Popcorn?"

Mum laughing. The last time I'd been sick was two or

244

three years ago on holiday in the caravan. Shona had nearly set fire to the microwave as we both binged on popcorn – and I'd come off worst.

"I know. I must have been really tired or something. I can't even remember coming to bed."

"Well, you had a nap downstairs next to me but as soon as the film finished you woke up and said you were going upstairs."

"Mhmm."

"Had we better check your sugar? Just to be on the safe side?"

"I can do it. But thanks, Mum."

"Right. If you're sure you're ok now."

"Yes."

Goodnight kiss. The stress of everything must have really knocked me for six. I checked my blood to make sure it was ok. That's when I realised I'd forgotten to take my insulin before climbing into bed. I jabbed myself, cursing my stupidity, then lay under the sheet thinking of Shona, thinking of life, thinking of Levi and Cody actually. Somehow I was getting to know them better, but without really wanting to.

CHAPTER 40

SUNDAY during term time is usually homework day. I slept in until well past eleven. I texted Lucy – no news – had a shower then put on my oldest, most comfortable track-suit and started on my Biology diagram of photosynthesis.

Mum had invited Aunty Grace round for Sunday dinner. Dad and Uncle Andrew were going clay pigeon shooting and weren't due back until late. She's really sweet and I do feel sorry for her even though I know all about her dark secret now. She'd brought Mum a bunch of flowers and got me a £15 voucher from HMV.

"Late birthday present, love. We forgot all about it."

"That's ok. Thanks."

"Your mum says you were poorly in the night."

"She's looking a lot better now."

Mum can't help intervening.

"Well, that's good news."

I gave them a hand laying the table. I was famished.

"I hear you've got yourself a boyfriend."

"Aye, but it's hush-hush. She's told me nothing."

"Mum!"

"And what's his name?"

"It's Kevin. But we've not met him yet."

"That's nice."

"He's a student in the Art College. You know. That big glass building behind the bus station in town."

"Right. You're not seeing each other today then?"

"No. She's not. She's having her hair done so she's going nowhere."

"What are you having done?"

"She says she wants some blonde highlights but I don't like the idea."

246

"Oh, I can't keep up with all these latest fashions."

This whole cross-examination was doing my head in. Aunty Grace firing questions and Mum supplying the answers on my behalf.

Then the topic of conversation turned to Stacey.

"Did ye hear about that wee lassie getting attacked on Friday? It was on the STV this morning. It said a nineteen-year old man from Lochend is helping police with their enquiries. They always say that but it sounds as if they've got the right one."

I was praying they hadn't given out his proper name yet.

Mum looked at me but I kept my lip buttoned. No secrets round this table.

HEATHER turned up just after three She'd been in school with our Shona and her granddad lives two doors down from us. She does all our hair – me, Mum, and even Shona's when she's home. We went into the back room once she'd said hello. I was hoping that Mum and Aunty Grace would stay in the kitchen because I didn't fancy an audience.

I'd decided to have about three inches taken off as well as the highlights. I had to start looking more sophisticated now I was actually dating somebody.

"Ah haven't seen ye roond much this summer. How ya feelin' after losin' Farran an' all that?"

"Bit better now. Holidays went too quick though."

"They alus do."

"Shona's away to New York. Did you know?"

"Ah had heard, aye. Ah keep promisin' tae call roond an' see her but, well, ah dinnae get a minute's peace."

She's got two wee bairns. One's two and the other's only four or five months old.

247

"So was thit the boyfriend ah seen you wi this last week?"

"Where?"

"Monday it must huv been. The back of two o'clock. Ah'd jist bin roond tae ma granddad's wi' the weans an' he was stood ootside yir front door."

Shit.

"Yeh, sort of. But Mum doesn't know he's been round here."

"Right. Thit's ok. Ah'm no gonna breathe a word."

I was fairly sure she wouldn't.

"He come round for his breakfast and then we just listened to some CDs."

"Breakfast? Thit's a new name fir it."

I was actually relieved when Monday came round – even though there hadn't been much time to prepare for the ritual humiliation facing me. Stacey and Casey were the talk of the school obviously. Most of the looks I got were pitying, and not because of my new hair style. But one or two couldn't resist saying some really vile things. Why are some girls so mean? We even had a five minute talk off Mrs Casket, Fifth Year Tutor, about under-aged girls going out to nightclubs and so on. How they needed to be careful.

Lucy came up to me as soon as she saw me at break.

"Oo. Look at the hair."

"Mhmm. I know."

"You heard anythin'?"

"From Casey? No. I feel awful."

"Same here. I keep expectin' Kenzie to phone us."

Trudy King was hanging round the loos as if she had something on her mind.

"What you after? Something you wanna say? Cause

I'm just in the mood to slap somebody."

"No, Luce. But I were there, on Friday, you know?"

"So?"

"Well nobody got raped fir starters."

"What?"

"It's such a joke. I mean, we was stood in the queue waitin' to get in an' somebody pinched ma arse. Sae I turns roond an' there's a couple a draftpaks behind us lookin' aw innocent."

"Was Casey there?"

"Och aye. An' thit knob Jaker was with um."

"Right."

"Then somebody must of tried to do something to the strap at the back of Stacey's dress 'cause her top suddenly falls down an' her tits are on display an' everybody's cheerin'. So she turns round an' slaps Casey across the gob then the next thing she's like layin' on top of him screamin' blue murder. One of the doormen came an' pulled her off um an' grabbed Casey an' said he was callin' the polis."

"So who says he raped her?"

"Dinnae ken. There was people with their mobiles takin' photos of Stacey with her boobs hangin' out an' her skirt up around her waist showin' her arse an' everything else she's got. Then soon as the Five-O's come an' we seen the blue lights everybody did one. Me an' Leslie nashed off an' all."

I felt a bit better now. Even if Casey had been larking round with Stacey it wasn't anywhere near as bad as what everybody was saying.

Lucy even managed half a grin.

"They've got to let him out. I mean they can't lock him up for something like that. Can they?"

"Hope not."

It was dance class after school at the Leisuree. Casey
and Kenzie were outside the school gates waiting for us.

CHAPTER 41

AS soon as I saw him my heart swelled up until I thought it was about to burst. He grabbed me and kissed me in front of all the rest of the girls. And he gave Lucy a hug and she kissed him too, and Kenzie kissed her then he kissed me as well. It was like the best ever.

"God I been so worried."

"Ah was gonna phone you last night but I just wanted to get home, get showered, fed an' watered, an' get my head down. An' I had to go to the college this afto so I thought I'd meet you here."

"Last night?"

"Well aye, but it was late on. About ten past eleven, an' I was fair knackered, I'm tellin' you."

We started walking towards Lochend.

"'S ok. So what's the police said?"

"Let me off, no charges."

"Oh my God. That's so fantastic."

"They had a deek at the CCTV cameras an' they realised it weren't me like I'd been sayin' all along."

"So who was it?"

"Feckin' Jaker, the dipshit. He flips her top open an' I'm the one gits gubbed. Couldn't believe it."

"So didn't you tell them that when they arrested you?"

"Jaker's a top man, kenlike? You don't grass up yer mates."

I couldn't believe it. But I was too thrilled to care.

"Anyway, he's claimin' drunken immunity, an' I've got to go back to the station on Wednesday. They're askin' if I'm pressin' charges against the stupid cow."

"Against Stacey?"

"Well, aye. Ah mean, she's the one what attacked me, right?"

"I s'pose."

"But I'm gonna leave it. She's got enough problems with her tits on show all over the You Tube."

"Honest?"

"Och aye. She's been well moded. The lassie's a right porno star now."

"Wow."

"Anyway, Rubes. What's happened to your hair?"

I danced like my life depended on it. We were practicing our solo pieces ready for the mid-term concert and I'd been working on a routine all summer in my bedroom. Massive Attack. 'Paradise Circus'. Shona had downloaded some new mixes off Amazon and I'd had that one blaring from my iPod most evenings until Mum asked me if the needle was stuck. But I love it – that slinky tune and that girl's sexy voice like a drifting spirit singing from beyond the grave. Lucy watched me try it out a couple of times and I was soon drenched in sweat.

"What's got into you?"

"Nuthin'. I'm just made up that Casey's ok and that all those horrible rumours were wrong."

MUM noticed the transformation as well as soon as I walked in.

"Somebody's managed to stick a smile back on your face then. Dance class ok?"

"Brilliant."

"Well, that's good."

"And the police have let Casey go."

"Oh?"

"It wasn't him after all. Somebody else was messin' about, pinching girls' bums, and Stacey turned round and

252

smacked Casey in the face 'cause he was the one standing behind her."

"I see."

"And I mean, if they'd checked the CCTV cameras straight away they'd have realised they were wrong."

"Right. So that's why you're looking like you've just won the lottery."

"Sort of. And I've been invited out Friday night. To a big do at the Art College?"

"Oh."

"With Kevin. Lucy and Casey are going an' all, and they want me to go 'cause Kevin's paintings are in this big exhibition with the other students."

It was getting quite tricky remembering that, as far as Mum was concerned, Casey and Kevin were two different guys.

"Sounds nice."

"So can I, please? It's a proper reception so I'll need to dress up, and Kevin said he'll sort out a taxi to pick me up and fetch me home. Please?"

That's all I'd been thinking about since he told us – just before we went inside the Leisure Centre. The four of us were going together and it was going to be soooo cool.

"I'll have to ask your dad, but I don't see why not. What time's it start?"

"Half past seven 'til about eleven o'clock. So I'll be home at a sensible hour, and it's not like it's a rave or some wild all-night party. There'll be teachers there from the college as well."

How could she say no? I'd already said yes to Casey and she could see my heart was set on going.

"Well, your dad might want to drive you there and back rather than have you crossing town in a taxi on a Friday night."

253

"Does he have to?"

I could actually live with that as long as he dropped me off outside then disappeared smartish.

"I think it's best. Have you decided what you're going to wear? Because we're not splashing out on some expensive frock that you'll more than likely never wear again."

I'd already picked out one of Shona's. An off the shoulder silvery dress with cream fringes running diagonally from one of the shoulders down to the waist. It was probably six inches too long, well below my knees. And it was low cut as well. But I don't mind flashing a bit of cleavage as long as it's done tastefully.

I was too whacked to think things through for now. And I could smell my leotard under my sweatshirt. Shower emergency.

I switched on my laptop for five minutes.

YouTube.
'Scots Wildcat Strike'.

Somebody had posted a 37-second clip from their mobile. It was a bit jumpy but you could see Stacey like some cave woman laying into Casey who was sprawled on his back, both arms trying to fight her off.

Her right boob was clearly visible and her skirt was bunched up so high that you could see her purple thong. I was dying to laugh but she looked pathetic really. And she's such a lying bitch. There were more white bits than tanned – top and bottom.

But, OMG. What if Stefan had been able to store images of me flashing the flesh on his computer? I might end up like Stacey on YouTube. Millions of people watching me posing in the bare scud.

CHAPTER 42

MUM and Dad both said I looked stunning. I'd tied my hair up and Mum had given me her short, navy blue jacket to wear over Shona's dress. It fitted like a second skin and I felt like a million dollars.

Lucy and Kenzie were waiting outside the main doors. Fortunately there's no parking allowed there so I jumped out of the car and Dad was gone again within a matter of seconds.

"Don't forget. Text me half an hour before you need picking up."

"Ok. Will do. Bye, Dad, and thanks."

Lucy had on a chocolate trouser suit and black blouse and wow, she looked gorgeous.

"Look at you, girlfren."

"And you too. O-migod."

Kenzie gave me a hug then he led us inside and up the stairs.

"Casey's gone to make sure his pictures are set up properly."

"Ok."

It was much more classy than I expected. Like one of those awards ceremonies they have on TV with real celebrities like Ant and Dec. There was a huge reception area at the top of the stairs and there were people everywhere. Most of them had on suits and evening dresses. But you could tell which were the students – crazy hair styles and make-up, and clothes you'd normally see on a second-hand stall or inside a charity shop.

"Wow, Rubes. You look like a film star."

Casey in his funeral suit but looking dishy and just as sophisticated. He put a hand on either shoulder and pulled me towards him for a cuddle and a kiss. No snogging of course.

"You wanna drink?"

"Ok. Not wine though."

"Ah ken. There's fruit juice or fizzy water, or I think they've got Diet Pepsi an' Sprite as well."

"Err, have they got apple juice or something?"

"Comin' up."

Casey had warned me that I might be in for a shock. Not just the crowd but the exhibition itself. Well there was classical music playing in the background which wasn't too bad but most of the stuff on display was a bit hard to understand. Lucy was staring at a collage made out of bits of driftwood and barbed wire then sprayed all over in black.

NIGHTSWIMMING

"D'you get it?"

"Not really."

Then there was a massive batik in loads of bright, glossy colours, showing a boxer in just his shorts, standing in a large oyster shell inside a boxing ring.

VENUS #17

Weird.

Of course, there were normal pictures as well. Proper paintings of the city streets with buildings piled all on top of each other like those going up Chambers Street. A dilapidated boat shed. A strange old woman with wrinkled brown skin, and a white clay pipe in her mouth.

There must have been twenty or thirty people crowded round Casey's display. You could tell they were

256

impressed. I mean, it even blew me away and I'd already had a sneak preview. Of sorts.

Four pictures in proper frames now. Thin, black plastic frames and mounted on cream card. Four girls' faces with their titles embossed underneath.

GIRL ONE the beauty products picture with the face of that unknown model he'd copied from one of Lucy's magazines.

GIRL TWO Lucy and them horrible words.

GIRL THREE moi, naturellement. God, it felt odd seeing me here and having all these strangers eyeing me up. One or two had already spotted me and Lucy there in the flesh and made the connection.

GIRL FOUR Casey squeezing my hand tight in his. It'll be ok. He'd warned me but it was still a splinter in my heart seeing her there. Who else? Farran. Looking like a sweet, innocent child with her black curls and dreamy eyebrows and rosebud mouth. Half her face was swathed in tendrils of seaweed – like a beautiful mermaid drowned and washed up on the shoreline. And the words printed across the entire picture in more exquisite lettering.

HEROIN - CANNABIS - PCP - COCAINE - ECSTASY - MEOWMEOW - METHAMPHETAMINE

I felt like crying it was so moving. But I also felt this huge welling-up of love and admiration and pride. Kenzie and Lucy were stood alongside us, each struck dumb – presumably for differing reasons.

"So, what d'you think?"

The tears in my eyes and the stupid grin on my face said it all.

"No as bad as ah thought," Lucy muttered – still scanning the graffiti of anger and frustration splattered across her own image. He'd forewarned her that she was one of the exhibits, and that she might not take too kindly to the way she'd been portrayed.

"It's phat, man," Kenzie. "Ah mean, to-tally phat."

I turned to face Casey.

"She'd love it. Farran, I mean."

Someone next to us started clapping. It was Mr Allman from school. He reached out to shake Casey's hand then some other people started clapping as well and soon there were about thirty standing there giving polite applause as they realised they were in the presence of the great artist himself.

"It's good to see you've brought your friends along."

A middle-aged man with a bow tie, and glasses on a string.

"Hi, Mr Neil. Err, this is my pal Kenzie, an' Lucy; an' this wee lassie is Ruby."

"Ah, the girl with the rubies. So are you comfortable seeing your egos exposed to public scrutiny like this? I mean, it's a phenomenal piece; remarkable. And it makes a set of very bold statements, but it can be quite unsettling, don't you think?"

"I don't mind, really." But the look on Lucy's face gave away the game. If Kenzie hadn't been there with her I'm fairly sure she would have walked out.

"And Ruby?"

"I love all four, so it's not just about seeing me

258

looking like this. I mean, Farran, she was my cousin. And I know she would absolutely love this one even though it's really sad."

Casey gave me a tender hug. And we spent the rest of the evening practically glued to each other's sides. It just got better and better. One of the lecturers told Casey he'd had an art dealer from one of the galleries in town asking if he was interested in selling. And there were loads of students who came up to him and said how fantastic his display was.

Then Dad walked in, and I almost burst out laughing at how out of place he looked until I saw the stunned expression on his face as he searched for me in the crowd.

"It's my dad."

"Where?"

Then Casey must have noticed the weird guy in a raincoat looking as if he was balancing on a ledge high above the street.

"Come on."

He led me towards Dad like a matador about to address the bull.

"He's not gonna kick off is he?"

"Well no. I mean…"

"Oh, Ruby, sweetheart. There you are."

I'd never seen Dad look so relieved.

"I have to get you home. Please, darling. No questions, eh?"

"What's the matter?"

"Is summat wrong?"

Dad turned to Casey.

"I'm really sorry. It's just, something's happened. Ruby needs to get home. I'm really sorry everybody."

"Right."

Casey gave me the gentlest of kisses.

259

"Text me, ok?"

I felt like Cinderella stolen away from the magic of the ball even before the first dance.

"Dad, you're scaring me."

"Let's get away from all these people. I'll tell you in the car."

He'd parked right outside the front steps, half on the pavement. As I got inside our car the bright lights and razzamatazz of the evening drained away like dishwater and I was left to shiver in the dark metal cage of this prison as Dad gripped the steering wheel and tried to explain what had happened.

"Ok. We had a phone call. Laura's mum and dad, in Newcastle."

"And?"

"It's Shona, love."

Such a wonderful night. Such euphoria and then, like a lancet piercing a blood-filled bubble. All destroyed in just three words. Dad sobbing as he forced them between his lips.

"She's gone missing."

CHAPTER 43

IT didn't take me long to figure it out.

Girl One   – Levi.
Girl Two   – Cody.
Girl Three – Shona.
Girl Four   – me?

You don't need me to tell you what it was like when I got home. Mum was a complete wreck. As soon as she saw me in Shona's dress looking all grown-up but weeping like a little child she held on to me until Dad intervened and said we should both have an early night so we could face this all together in the morning. He was going to our local police station with a recent photo of Shona so they could e-mail it over to America.

But I don't think either of us was expecting to get much sleep. Mum said she couldn't face going to bed without knowing what was happening. I went up to my room, took off that dress, checked my oil and water and put on my dressing gown.

I thought about sending God an e-mail.

God, please protect Shona. And look after mum.
Hold her in your arms this dreadful night and help
her float away on sweet dreams to some safer
place where none of this has really happened.
Rube xxx

But in the end I scribbled a few bits in my journal then went downstairs for a couple of crackers and to keep Mum company. I'd been so looking forward to recording every detail about Casey's exhibition and the fabulous night but things had gone rather flat. I didn't even have the heart to text him or Lucy to tell them the bad news.

THE smell of the river doesn't reach here. No salt spray, flaking rust or rotting sea weed and crab shells. Just diesel oil, the baking aroma of hot metal and exhaust fumes. Everywhere you turn exhaust fumes.

And there's a tide of people passing on their way from Central Park along this busy street with that old building on one side looking more like an ancient monument. Curved balustrades of weathered stone and windows with fancy mullions. And on the other side of the road a block of new red-brick apartments with every window caged and housing an air-conditioning unit like security lockers bolted onto each frame.

There are green canopies outside the front of the next long building. A smell of beer wafting from the open doorway. Cigarette stubs outside in the street like the spoor of some stricken beast. An old jazz tune spilling the detritus of a more innocent past into the street – 'Dream Blues'.

Scaffolding fronting the building opposite. A large entrance with a red 'TJ' above the doors. No it's actually a name – 'TaJ Mahal'. Somebody's ruck-sack left inside the entrance. The heady fumes of freshly brewed coffee and unwashed bodies. Our room is on the third floor with the other dorms – right at the back where there's hardly any traffic noise at night. Six bunk beds. Maroon eiderdowns and hard pillows and crisp white sheets. Maia and Doreen from New Zealand, two stand-offish girls from the West Coast, Laura and me all sharing one bedroom.

"So who's going for the Hungarian pastries?"

It's me who draws the short straw. I've got my new

262

Nike running shoes on and my money-belt and I'll be back in less than an hour, once I've had a run in Central Park...

...and it's like I've stepped off the kerb and there's nothing there to stop me falling.

Mum was still slumped in the chair. An empty wine glass on the floor kicked over at her feet. I'd brought her duvet down but she held it on her lap like an over-stuffed teddy bear instead of getting under it properly. I was flat out on the couch under an old throw. The room was still dark apart from the stagnant orange glow creeping through the blinds from the street lights outside and the ever-present red eyes of the TV and DVD-player on stand-by.

She hadn't noticed the way I'd jumped. Just as well perhaps. I tried to get comfy again but I kept thinking back to the dream. It was New York, obviously. But it didn't make much sense. Was it Shona? The girl through whose eyes I'd seen everything? All those strange buildings? And the smells – they seemed so real.

If that was the case, could I possibly search the dream some more and pinpoint exactly where she'd gone? I was dreading finding out that maybe I already knew. That cellar with the plastic bucket and the dog chain and the man with the blade.

IT was late when Dad got back. Sometime after one. He looked worn down and was desperate to get to bed. But not before he told us all his news.

"Well, they've e-mailed Shona's details across to New York. The polis there say they're doing everything they can to look for her. But they said tourists sometimes wander off into parts of the city where they shouldn't and end up getting mugged. They're checking all the hospitals

263

and stuff like that. It's only been seven or eight hours, love."

"Only? Only? I keep thinking…"

He tried to calm her.

"I keep thinking we should never have let her go."

"I know. But we can't keep her wrapped in cotton wool for ever."

"Oh, John. I'm scared something bad…"

Dad looked across at me and our eyes met. I took the hint, gave them each a hug and a kiss and went to bed. And somehow I managed to sleep – no dreams, no nightmares, no nearer finding my sister.

CHAPTER 44

SATURDAY morning, not even 07:00. All I wanted to do was turn over and go back to sleep. But I was desperate for news. I could already hear Mum and Dad shifting about, and when I sneaked into the kitchen neither looked like they'd slept much.

"You ok, sweetheart?"

"S'pose. You heard anything?"

Dad shaking his head. "Nothing. But your mum and me have been talking to Laura's dad. He thinks we should go to New York and... well, we'll be a lot nearer if anything..."

"Nana Mac's coming to stay here with you while we're away. It makes more sense than dragging you all the way to Penicuik. We'll phone you soon as we get there. And we'll let you know what's happening every day. I promise."

Laura's dad had offered to pay. He'd already booked their tickets on a flight this afternoon. There was no way Mum and Dad could afford the air-fare. Laura was going to meet them at the other end and they were going to stay in the same hostel her and Shona had been staying in. Mum said she couldn't bear to spend another night here just doing nothing.

So as soon as Nana's taxi arrived they were gone and I suddenly felt abandoned; washed up on a cold, misty beach without a single footprint in the sand. Their flight was from Edinburgh to JFK, New York via Amsterdam. 12:40 departure – 20:00 arrival. Things were happening so fast. I phoned Lucy and left a voicemail for her to ring as soon as she was up. Then I sent Casey a text saying sorry and telling him all about Shona.

Comin round 2 c u, xxx KC

I couldn't stop him, I know.

Lucy rang just as I finished getting dressed. I could hardly get the words out, trying to tell her all that had happened in the last twelve hours. I told her Casey was on his way round and she said she was going to come as well. Of course. I needed as many friends around me as possible. I mean, if Shona was to leave us I don't think I would ever recover.

Nana was wanting to fuss over me and tell me all about the old times when she'd been a young girl in Glasgow but I wasn't in the mood. I told her I'd asked a couple of mates round and to give her a bit of peace and quiet we'd hang out in the back room. I was hinting that we would appreciate being left alone.

"Shall I make you all a bite to eat?"

"No, Nan. We can help ourselves to coffee and a biscuit, honest."

I realised that she was just as upset as the rest of us. Trying desperately to find something to take her mind off the crisis. But I wasn't feeling particularly grand-daughterly.

"So what's the crack, Rubes."

I told them what little I knew.

"What do the polis think?"

"Well, they told Dad she could have got mugged or been in an accident. Laura told them that Shona'd gone off on her own, for a run or something, and just never come back. She waited for a couple of hours then went round Central Park herself to see if she could see any sign of her. But it's so massive, and in the end she started panicking and rang her dad. He said she should go to the police and tell them what happened."

"God, that's awful."

I snuggled up to Casey on the old couch in the back

266

room and he was holding me as close as he could. Lucy
kept giving us the evil eye but she was doing her best to
be positive at the same time even though I knew her heart
wasn't in it.

"They're bound to find her, Rubes."

I nodded. I knew she would be found. Sooner or later.
But I was worried what it was they might find – my sister
or just her body.

"Remember those dreams I told you about?"

Casey nodded.

"Well I'm sure they're something to do with Shona
going missing. I dreamed that I was in New York last
night and…"

"Hon, you're just upset. You've got all these horrible
thoughts tangling up your brain. No wonder you're having
nightmares."

"No, Luce. Listen. It's not the first time. Remember
that girl I told you about? When I had that hot dream, ages
ago."

"Mhmm?"

"Well I had more dreams about her. Her name's Levi.
She was chained up inside this room. An' I think she was
murdered. And then I had other dreams about another
girl called Cody. An' she was killed as well in the same
place. I don't even know how I know their names. And I
think that's where Shona is now. An' if I don't find out
exactly where she is she's going to be killed next. I know
it."

Casey gave me a hug. "Calm down, Rubes. Ah already
told you. It's just your imagination."

Lucy snorted.

"For God's sake, Casey. You tellin' me you already
know about this shit?"

"Some of it, yeh."

267

She laughed as I fought free of his arms and got to my feet.

"But I'm sure if I can find out where Levi and Cody were taken I can help them find Shona. I mean, that first girl – Levi. I've found the school she went to an' everything. It's in New York – Harlem. Exactly like she said."

"Whatchu talkin' about? You're really startin' to freak me out now, Rubes."

"It's all real. I went on 'Google Earth' an' it was there."

"What d'you mean it was there?" Casey also looking at me with mounting disbelief.

"Her school. I know it sounds mad. But I know what I dreamt. An' why would I make up something so crazy?"

In the end I had to show them on my laptop. After getting lost a couple of times I finally managed to zoom down onto that big, colourful mural I'd found outside that building.

"I just know that's the place."

"But it doesn't even look like a school, doll."

I couldn't explain how I knew. There was that writing about Excellence in Education outside but it was more than that. Somehow I was able to tune in to Levi's memories from when she was a student there. I was 100% convinced.

"We can check out this 'Home ay the Jaguars' I suppose," Casey said. "But I dinnae ken…"

He Googled it. But it was hopeless. There were hundreds. One in Florida. One in North Carolina. Mostly football teams or basketball.

Lucy looked like she was desperate to leave.

"We've told you, Rubes. Your brain's just got over-excited. You need to chill out."

But I wasn't about to give in so easily.

"Put in Harlem as well."

Casey looked at Lucy as if he agreed with her about this all being a waste of time. Then there it was. Public School 180. The exact same address in New York City.

Lucy huffed a bit. "You probably read about her somewhere else on the internet, this Levi."

I shook my head.

"You could tell the polis, ah s'pose."

She gave Casey a bewildered look.

"Are you friggin' mad? They're not gonna take any notice of some crazy kid who has weird dreams."

Lucy was right. If I couldn't convince her I wasn't going off my head I had no chance getting the police to take me seriously.

"An' as soon as they realise you're Shona's sister they're just gonna' think you're over-reacting."

It went quiet. The matter was closed. They were both humouring me because they felt sorry for me. But secretly they obviously thought I was unhinged.

I shut my computer down and made us all another coffee then Nana came in. I introduced her and we made polite conversation for about thirty seconds. Then they left. Casey had suggested I go out with them but by now it was mid-afternoon and I was in no mood to go into town or round the shops or even for a coffee and a smooch. He promised to text me later.

I retreated to my bedroom like a wounded animal and lay on top of my bed. Had I really imagined it all? Was this business with Shona totally different? Me seeing connections that weren't really there?

I dug out my diary. My journal. My Bible. My confessional. It was scary because I knew that once I did write anything in it about this, about Shona, then it would

269

suddenly become real. From a faint possibility that she might be in trouble, writing it down in black and white would confirm she was.

Can I stop time? Turn it backwards? Wish I could.

I could stop those dreams even before they started and avoid Shona coming to harm. Because I'm certain that guy who's grabbed her has taken her to get back at me – he thinks I know who he is.

Or perhaps time works both ways anyway – present to future and present to past. He took Shona – but that was pure chance. She was in the wrong place at the wrong time. And because she saved my life, fate has decided it's my turn to save hers. So those dreams were sent into my brain weeks ago in preparation for this moment.

Notmyfaultnotmyfaultnotmyfault.

Me having those dreams didn't put Shona's life in danger – it was Shona being in danger that caused the dreams.

God, please let that be so!

I mean, why is your universe so frigging hard to understand anyway?

I threw it back inside the drawer and wrapped myself up inside my duvet. I miss Shona terribly, and Mum and Dad as well.

WE didn't get the phone call until nearly two o'clock in the morning. Dad just ringing to say they'd landed safely. They were going to check into the hostel then go out for something to eat. He said Laura was upset but relieved to have somebody else there to help her cope.

Nana wrote their address and number down on the telephone pad then let me have a few words. I so wanted

270

to be there with them. But more importantly I wanted Shona to be safe.

"If there's any news we'll let you know, love. I promise you. Be good for your nana and try not to worry, pet. Now get to your bed."

I put the receiver down.

Nana's handwriting is really neat for somebody who's so old. I mean, her eyesight's not too great. She always says her eyes aren't what they used to be. And her hands sometimes shake when she pours a cup of tea. But she'd printed everything neatly in block capitals. The phone number and name of where they were staying.

TAJ MAHAL   001-212-646-9779

CHAPTER 45

WE both went straight to bed after the phone call. Nana was sleeping in Shona's room and she told me if I needed anything it was ok to wake her. I texted goodnight to Casey but there was no way I could get off to sleep. I switched on my laptop again like a drug addict desperate for another fix.

It took me less than five minutes to find it. Exactly where I'd dreamed it was – a hostel close to Central Park. There was the street with the fancy old building and the air conditioning units and the green canopy and the big red 'TJ' and the scaffolding. It was like I'd opened a door into that dream but this time I was still awake. Wide awake.

Mum and Dad would be sleeping there tonight. I felt like I was watching over them although Casey said all the images were at least a year old so I was kidding myself I'd spot Shona. He didn't really get it.

I decided I might as well sign into Messenger, click on my webcam and see if Stefan was still online.

```
*R    hiya
      r u awake
$*    o hi there
      wow u are a night owl
      but it's good to hear from u
      - and to see u :-)
      how are u tonight?
*R    really down
$*    oh dear
      you need a little hug
*R    I wish
      I mean I wish u were here
      and could give me a proper hug
```

272

$*   so what is wrong
        dear Ruby
*R   more bad stuff's happening
        Shona's gone missing in nyc
        an' I don't know who to talk to

He could see me. I knew that, but I couldn't care less how much of a mess I looked. My face was shiny with tears and there was snot dribbling from my nose and I kept trying to wipe it with the sleeve of my nightshirt.

$*   that's dreadful -
        you poor thing
        you must be worried
*R   yeh i am - but a few weeks ago
        I thought u were a MURDERER
        did u know that?

That got his mind off whatever sexual fantasies might have been germinating inside his seedy little skull. He thought it was a joke I was making but I told him everything. I confessed the lot as if I was to blame for those poor girls going missing and for Shona's disappearance. Then I asked him what he thought I should do.

$*   you have shocked me
        what you have told me tonight
        sweet ruby
        but I know you are not a girl
        who plays games
*R   what do you mean
$*   I can see you believe
        everything you say

273

```
        and so if it is true for you
        there must be something behind it
*R      you mean you trust me
$*      of course
        why not?
```

This was more than I'd been expecting. I had assumed he would tell me I was imagining everything and should stop being so stupid and just take off my t-shirt and give him the goodies or get out of his face.

```
*R      I thought u'd think I was mad
$*      have u told anybody else?
*R      a couple of friends
        they said go to the police
        but the police won't believe me
        I shldn't think
$*      no but if you trust me
        I can perhaps try to get in touch
        with someone in New York
*R      really?
$*      well
        if you write everything
        you have told me - in a e-mail
        I can maybe send a copy
        to someone there who listens
        and if any of the things in your dream
        have really happened
        then the police will have to believe you
*R      oh thank you
        thank you
$*      I will need your name and address
        - the police may need to contact you
        - and the telephone of your house
```

but I will stand by everything
you have said.
    Ruby, I will always
    be a good friend
    I hope you know that
*R   I do now

    I spent the next hour scribbling down everything I
could remember about those dreams, every trivial detail.
Then I e-mailed it off to him as soon as I'd finished. It was
nearly half past four when I finally snuggled under the
duvet. I even said a prayer but I've never been sure how
they're supposed to work. I mean, why does God let bad
stuff happen to someone as sweet and kind as Shona then
wait for someone else to ask him to put things right again?
If he had any sense no bad things would ever need to
happen in the first place.

CHAPTER 46

THE e-mail arrived on the 24th Precinct's server at 01:37 Sunday morning. The dispatcher logged it as 'UNKNOWN SENDER', had it checked for viruses and the like then cleared it to Homicide.

It sat in limbo for over 32 hours because Sunday was Garcia's day off. So it wasn't until 10:18 on Monday when he got around to logging in and checking his in-box that he found the strange e-mail which had been flagged as one he might care to look at.

> **To:**   NYPD Homicide Precinct 24
> **From:**   dukes@spazmoid.nl
> **Subject:** Harlem murders
>
> This is not a hoax. Please read this all through and if any of the facts relate to something you are investigating then contact me as soon as possible. I repeat this is a genuine message not a hoax.
>
> **Stefan Scheppers, Haarlem, Netherlands**

He buzzed Iversen and his partner joined him to scan the screen and scrutinize the e-mail's attachment. The more they read the tighter the tension grew inside their cramped office.

"What the hell's going on? Has this guy got some sort of crystal ball?"

"Perhaps he's hacked into our database."

Iversen seemed to believe otherwise.

"Could be. But it's more likely he knows who the killer is and wants to rub our noses in it. Let's take a look at everything he's given us. Check how many of the facts we kept from the Press are included."

On their own none of the fragments made much sense. But once the pieces of the jigsaw were fitted together Garcia grew increasingly unsettled.

1) Levi – 13-16 y. o. girl – wearing grey vest and panties – white plastic belt/torn jeans/blood – poss sexual molestation (?) – attended Public School 180 (Harlem?) – Special English classes – chain (?) dog collar (?) tied around her right wrist – dirty cellar – man with a knife – died on June 20th (suffocated?)

2) Cody – wearing one pink woolly sock and green slip – Anita (?) – Rami (?) – cuts on her legs – a cross or the letter 'X' as well (?) – bruising around the mouth and a cut lip – Peligrosas (?) – chain/dog collar again – same cellar – plastic bucket and old blanket – noisy machinery – dirty windows – died on August 16th

Within a half hour of analysing the information Garcia sent an e-mailed reply instructing Scheppers to report to his nearest police station. Interpol had already been asked to apprehend him and interview him, with a possible view to holding him on suspicion of double homicide.

"So you're thinkin' the same as me now, Reub. This Dutch guy's involved even though he's thousands of miles away.?"

"Well he knows as much as the killer, so if he's not involved it's one hell of a coincidence. You know how these whackos like to demonstrate how smart they are. Maybe this guy's looking for a little notoriety. I don't know. Let's see how good the Dutch police are at applying the thumb-screws."

277

To: Detective R Garcia
        - NYPD Homicide Precinct 24
From: Chief Inspector Hans Riggard
        - Police Station No. 5 BV, Amsterdam
Subject: Stefan Scheppers Statement

23.00 Monday September 7 - following 3 hours
intensive interview SS has been able to provide
water-tight alibis for both dates and appears to
have no motive regarding this initial contact other
than to assist you with your enquiries. At present
unwilling to reveal source until NYPD are able to
confirm girls described are genuine murder victims.
In our opinion forcing SS to reveal the source of his
information would be counterproductive. Suggest
direct contact made between NYPD and Scheppers
- who might then agree to providing further details
once he is accepted as a trusted and reliable
source. Suspect released pending further
investigation. If I can be of any further assistance
do not hesitate to contact me direct.

C. I. H Riggard

CHAPTER 47

I'D gone for a couple of runs in Central Park on Wednesday and Thursday with Laura and the two Australian guys from the hostel. Doreen warned us off them. Told us they were only interested in two things – and women were third on that list after booze and more booze, so we were wasting our time.

Well, they certainly like a drink. They actually took us on a summer pub crawl as it's called. A slug in every bar between the Park and the riverside. Smokey dives. Cocktail lounges where a Martini costs more than a bed for the night. Piano bars with moody music and a clientele like something out of a Scott FitzGerald novel. A club with a floor-show – exotic dancers. Silver paper stars taped to their nipples. Ouch. We didn't get back until after two in the morning and the two LA ladies made such a fuss about us disturbing their beauty sleep. Mardy cows.

Friday was meant to be a 'Zen' day. Unwinding in preparation for a wild weekend of booze, boys and bed. Bagels for breakfast. Lots of fluids. Playing pool and table football. Lazing about on the patio – glad of the shade thrown by the high walls enclosing it. Tiny cast-iron tables. Everyone just chilling out. Then I said I might go for a half-hour run even though I was still feeling hungover.

Laura wasn't up for it but when she asked someone to call at the Hungarian Pastry store I volunteered. I could drop in on the way back – if I could remember where it had been. Maia offered to draw a map on the back of my hand to make sure I found my way home.

$40 in my bumbag. Radiohead on my iPod. My new Nikes like winged shoes. The pavement gliding beneath my feet in a blur. Sublime. Forty minutes in the park with the

rest of the conditioned hamsters on our treadmill then off in search of that little shop on Amsterdam Avenue. Morningside Heights. Well I was unlikely to forget the name. Viennese coffee the last time we'd been there. A dark, dingy place: such a tight squeeze, with so many customers in there and the waitresses as rude as you like. No need for a map. 3 blocks West then 5 blocks North. Easy peasy. Two takeaway baggies in my back-pack. I'm returning by way of Morningside Park rather than taking the main streets that are forever crawling with traffic. The exhaust fumes make the heat unbearable. I can see mothers pushing their babies in buggies and Japanese tourists with their cameras and I'm pausing under the trees to tighten one of my laces and...

...something fires a buzzing jolt through my left shoulder and I can smell her lilac body spray. The one Nana Crozier always gets her for Christmas. And I'm thinking 'Am I dying? Is this what death is really like – remembering those closest to you now your time is up?' And then the screech of that door and he's back in this room.

CHAPTER 48

THE same basement room with its stifling heat and constant throb of machinery. And the screech of that door waking me up like it always does.

09:07. I needed a wee but after that I crept back into bed. Too shattered to go through my daily routine just yet. Lurching from one dream world into another. Trying to get in touch with Shona again but she was gone. Instead I was with Farran:

The pair of us floating high on happier times not heroin. Like those two penguins in Stefan's photos – me clamped next to her mermaid curves with the tide along Dunbar beach teasing our flip-flops. Feet slapping on the wet sand as we raced to find the exact spot where the Statue of Liberty lay buried in the dunes. Farran loving every moment of it. Then she stopped and turned her china doll face towards me and I saw her cold, empty eyes and that rosebud mouth, chewed red raw and slick with slobber. I tried to catch her before she slumped to her knees. But we were both complete shipwrecks.

By the time I decided to get up my blood-sugar was all over the place. My whole timetable had gone to pot. I could tell from the dull ache in my tummy that I must have picked up a slight infection as well. I found myself having a lazy Sunday by default, desperate to hear from Stefan yet increasingly nervous now that the police were presumably involved.

Nana suggested I take a day off school if I was feeling really poorly. She would be glad of the company. I was happy to wag it anyway with everything else that was going on in my life, but I realised if I was really coming down with something I'd need to switch to 'sick day rules'. That would mean keeping a close check on my sugar levels every hour or so and taking extra food and insulin as necessary. Just what I needed on top of this: up and down to the loo all day like a ruddy yoyo to check on my wee.

Grossness squared.

IN the end I didn't take much persuading to stay home on Monday. Casey kept texting during the day but I wasn't in the mood for any lovey dovey stuff to be honest. Every time I went upstairs to the bathroom I checked my e-mails for news from Stefan. Nothing. And when Mum phoned late at night, tearful and incoherent for much of the time, I told her I was fine – not a word about what was really going on.

Her and Dad had been to the local police station to give a proper statement. But they had been warned it could just be a case of Shona choosing to drop out of circulation for a long weekend. It often happens – young girls on holiday in an exciting city. She might have met some hunky guy and decided to hook up with him for a few days.

Total crap of course.

Sunday's dream had already confirmed that. The only guy she was hooked up with was the shadow man.

And later, in the darkest recess of Tuesday morning, Shona was there inside that same basement, chained to the wall and at the mercy of a psycho telling her he loved her. I heard her whimper as he began to cut her. Just once.

It was enough to wake me. 03:15. I was limp with

fatigue but couldn't get back off to sleep. I sat on the edge of my bed and checked my sugar for the millionth time – sky high. So I took a little more insulin, put on my stripy bed-socks because my feet were cold then lay awake counting the seconds. I finally clicked on my laptop for the hell of it and there it was – the latest e-mail from Stefan that must have arrived sometime after midnight. God, I was dreading reading what he had to say.

Ruby,
I think the police finally believe what you have told
me. Do not be scared but someone from the NYPD
might telephone you later today. I have told them
everything so they know all about the dreams -
and about your sister disappearing.
Keep strong, catch u soon,
S x

CHAPTER 49

THE police car turned up sometime after 'Countdown' had started. Nana rattling her brain to come up with 9-letter words. Me half-awake, half-asleep on the couch. Feeling like shit.

"Is it possible to speak to Ruby MacGregor?"

Nana terrified when she first opened the door that they'd called with the worst news possible. News too terrible even for Mum or Dad to pass over the phone.

"But what's this all about?"

"It's nothing to concern yourself with. We're acting on information we have been given by an acquaintance of Ruby's. If we could just come in and have a few words with her. Is she home?"

Nana left us to it – I could hear her pottering about in the kitchen: filling the kettle, clinking the teaspoon in the sugar bowl, the clatter of the lid on the biscuit tin. Chocolate Bourbons. This was still the same house I'd lived in all my life, yet the lounge suddenly seemed unfamiliar. It might have been the dark uniforms they were wearing. Something about the contrast between those and the bright orange cushions on our settee. It made the room appear smaller – claustrophobic.

There was no way out once they closed the door, thanking Nana for the refreshments than asking her to give them some time alone with me. I was bricking it.

"We need to ask you a few questions, Ruby."

The policewoman never taking her eyes off me as she began. The look on her face signalling that she knew I would do a runner if given half a chance.

I could hardly catch my breath as I began to tell them everything I knew. The same facts I'd passed on to Stefan basically. I tried to give them a clearer description of the basement room. The oil patches on the floor. The metal racking. The discarded clothes and tatty trainers. Those dirty windows high up beneath the ceiling and the noise of machinery.

I was busy digging myself into a bottomless hole but didn't realise it at the time.

The policeman sitting in Dad's chair kept making notes and it seemed that they were taking my story seriously.

Huh.

Then he began with his set of questions – really grilling me.

"Can you tell us how you know this Stefan?"

The faintest flicker of an eye, searching for the lie in my statement.

"Oh. It was just in a chat room I'd joined. Chatterteens. About three months ago."

"And you've been in regular contact?"

"Well, no. Not regular. Only about half a dozen times really. He's been away a lot."

"And was it just chatting, Ruby? We need to know as much as you can tell us about your relationship with Stefan. There's nothing to worry about but you're best being honest with us."

I was shaking with embarrassment even though I didn't dare reveal the very worst bits. I think the policewoman knew what I was hiding. She turned to face her colleague who gave the faintest of nods before changing tack.

"Ok. Now is there anyone else you're in contact with? Over the internet?"

"Well, my nana, Shona an' a couple of mates. Lucy an' Leesha."

"I mean, any other strangers? Anybody in New York for example?"

285

"Course not. I mean… why?"

"Well all this detail you've given us. It doesn't make much sense unless you've seen that room with your own eyes, does it? Everybody's finding it really difficult to understand how you know so much about a place that's on the other side of the world. The only plausible explanation is that you're in touch with someone over there. Perhaps some guy with a webcam set up in his basement. Perhaps that's where you saw Levi and Cody and you're too embarrassed to tell us the truth. Frightened perhaps because the situation has got out of hand and you don't know how to get out of it."

I was so stunned I could hardly make sense of what he was suggesting at first.

"Perhaps if we take a look at your computer. Put this business to bed right here and now."

I got up off the sofa and sleepwalked my way up the stairs. They followed me to my bedroom and I could feel my stomach churning with each step. I was dreading what they might be able to tell from just looking at my laptop – all my undeleted e-mails, my list of contacts, some of the snidey Facebook comments about Stacey that I wish I'd never posted. I knew I'd done nothing to be ashamed of but it was almost as bad as having someone rifle through my underwear drawer.

I still couldn't come to terms with the thought that these two police officers assumed I was in contact with the killer. They actually believed I'd be up to watching this psycho torturing and murdering girls on his webcam. I felt sick to the stomach that anyone could even consider I'd do anything of the sort.

"It's a dream. Everything I saw I dreamed. And then I went on 'Google Earth' and the places looked familiar."

I clicked onto Internet Explorer. They started checking

my internet history and stuff and it went quiet for about twenty minutes. If they got it into their heads that I'd been hiding stuff from them or was friends with the killer there was no way they'd listen to my story about wanting to help find Shona. Eventually they let me log out and the policewoman looked at me as if she genuinely felt sorry for me.

"Are you sure you didn't dream all this New York stuff after stumbling across it on the internet? It can happen, you know – forgetting things you've already seen and then dreaming about them and thinking it's some kind of… some kind of sixth sense."

She had me doubting my own sanity. Like Lucy and Casey had when I'd told them about Levi's school. Even though I knew what the truth was it was a struggle to squeeze the words out so they sounded convincing.

"I already told you. It's nothing like that. I just want to help. I know he's got Shona. I want to find her."

"Ok, Ruby. We'll leave it there for today. But we might need to interview you at the station later and take your laptop in for forensic tests."

God, what next? Did that mean they were going to arrest me? Get a search warrant?

I couldn't hold my feelings in check any longer; my heart racing away with itself as the dam burst. I knew it made me look as guilty as hell but I couldn't stop the tears.

"Ok now, Ruby. Don't go upsetting yourself. This business with your sister. It must be very hard on you, we realise."

Understatement of the century.

"Just to let you know, one of the detectives from New York might decide to telephone you this evening. Once we've reported back and told him everything you've told us."

Shit shit shit, what had I gone and done?

I asked if they could tell him to ring me on my mobile. I didn't want Nana finding out about this Stefan crap or about the dreams. Not yet anyway.

I was still a bit shaky after Nana had shown them out. When she asked what they wanted I made up some story about how the police were still investigating that so-called attack on Stacey. Someone posting malicious comments on-line about her being a slag and so on.

"Poor wee lassie. How could anybody do such a terrible thing?"

Easy. Anyway, I didn't say another word. She could see the state I was in and sat on the arm of the chair to give me a hug. It was like someone cuddling a suitcase of dynamite.

"I'm sorry Nana."

"That's all right, pet. You haven't done anything wrong. I know you're fretting about Shona. All of us are."

I retreated upstairs soon after tea and left Nana to watch her soaps. Detective Garcia telephoned during some reality programme about cowboy builders. He sounded just like Columbo off the telly.

"Hi, am I speaking with Ruby MacGregor?"

"Yeh."

"Hi, Ruby. And how are you today?"

"Hmm, not too good I s'pose."

"Yeh, well. I want you to know we're all pulling together here, doing everything we can to find that sister of yours. Right?"

"Ok. Thanks."

"First of all, everybody calls me Reub."

Rube. Hilarious.

"And just so you know, we're going to record this

conversation. It's normal procedure. Are you comfortable with that?"

"S'pose so."

"Ok, now there's nothing to worry about. But I guess you know that I need to ask you a few more questions about these... these dreams you've been having."

"Yeh. Well, Stefan was s'posed to find out if the stuff in my dreams had really happened. Those girls."

"We need to check out a few things first. I just need to ask you a few personal questions. Are you happy to go ahead?"

"Well everybody prob'ly knows what me an' Stefan have been doing anyway. An' I haven't made the dreams up, you know."

"Nobody's saying you have, honey. Let's take things step by step. So first of all, can you tell me a bit more about what was happening right before these dreams started? Were you on medication for example? Taking drugs? Getting a little high maybe? Drinking alcohol? You know why I'm asking these sorts of things don't you?"

There was no way I was going to mention that evening at Lochend Park. Surely one spliff hadn't caused all this? Or my insulin maybe? I gave a slight gasp and explained to him about my diabetes. How I'd been injecting myself for nearly seven years.

"Ok, Ruby, so tell me. How were things at home? Or at school? Were you being troubled about something? Something playing on your mind?"

I could think of nothing out of the ordinary. Other than Shona going to university and Farran running away from home. But feeling a bit lonely wouldn't...

"Well no. I mean, I just remember having that first dream and it sort of came out of nowhere. Then I started having other dreams. Nightmares really. First Levi, then

289

Cody, and now Shona and I'm really scared."

"I understand that, Ruby. Is there anything you've remembered that perhaps you didn't tell the officers this afternoon? Anything that sticks in your mind that you believe might be important?"

How many times did I have to repeat the same story to them?

"Not really. It just seemed like I was seeing things through everybody else's eyes, you know? Levi's school. The store and that sign. 'Peligrosas' or whatever it was. I thought it might be the place where Cody worked, or the place where she was taken, you know, when the man grabbed her."

"Maybe. Maybe not. You know what that word is, Ruby?"

"Peligrosas?"

"'Peligroso'. It's Spanish, honey. The Spanish word for 'Danger'."

DREAMGIRL

GIRL FOUR : DREAMGIRL

CHAPTER 50

STATISTICS. My least favourite subject in school. I soooo hate it. Hate the way it converts everything in this beautiful world into boring figures. Then chews them up and reduces the whole lot even further into one pointless number. One value. Mr. Poulson says statistics simplify the world we live in so we can understand it better. Make order out of chaos. But they also tell lies. His example – the average family has 1.7 children – says it all. Think about it.

But that Reuben guy had rattled my cage. Asking me to think of a reason why I'd started having these dreams in the first place. Why me.

So as soon as Mum and Dad had phoned to say goodnight I went back up to my room and took out my journal and my Diabetes Diary to compare dates. And there it was – the pattern revealing the order in the chaos. Each time I'd had one of those dreams my glucose levels had been much higher than normal. There had to be a link.

My blood-sugar was already at 10.1. Higher than it should be. Taking my insulin before going to bed would bring it down overnight – but not enough to make it fall so low that I'd sink into a coma while I was asleep. But if I didn't have my jab the food still inside my stomach would continue to be digested, eventually clogging my blood with sugar. I could end up having Diabetic Ketoacidosis. It sounds nasty but it's survivable. And since it's my body I get to do what I want with it. Shona had already saved my life once. The least I could do was try to do the same for her. This might be my only chance.

So I went to the loo, brushed my teeth then got undressed. I put on Mum's black and pink silk bath robe. It was too hot for pj's or a nightie. And it was the next

292

best thing to having her here. Nana said there was a storm forecast. I would give it an hour. Let my own internal storm build up before exploring z-land. Then hopefully my dreams would take me to where Shona was being held. I might be able to uncover more clues to pass on to Reub before it was too late. I mean, the worst that could happen was I'd black out and Nana would find me here in the morning and get me rushed to hospital. Or I'd have a nightmare so bad it would wake me up. And then I could take my jab and I'd be fine again. It was a no-brainer.

I switched on my laptop out of habit really. No e-mails. There had been no texts either. Nobody loves me tonight. Even Casey had taken the hint and left me to sulk alone. I jotted down a few rambling notes in my diary – cursing those two police officers for the way they were handling the case. Then I sent a quick message to Stefan while I was at it. Letting him know about the tough time they'd given me and to thank him for everything he'd done. Finally I decided to take one more trip into the heart of the Big Apple to get myself prepared for possibly the most important dream of my life.

I remember reading somewhere that New York is the city that never sleeps. Well on the internet it's always buzzing with people and traffic and life itself. I wandered past Levi's school and zigzagged along a couple of blocks either side. Then I hung around outside Mum and Dad's hostel for a few minutes before crossing Central Park and heading North towards Morningside Park. It was the same as always. Locked into an endless summer filled with greenery and baking sun. I could smell the exhaust fumes and the pavement sizzling underfoot. Then I found those overflowing trash cans: the nauseating stench of stale food rotting in the summer heat, and it all came back to me.

I retreated a couple of blocks. There was the cheap

store occupying one entire corner. Coloured lettering above the windows.

ColdBeer&SodasCandies&CigarettesHot&Cold SandwichesCoffeeTea&ChocolateFreshMeatFr uit&VegFrozenFoodIce&IceCreamSchoolSuppl ies

Oh, Cody, sweetheart. This was the place. Without a doubt. This was where she had worked. Where I'd watched her serving Laura and Shona that time even though she was already dead by then. I zoomed higher to get my bearings. There were dark little alleys hidden away at the back. No street cams there so no way to get a proper look. I hovered above each block. Everything began to blur at the edges as my eyes hazed over. I was so weary.

One building began to look pretty much like another...

...then he made her take a left turn and they ducked under the scaffolding and loose, rusted pipe-work cluttering up one side of the street. It was barely wide enough for them to walk along. The narrow alleyway ran parallel to the main street and as she snatched a final glance towards freedom she saw the large metal sign attached to the fence closing off the building site. I didn't need to zoom in any closer. This is what Cody had read before she was dragged into that basement. The same basement where Shona lay tonight.

PARA REPARTAR CONDICIONES PELIGROSAS EN UN SITIO DE TRABAJO LLAME AL 311 NO TIENE QUE DAR SU NOMBRE

CHAPTER 51

I was lathered in sweat, frothing through my paper lips, gasping for air and light. It was either this hot, humid night or my blood boiling with the glucose overload. I opened Messenger and prayed my knight in shining armour was still up and on-line.

*R   Stefan u there?
$*   ruby
       there u are
       I got yr mail
       u are feeling better now?
*R   can u help me
       do u know spanish
$*   what do you mean
       is this homework
*R   para reporter
       condicions - peligrosas
       sito de trabaio
$*   that is Spanish?
*R   don't really know
       thinks so
$*   u are not very well?
       u look fevered
*R   theres scaffolding outside
       and that were shona is
$*   ok but should u cover yourself maybe
       with your gown
       I can see everything
       u know what I'm telling you?
*R   don't care
       tell ny police
       = checkit out

             hurry plse
$*   ok
       I shall try to find a friend
       maybe who can translate
       will you wait for me?
*R   course
       thnx
       xxxxx

*It was a back-to-front dream, if there is such a thing.
Shona lay on the concrete floor, her legs tucked under her
as if she was asleep. But even in the low light I could see
her eyes, darting into each corner, searching to make
sense of where she was. One arm lay across her lap. The
other was held up like she was asking permission to leave
the room – held up by the chain attached to the wall.*

*Her face was unmarked. But her hair looked stiff with
sweat and I could see the familiar scarring on one of her
legs. His blood red kiss. His 'X' etched into her flesh. She
was barefooted, wearing just running shorts and a sports
bra. Her breath was ragged as if she had a stitch but I
knew that was more from fear than pain. I could smell fear
in the air like flowers dead in the vase and turning to
black, rotting skeletons. The fear that he was going to
come and stick that burning thing back against her body.*

*Then suddenly my eyes locked onto hers and she was
looking at me... and I was looking... at the room through
her eyes. The same hot, stifling cell with the sepia light
and the sounds of machinery and the cloying stench of
evil, but with the faintest hint of lilac blossom now. The
door opened and we were in the alley with the Spanish
sign. And I was still high from the weed. High as a white
island of cloud floating over Leithend Park, and there
were the mothers with their buggies and a couple of kids*

296

playing with a Frisbee and me and Casey canoodling under the trees and my running shoe came undone and I felt a jab in my shoulder like I'd been stung. And my whole body twitched like a puppet going crazy. Then his arms caught me and he held me close as if we were lovers yet his skin smelled nothing like Casey's and he kept telling me everything was ok. He was gonna help me home, sweetie.

I so wanted to find Laura and tell her to phone my folks. Tell them I loved them. Then there were the waste bins again filled to overflowing with garbage; fire escapes like metal hanging gardens. He was taking me under some scaffolding and past all that rusted pipe-work and I could see the sign there before we got deep inside the basement inside the basement inside the basement where the air grew thick and toxic, with just the muffled sounds to mark the way...

...muffled sounds like we were inside a narrow passageway. Clammy air all about us. Shoes slapping on stone steps. A screech from an old, metal grating being pulled to one side.

Sounds growing fuzzier; more distorted as if I was underwater.

Something loose clattering above my head.

A flickering light like when the tube in the garage sometimes doesn't quite come on properly no matter how many times you flip the switch. Coils of heavy chain and light-sucking puddles of oil on the concrete floor. A shadow thrown across it like a forgotten item of clothing.

And either side of the fallen shadow those two penguins in the photo somehow ending up on the beach at Dunbar. I'm there with them, an inside out crab with a hard shell encasing my useless pancreas and this white, baking flesh melting in the Pentland sun. Half my face has already gone, don't you see? Transformed into crystal red rock and dead leaves and desiccated desert hardpan and seaweed and I'm a mermaid turned inside out with turtle-skin and sea kelp smelling of lilacs and popcorn.

It's a loop >> some dark tunnel like under8water with the humid air becoming more and more like plastic as I try to claw life into my lungs. A horrible grey membrane pressed against my face, shutting off my mouth and my nose, and I'm sucking desperately for breath and even with my eyes open all I see is this fog of death. Colours washed out like watered down milk.

But he's there/ oh I can smell him and his ro|tten o|dour. Shona crouched underNeath him and he#s holdin that thing against her body – u want more of this, bitch? – p[ressed down on top of her And he says heLOVEs her and he's here inside me like in that very first dream and theSCREEch of that FUCKINGdoor again and like a scalded cat he jumps away from her and in my guts this burningFIRE

$*   ruby ruby
      look at me
      ruby

"Reub, hold on buddy. Hold on. Try to stay awake, man. They're gonna get you fixed up, ok? We got him, man. We nailed him."

And I look back towards her heaving body – the plastic bag torn from her head and her right arm cut loose of that chain, sobbing and throwing up all the poison that had been fermenting inside my guts and it's all over the front of my body and my robe opened wide like the wingspan of a pink and black butterfly pinned down in a

298

glass case, bathed in sweat, and he presses that horrid thing against me again and in the distance a voice says 'Clear' and my heart hip-hopping and it's Massive Attack and I'm dancing the dance spread-eagled on my bed and my muscles are on FIRE and BURNING in my guts through to my kidneys

and "Reub, Reub, hold on buddy

$*   ruby ruby
        look at me
        ruby

hold on"

but I'm already in 'Google Hell'. Couldn't reach the keyboard to send him a goodnight kiss. Couldn't hear the telephone downstairs as he rings our house. Trying to get someone to come and check on me. Nana taking forever to wake from her own butterscotch dreams to the insistent doorbell and those blue flashing lights in the street... an'
den my nose done bleedin all down my front an over my jeans. Den I feel engine vibrations through da floor an gentle sway wid truck as it moves. I bad scare...

...and then they pump me full of Buckie and all is well with the world.

THERE'S a huge Get Well card from Casey. One he made himself with a cartoon of me dressed like a regular Powerpuff Girl with sparks coming out of my fingertips. If only he knew the whole story. And there's lots of beautiful flowers – even a bunch of white lilies from some stranger called Reuben Garcia.

And slowly it comes back to me like fast-forwarding a movie and I'm so glad Reub survived. The electric shock. The killer brandishing a Taser and that sting like a million mosquitoes sending him into cardiac arrest. Both of us linked by this invisible umbilicus, these writhing tentacles of internet. He recovered. We all did.

Me on my back like a crab shell turned inside out and rotting on the beach. Asleep beside the soothing pulse of tide that washed through my veins, rinsing away all the poison and scum of my wretched life. Shona, scarred and shaken but safe. Mum and Dad like refugees in a new country, scarcely believing all that had happened in the past five days. Stefan. I'll need to thank him properly once I'm out of this dire place. This ward with the smell of disinfectant and lilacs and potential death.

There are charts at the end of my bed. More statistics. More meaningless numbers. But you don't need to look any closer because there's nothing complicated about any of this story when you analyse it. It's just two sides of the one coin – synchronicity:

Doctor Jekyll – Mister Hyde
Hyperglycaemia – Hypoglycaemia
Reuben – Ruby
2 Harlems
2 Amsterdams
2 Morningsides
2 sets of Girl One, Two, Three and Four
2 sides of the Atlantic
2 ends of the internet
2 injections a day

and two endings unfortunately. If you favour happy endings then this is the one for you. Stop reading now…

…but as Shona once told me, people don't usually live happily ever after.

CHAPTER 52

THIS house can never be the same again. Not with that empty bedroom still echoing with her crazy laughter and the scent of her body spray and her photos stuck everywhere having some good craic with her mates. A room that was once filled with fun and colour and life and hope.

Mum couldn't bring herself to go in there for weeks. It was left to me. And I did so gladly. I still sneak in there even now when I'm missing her most. Those grey, out-of-focus nights when I end up climbing inside her bed, desperate for her touch but knowing it has gone for good.

I know I will never get over losing my sister. She saved my life after all, yet in the end I never got to save hers. Every breath I take is such agony when I remember that she will never draw a single breath again. My eyes blur when I realise I'll never get to watch her grow into an amazing young woman. Because she would have done, mark my words.

It's so unfair. This is not the way the world is meant to work. But perhaps that's all part of growing up. One of the hardest lessons we have to learn. Accept that most of our illusions are destined to be broken into smithereens sooner or later. But like a perfect mirror that breaks into a million glittering shards, a million diamonds, the underlying beauty of life is never destroyed. And so the beautiful memory of my sister will never wane for me.

FORGIVE me. This was written to honour her life not wallow in the grief of her loss. Much of the actual story I've recorded is pure guesswork but there were enough bits scribbled in her private diary for me to come up with the basis for this. And, of course, the news clippings from the New York Times, what those police officers let slip. The two who found me in that basement – the ones who probably saved my life. And the dozens of notes and undeleted e-mails on her laptop. It was as if she could never bear to throw away a single memory.

That's how I first came across Stefan's name. She'd never mentioned him to us, obviously. I was debating whether or not I should contact him – let him know what happened. In a way I'm glad I did even though it made my flesh crawl imagining what sort of guy goes on-line in search of young girls. He said a lot of nice things about her. He was the one who got in touch with the police the night they found me, also contacting the emergency services when he saw Ruby on her webcam and realised she was having some sort of fit.

He filled in most of the other blanks as well, though I realise more went on between them than he let on. But that's all in the past and this is no place to find fault with the way Ruby chose to live her life. We all have secrets we pray will remain buried after we die.

I also spent a lot of time chatting with Lucy and Casey. Even Stacey got in touch once she heard the news despite everything Ruby had written about her on Facebook. Again I found out a few things I'd never have guessed. But thinking back to when I was sixteen perhaps I should have been prepared for a shock or two. Casey was probably the biggest surprise of the lot. He's as much of a dish as she said he was. We met for a coffee a week or so after the funeral. He showed me the amazing pictures he'd drawn of her and I would have asked him for one but I could see how much they meant to him. He said he would never sell them. And of course, Mum and Dad know nothing of this so it would be difficult to explain where I'd got it from.

They're unlikely ever to find out what really happened. Mum likes her historical romances. Dad reads the racing results and that's about it. But even if they read this they would never guess. In case you haven't realised yet, our name's not MacGregor and there's no such place as Fingal Gardens.

The fact that she's gone is never going to change. Her illness got the better of her in the end. She sacrificed her life for mine – took a risk and lost. There was nothing the doctors could do. It's extremely rare for a teenager to die of DKA. And it's a laugh really because sometimes you can get it from binge drinking yet poor Ruby never touched a drop of alcohol.

Anyway, there's nothing anyone can do or say or write to bring her back. But this story might keep her memory alive a little longer, like a candle flame that will never blow out.

So if you've read this from start to finish I hope it doesn't make you feel so sad that you forget the good things in Ruby's life. Many, many people loved her. She taught me so much – that no matter what difficulties you are faced with you never give up. Love your family and keep them close to your heart no matter what.

Love life – the good bits and the bad. But most of all, love yourself...

END

ACKNOWLEDGEMENTS

Firstly I must thank Gill James and the editorial staff at Red Telephone Books for their encouragement right from the start. It's unlikely this book would have made it into print without their continued dedication and professional assistance.

I'd also like to salute my fellow-workers at the rock face – the regular members of the North-West Highland Writers' group who encouraged me to chip away and always gave constructive responses to my efforts.

In particular I owe a huge 'Thank you' to Mandy Haggith, whose expert guidance and ceaseless motivation led me to put pen to paper in the first place – and to Helen Simpson for her continued support. Given the unenviable task of exploring the uncharted territories of the complete first draft, Helen emerged unscathed and through her astute reading was able to suggest a number of revisions.

I'm also grateful to Patrycja and to Mary Kate for taking the time to read this during the final stages and for providing useful feedback.

Many of the enhancements are thanks to them. Any retained flaws are entirely my own.

CB

Other novels by *The Red Telephone*

Calling for Angels
by Alex Smith

Em tries to avoid the annoying clones – the girls in her year at Philiton Comprehensive who spend all their time thinking about clothes, make-up and boys. She worries about her aging grandparents and her older brother Ollie, who seems to be behaving in a distinctly odd way.

Then three new people come into her life: the mysterious woman who gives her a beautifully carved figurine, Kai whose own story has a touch of sadness, and Zak, the new guy who causes a stir amongst the girls.

And she discovers she needs to call for angels.

Alex Smith is 16 and lives in Hertfordshire, England. She started writing when she was just four and says, "to me, writing is like breathing." She finished her debut novel, Calling For Angels, at the age of 14, "as a way of relaxing".

Winner of *The Red Telephone's* 2009 novel competition.

Order from http://theredtelephone.co.uk
Paperback: ISBN 978-1-907335-09-9
eBook: ISBN 978-0-9568680-5-3

XY

by Shanta Everington

Fifteen-year-old Jesse lives in a society where babies are born neither male nor female – gender is assigned at birth. Will the secret she closely guards be found out? Boyfriend Zeus, mother Ana's Natural Souls, and new friend Ork, leader of We Are One, pull Jesse in different directions, forcing her to make her own mind up about who she really is.

"A highly original and thought-provoking dystopian novel. I don't think I've ever read anything like it!"
(Luisa Plaja, Chicklish, the UK's Teen Fiction Site)

"Though this book is a work of fiction, the plight of the intersexed that is so artfully brought to the forefront within its pages is quite real. There is a large group of the world-wide population living as members of the transgender, intersexed, community, who just want to live lives, love, and be accepted for their true selves. This book speaks to those desires in an eloquent and powerful voice that deserves to be both heard and understood." *(Amazon)*

Order from http://theredtelephone.co.uk
Paperback: ISBN 978-1-907335-32-7
eBook: ISBN 978-1-907335-34-1